"It se_____."

"You need a _____ housekeeper. _____ you would be agreeable to the arrangement, I would like to offer you the use of the apartment in exchange for housekeeping services. Two or three times a week would be sufficient."

Housekeeping? He wanted her to clean house? He was just like the rest of the rich people who lived on the hill. She should have known.

"Y-y-you—" Anna sputtered, trying to find words to dismiss the outlandish plan.

Ma took advantage of her fury to ruin everything. "That would be wonderful. Oh, Mr. Brandon, how can we ever thank you? It's perfect, isn't it, Anna?"

Perfect? Living under the thumb of Brandon Landers? Working for him as a servant? Living in what must be servant's quarters?

It wasn't perfect; it was humiliating.

Books by Christine Johnson

Love Inspired Historical

Soaring Home
The Matrimony Plan
All Roads Lead Home
Legacy of Love

CHRISTINE JOHNSON

A small-town girl, Christine Johnson has lived in every corner of Michigan's Lower Peninsula. She loves to travel and learn about the places she visits. That puts museums high on her list of "must see" places and helps satisfy her lifetime fascination with history and archaeology.

Twice a finalist for RWA's Golden Heart award, she enjoys creating stories that bring history to life while exploring the characters' spiritual journey—and putting them in peril! Though Michigan is still her home base, she and her ship captain husband also spend time exploring the Florida Keys and other fascinating locations.

Christine loves to hear from readers. Contact her through her website at http://christineelizabethjohnson.com.

CHRISTINE JOHNSON

Legacy of Love

Love Inspired

™ LOVE INSPIRED BOOKS

ISBN-13: 978-0-373-82941-5

LEGACY OF LOVE

www.LoveInspiredBooks.com

Printed in U.S.A.

If we confess our sins, he is faithful
and just to forgive us our sins, and to cleanse us
from all unrighteousness.
—*1 John* 1:9

For my nieces, Jennifer and Sara.
May you find adventure around every corner
while enjoying the solid foundation of home.

Chapter One

Pearlman, Michigan
December 1922

"I had to resign," Anna Simmons explained to her sister-in-law, Mariah, as she pushed open the mercantile door. Her red knit glove looked like a splash of paint against the darkened oak.

The bell on the door tinkled, announcing their arrival to the handful of customers shopping that afternoon. Most looked up to see who'd entered. That's the way it was in Pearlman. Everyone kept track of everyone else. Sometimes that was good. Other times gossip had a way of taking off and running around town until it had wrung the life out of everyone involved.

Anna knew full well that word of her leaving the Neideckers' employ would race through town like wildfire. Best douse that flame before it got started.

"I had no choice," she announced loudly enough for everyone in the store to hear.

"Why?" Mariah's brow puckered into a frown as she picked up a shopping basket.

"The uniform she wanted me to wear was positively indecent. Why, the skirt didn't even cover my knees. It was as short as a bathing suit."

Mariah shook her head. "It couldn't have been that bad."

"It was horrible, with a frilly white apron and cap." She lowered her voice when Mrs. Butterfield glanced her way. "How am I supposed to clean in that? Especially with Joe Neidecker looking at me like I was some floozy." She shuddered at the memory of the oldest son's stare. Everyone knew he frequented the speakeasy. "I can imagine what he was thinking. I've read books."

"Dime novels," Mariah pointed out.

"Books," Anna stressed. "In the last one I read, the maid fell in love with the duke's eldest son only to be thrown out on the streets."

"The son didn't rescue her? Usually those stories have happy endings."

"That's not my point. They threw her out."

Mariah clucked softly. "So you took matters into your own hands."

"I'm not wearing that uniform. I clean houses. I am not a servant." She'd told Mrs. Neidecker the very same thing, but the woman didn't take it well. Her tirade still rang in Anna's ears.

"We are all called to serve," Mariah pointed out. "Jesus washed his disciples' feet. There is no shame in working as a servant."

"Maybe." Anna did not need a lecture. Mariah might be thirty-one years old to her twenty, but that didn't give her the right to scold. "I'd rather be doing something exciting, like exploring ancient ruins."

"That requires connections and a great deal of money."

"I'll get another job."

Mariah looked unconvinced as she placed four cans of

beans in her basket. "Jobs are difficult to find. I haven't seen a posting anywhere in weeks."

"The cannery in Belvidere is hiring."

"And spend half your wage on train fare?" Mariah's brown bobbed hair peeked out from under the brim of her blue tricorn hat. "I wish the orphanage could afford to pay you."

"I wouldn't take a nickel." Anna knew how tight Constance House's finances were. As director of the orphanage, Mariah scrimped and saved and solicited donations, but she could never make ends meet. The number of children had grown but not the funding.

"Thank you, dear." Mariah lifted the lid on the barrel and examined the flour. "No weevils today. I'll take five pounds," she said to the clerk, who'd finished waiting on Mrs. Butterfield.

Anna noted Mariah's long grocery list. "What can I get for you?"

"Would you ask the butcher for a five-pound beef roast?"

Anna strolled down the aisle lined with barrels containing flour, cornmeal, sugar, dried beans and oats on one side and shelves holding one-pound bags of coffee beans and packets of tea on the other. Rolls of butter sat on ice, while wheels of cheese and the lard can stood nearby.

She passed by the candy display without the slightest interest, but when her eye caught a headline on the *Pearlman Prognosticator*'s front page, she gasped.

"Mariah, come here." Hands shaking, she unfolded the newspaper and scanned the single-column article entitled, "Treasure Tomb Unearthed."

"What is it? What's wrong?" Mariah hurried to her side.

"Look." Anna pointed the frayed tip of her knit glove at the article. "A Mr. Carter found a pharaoh's tomb filled with gold and riches. He says it's so full of artifacts that it'll take months to clear."

"Is that so?" Mariah sounded unimpressed.

"It's the tomb of a young pharaoh, King Tutankhamun." She stumbled over the unfamiliar word. "Can you believe tomb robbers never found it? Mr. Carter is the first person to step inside since it was closed up centuries ago. Oh, Mariah, if only I was there. If only I could find a treasure like that. Imagine. We'd be rich. The orphanage would have everything it could ever want. Ma could have a big house on the hill. You and Hendrick too. Wouldn't it be wonderful?"

"Oh, Anna, you're such a dreamer." Mariah smiled softly. "It would be wonderful, but what would be even better is to finish my shopping before school lets out. Will you pick up the meat from the butcher?"

With a sigh, Anna refolded the newspaper. She wanted to buy it, but, as Mariah would point out, that wouldn't be prudent now that she had no job.

As she walked to the butcher counter and requested the roast, words from the article bounced around her head. Valley of the Kings. Boy king. How she wished she could have been there when Howard Carter opened the tomb. Had the centuries-old air rushed out? Did it smell stale? Did he gasp when the torchlight danced off glittering gold?

Her imagination raced as she absently accepted the paper-wrapped package of meat from the butcher. One day she would discover an even bigger treasure. The press would swarm around her, eager for just one word from the famed Egyptologist, Anna Simmons. Cameras would flash as the reporters asked what she'd found. She'd shield her eyes from the glare and answer mysteriously, "You'll just have to wait."

"Excuse me?" The irritated question came from a very tall and very distinguished man.

Blinking, she pulled herself out of the fantasy to take note of the stranger. He must have been in the store the whole time, but she'd been too preoccupied to notice him. What a mistake. Judging by the quality of the stranger's clothing, he had money and lots of it. His straight nose and commanding jaw made her tremble. He looked exactly like how she'd imagined Jane Eyre's Mr. Rochester.

"I thought you were finished," he said in a rich timbre that resonated clear to her toes.

"I, uh, uh…finished with what?"

"You said I had to wait." He pointed to the paper-wrapped package she cradled in her arm. "Since you walked away, I thought you were done." He swept a magnanimous hand toward the counter. "Please, go ahead."

"Oh, no." Anna felt heat infuse her cheeks. When she'd imagined telling the reporters to wait, she must have spoken aloud. "That is, I'm done." The words came out all awkward, like a dumbstruck schoolgirl. "Go ahead."

"Thank you." His lips curved slightly, greatly softening his appearance. "If I might correct you, the seals had been broken."

"Seals?" She stared blankly. "What seals?"

"Clay seals. They are affixed to the entrance of any pharaoh's tomb. You said the tomb had never been opened before, but the seals at the entrance had been broken sometime in the past. Fortunately for Mr. Carter and the Cairo Museum, the contents appear to be largely intact."

Anna could hardly breathe. Not only did he look distinguished, but he knew everything about the excavation. He must be a professor. Or an archaeologist. Maybe he'd take her to Egypt. Stupid idea. He'd never trust a girl who stammered and talked to herself. He certainly wouldn't take someone poor. Expedition members had to pay their way.

She bit her lip to force away the disappointment and

tried to say something intelligent. "Why is it fortunate for the Cairo Museum?"

His smile deepened. "They will receive the tomb's contents after Mr. Carter inventories them."

"How do you know so much?" She was gushing, but how could she help it? A pharaoh's tomb had been discovered, and this man knew all about it.

"I read the archaeology journals and reports."

"You do? Do you think...?" She hesitated, but the twinkle in his eyes persuaded her to ask. "Do you think I might borrow your journals someday? When you're done, of course."

"You may," he corrected. "Come by my new bookstore, The Antiquarian, when it opens next month."

Next month? January was two weeks away. She didn't know if she could wait that long, but she had no choice. He hadn't offered to loan his precious journals a moment earlier.

"Thank you, oh thank you," she said a bit too eagerly.

If he found her schoolgirl reaction amusing, he had the kindness not to mention it. "I suggest you begin with Dr. Davis's book on Tutankhamun."

She nodded dumbly.

"Until then." He turned to the meat counter.

"Until then," she whispered, unable to tear her gaze from him.

"Oh, good, you got the meat. Thank you." Mariah gently took the string-tied package from her hands. "We should be going. I just need to sign the account first." She tugged Anna toward the sales counter where the rest of her purchases were already piled into a crate.

Anna reluctantly followed, but her mind lingered elsewhere. She glanced back at the butcher counter. This fascinating man was opening a bookstore. And he read archaeology journals.

"Deliver it to the house with the rest," the man said to

the butcher. He grasped an ivory-headed ebony cane in his right hand. A cane like that could only have come from Africa. The Dark Continent. He must have traveled the world. She would do that one day.

He limped toward the sales counter, and Anna turned away so he wouldn't notice she'd been staring at him. The cane. The limp. Perhaps he'd been gored by a rhinoceros or barely survived a tiger attack. Maybe natives shot a poison dart into his calf, and he'd lost the use of his foot.

"I'll have Josh drop this off," the clerk said to Mariah.

After thanking the man, Mariah asked Anna if she wanted to come over for a cup of tea.

Anna shook her head. "I'd better go home. Ma wanted me to make supper." She sighed. "Cleaning and cooking. Does it ever end?"

"When you're doing it for your loved ones, it's a joy," Mariah started. "Goodness, is that the school bell?" She hastily buttoned her coat. "I'd better hurry."

"Go ahead. I want to look around a little." And read more of the article.

After a final farewell, Mariah left.

Before Anna could drift back to the newspapers, the door opened with a rush of icy wind, and none other than Sally Neidecker entered. Sally had graduated from high school a few years before Anna and went to college the following year, which is where she should be now. Mrs. Neidecker hadn't expected her daughter's return until the end of the week. Her appearance now meant trouble.

Anna pretended to be engrossed by the candy selection and hoped Sally wouldn't spot her.

No such luck. Within seconds, the girl had ferreted her out.

"There you are." Without so much as a greeting, Sally flounced toward her, the hem of her scandalously short skirt barely peeking out below the bottom of her fur-trimmed coat. "How could you leave Mother without help on the day of her Christmas party? She was beside herself. Absolutely hysterical. I thought we'd have to call in Dr. Stevens."

Anna's tongue stuck to the roof of her mouth. "I, uh—"

"Is that any way to treat a friend? I thought we were friends, Anna. Haven't I always helped you?"

Not always. True, she'd looked up to Sally when she was younger, and Sally had taken her under her wing, but not like a friend. More like a foot soldier.

"I, uh, thought you were still at the university. Your mother said Michigan didn't let out for the semester until the end of the week." It wasn't much of a distraction, but it worked.

Sally lifted her nose even higher. "I finished my coursework early, and my new guy drove me here."

The familiar way Sally mentioned her beau made Anna's skin crawl. She acted as if he was some swell from the big city. Maybe he was, but driving all the way from Ann Arbor alone with a man?

"He's perfect," Sally continued, her stained lips bright against the fox fur, "much too good for the girls around here."

Anna didn't bother to point out that Sally came from here. Instead, she glanced toward the newspapers.

That reminded Sally of her purpose. "You have to come back to work."

"I'm sorry. I can't."

"But then who will clean up after the party?"

Anna stared at the candy jars. "I don't know."

"What is wrong with you? It can't be the wages. Mother pays better than anyone else in town."

"I'm not a servant," Anna said through clenched teeth.

Sally snorted. "You're a maid. Maids are servants."

of the house arrived home from work. Until then, he'd look over the storefront where he planned to open his bookstore.

He hurried along the boardwalk, shoulders hunched against the wind. The leaden sky hadn't yielded snow yet, but it threatened. The cold weather had frozen the puddles and forced him to spend more for coal than he'd anticipated. At this rate, he'd run through his meager savings before spring. He needed to get the bookstore up and turning a profit soon, but the storefront required work. A lot of work.

To turn the old harness shop into a viable bookstore, he needed to replace the front window, install bookshelves and build a sales counter—none of which he could manage himself. That meant hiring a carpenter or handyman.

He unlocked the door and stepped into the dim interior. It smelled like a tannery. Dust, dirt and debris filled every corner and crevice. He poked his cane into the wall, and the plaster crumbled onto the plank floor.

"I need help," he muttered.

"I might be able to assist you with that," answered a painfully cheerful voice.

Brandon turned to see a man of middling height with unruly hair standing in the open doorway. Informally dressed in a mackinaw coat, he looked every bit the workman Brandon needed.

"You're looking for work?"

The man laughed and shook his head. "I already have a job as pastor at the church across the street, but I know pretty much everyone in town and can put out the word for whatever you need."

The man sure didn't look like a clergyman. "Aren't you dressed a little informally for a minister?"

The pastor laughed again and extended a hand. "Call me Gabe."

Brandon stared at the outstretched hand. Ever since the

war, he couldn't set foot in a church. Too much had happened—things he didn't want to remember, things no one could forgive. But he also couldn't deny basic civility.

"Brandon Landers." He completed the handshake. "I'm settling my father's estate."

"My condolences. We heard he'd passed away unexpectedly. Will you be staying in Pearlman?"

"At the family home." This conversation was already taking too long. Soon the man would invite him to church, and he'd have to make up an excuse. He eyed the dark street with its glimmering streetlamps and checked his watch. Five o'clock. Best get his unpleasant task done before it got too late. "I need to leave."

"But didn't you want to hire someone?"

An inquiry couldn't hurt, if the price was right. "Do you know a young man who needs a job?" A youth would cost less than a skilled carpenter.

Pastor Gabe glanced at the filthy interior. "I'd think you'd want someone to clean the place first. I know a lovely young woman who could do the work for you. She's a first-rate worker and could use the money. The family is struggling to get by, and I learned today that her widowed mother had her hours reduced."

"I beg your pardon, Pastor. I feel for them, but it's not a job for a woman. I need shelves built and the window replaced."

"I see." The minister tapped his chin. "Her brother and foster brother are excellent with their hands. I'm sure they'd step in for any construction required."

"That means hiring two people when I could simply hire one."

"I doubt either one would take money away from their sister. Hendrick Simmons is busy starting up his new aeroplane-engine plant, and Peter is managing the garage, but I'm sure one or the other could make time for a little construction."

Simmons? Brandon stiffened. That was the last name he wanted to hear. Once he delivered the envelope, none of them would have a thing to do with him. They certainly wouldn't work for him, not at any price.

Chapter Two

"You quit?" Ma froze, her soup spoon poised in midair.

Anna pushed her chair away from the rickety kitchen table. The potato, rutabaga and salt pork stew that had smelled so good minutes before now turned her stomach.

"You can't just walk out," Ma insisted.

"I'll get another job.

"That's not the point, dearest. Mrs. Neidecker was counting on you."

Anna couldn't look her mother in the eye. "I finished the day's work. Everything's ready for her Christmas party. All she has to do is hire someone to clean up."

Ma shook her head. "A Simmons always finishes the job. I'll take care of the cleanup."

"You can't do that."

"Why not?" Though Anna's mother was short on stature, she was long on resolve. "I'm perfectly capable. Mrs. Vanderloo doesn't expect me until Thursday."

Anna hated that Ma was always right. "Well, you can't wear that skimpy uniform, for one thing."

"Evelyn would never ask me to wear something that wasn't modest."

Anna wasn't so sure. Mrs. Neidecker had got it into her

head that her house should look like the Rockefellers lived there. That meant maids in fancy uniforms and Graves, the butler, in a tuxedo. Apparently she'd seen pictures of some rich person's house in a ladies' magazine.

Ma squeezed Anna's hand. "We need the money."

That much was true. Ma's hours at the Vanderloo house had been trimmed, and the Williamses dropped her in favor of a girl who accepted half the pay. Now, Anna had quit her job. She ducked her head. "I'm sorry."

"Now, don't you fret. We still have the money your brother gives us each month. I hate to accept it, now that he has a family to support, but it can't be helped."

"I'll get a job at the Belvidere cannery. I heard they're paying a dollar an hour."

Ma's gentle smile faded. "But I need you here. You're my only daughter. What would I do without you?" She brushed a strand of hair off Anna's forehead as if she were still a child.

"It's only Belvidere." Ma meant well, but Anna hated being coddled. "I'll take the train back and forth each day."

"But you wouldn't be home as much. I hear the cannery works its people long hours and then the train ride on top of that. I'd hardly ever see you. Please stay. For me?"

That was the problem. All of Anna's friends had moved on to bigger and better things, but she was still stuck in Pearlman, living with her mother, with no future in sight. At the age of twenty, she hadn't even had a real beau yet. Oh, she'd fallen for men, disastrously, but they either didn't notice her or fell in love with someone else.

That man in the mercantile, the one opening the new bookstore, would turn out just like the rest. She couldn't wait for someone to sweep her off her feet. She had to take care of her own future. That meant getting a good-paying job.

"The only jobs that pay well are at the cannery," Anna

pointed out. "If I get a job there, we won't have to take money from Hendrick anymore."

Ma heaved a sigh, which signaled she'd come around to Anna's way of thinking. "I suppose we have no choice then, but I hate the idea of you riding all alone on the train every day. I wish your father were here. He'd know what to do."

If Papa hadn't died, Ma wouldn't have had to struggle raising two children, and Hendrick wouldn't have had to quit school in the eighth grade to take over the garage. Everything would have been different. Anna might have been able to go to college. She wouldn't have worn homemade dresses sewn out of the scraps from Mrs. Fox's dress shop. But Papa had died—horribly. She shuddered, and shoved the memory into a dark corner of her mind.

Ma must have been thinking about him too, because she sniffed and dabbed her eyes.

Anna hugged her. "Papa was the best of men. He would have taken care of us."

"He always did."

Anna was so caught up in the painful memories that the knock on the door didn't register right away.

Ma noticed it first. "I wonder who that is." Her eyes grew round. "I hope nothing happened at the plant."

Fear ricocheted. All that machinery at her brother's new aeroplane-motor factory. The open belts and whirling lathes. The infernal racket. What if a belt caught Hendrick's arm? What if a heavy machine fell on him?

A blinding memory—one she desperately wanted to forget—shot through her head. The truck falling, her father's body jerking from the impact, the cry... She pressed her hands to her ears and squeezed her eyes shut to make it go away.

"Are you all right, dear?" Ma asked gently.

Anna shook off the memory with a forced smile. "I'm fine."

The knock sounded again, loud and firm.

Ma rose. "I'll get it."

Anna's pulse accelerated. What if something *had* happened to Hendrick? She couldn't let Ma hear the bad news first. She leaped to her feet and reached the door first.

The next knock rattled the hinges and made the knob jump in her hand.

"All right," she snapped, yanking the door open. "There's no need to pound down the—" But the last word stuck on her tongue, for before her stood the distinguished gentleman from the mercantile.

This wasn't bad news at all. He'd come to talk to her. Perhaps he'd brought her the archaeology book.

"Oh. You." The minute the words left her lips, Anna blushed. A scholar wanted intellectual conversation, not some moony girl who couldn't string two words together.

Yet he looked as taken aback as she was stupefied. "You're Miss Simmons? Or do I have the wrong address? This is 502 Main Street?"

"Yes, it is." What on earth did the address have to do with dropping off a book? "I'm Anna Simmons."

If anything, he looked even more distressed.

"And I'm Mrs. Simmons," said Ma from behind her. "Do I know you? You look a little familiar, but I'm afraid my memory isn't quite what it used to be."

His discomfort eased a bit when he saw Ma. "You knew my father, Percival Landers. I'm his eldest son, Brandon."

"Little Brandon?" Ma pushed past Anna. "The last time I saw you, your parents still summered here. You couldn't have been more than twelve and barely reached my shoulder. You laughed all the time."

Anna lifted her eyebrows. Clearly, he'd outgrown the laugh.

"Then your parents stopped visiting," Ma continued. "Of course your father would come to town periodically to see how the garage was faring. He was such a kind man, always concerned for us, especially after my husband's death." She leaned closer, as if she wanted to tweak his cheeks. Thankfully, he was too tall. "My dear boy, I'm so sorry for your loss. Please accept my condolences. I couldn't believe my ears when I heard your father had passed. So young. He couldn't have been more than sixty. My dear Brandon. I'm so sorry."

So this was Brandon Landers. Anna had never met him, though Ma had mentioned once or twice that Mr. Landers had two boys. She knew about his father, of course. The elder Landers was a silent business partner of her father's, though Anna had only seen him a couple times after Papa's death. He always brought papers for Hendrick to sign and left her brother agitated.

"How is your younger brother?" Ma bubbled on, oblivious to Brandon's discomfort. "Reginald, is it?"

"He's fine."

"And your wife? You must be married by now."

Anna shot her mother a glare, though she had to admit she wanted to hear the answer. Why hadn't she considered that Brandon might be married? Because he'd done his own shopping. No married man shopped for groceries.

He shuffled uncomfortably. "No, I'm not married."

Ma, whose greatest joy in life was matchmaking, didn't let up. "A fiancée, then? A handsome man like you must be engaged."

"Ma," Anna hissed under her breath.

He cleared his throat. "No, I'm not. Please forgive me,

but this is not a social call." He pulled an envelope from his pocket. "Is the man of the house at home?"

"Hendrick?" Anna surveyed the envelope, but he held it so she couldn't see the address. "Why would you want to talk to him?"

Ma stepped aside. "Do come in, Mr. Brandon, and sit a spell. My son no longer lives here. He married this September and is living at the orphanage, Constance House, with his lovely bride. They're feeding the children at this hour, so I wouldn't recommend interrupting, but you can wait here with us and have a cup of tea."

Brandon Landers in their shabby living room? Anna choked. "I'm sure Mr. Landers has supper waiting for him."

"My business can wait." He avoided looking at her.

Oh, dear. The letter brought bad news. Hendrick had put everything into opening his new aeroplane-engine plant. He did not need trouble with the garage. It was their only source of income right now.

Brandon started to tuck the envelope into his coat.

No. Anna couldn't let him spring bad news on Hendrick. She'd do it. She grabbed the envelope from his hand. "I'll see my brother gets it."

Startled, he snatched for the envelope, missed and settled for holding out his hand. "I'd rather deliver it myself."

She pressed the envelope to her breast. What horrible news was he trying to keep from her? "I'm not a child. If there's trouble, I can handle it."

Ma fretted, "What is it? Did your father leave some instructions for Hendrick?"

Perspiration dotted Brandon's upper lip despite the freezing temperatures. "I'm sorry. My father should have informed you. Someone should have informed you." His gaze landed on Anna for a second before flitting away.

"Informed us of what?" asked Ma.

Brandon shifted uncomfortably. "I believe it would be best if *I* deliver the letter to your brother."

He held out his hand again.

Why did he want this so badly? He must be trying to hide something from her. Anna hesitated long enough to notice that the envelope came from a law firm in Detroit and was addressed to the Simmons family at 502 Main Street in Pearlman, Michigan. Well, she was a member of the Simmons family. She had every right to see this letter too.

She ripped open the envelope. Ma gasped and fluttered her hands with a cry of protest, but Anna would not be deterred. Brandon paled when she pulled out the single sheet of paper. She was right. He was trying to hide something.

"Anna," Ma reprimanded sharply. "That's meant for Hendrick."

"It's addressed to all of us, the Simmons family, and that includes me."

"Please don't," Brandon pleaded, his palm open.

Anna paid him no notice. She had to know what that letter said. She carried it into the kitchen where there was more light, but as soon as she read the first line, she wished she'd let Brandon Landers give the letter to her brother. She heard the front door open and close.

Ma joined her moments later. "Anna, that was rude. Mr. Landers meant that letter for your brother. I had to assure him I would deliver it to Hendrick tonight, but he wasn't happy, not at all."

"I don't care how he feels. He certainly doesn't care about us." Anna dropped the letter on the table. She couldn't hold it a moment longer. She'd thought Brandon Landers was a hero, but he'd turned out to be the worst sort of villain. "He's evicting us."

Brandon stared at the telephone dial while he waited for his father's attorney to pick up the line on the other end.

The letters and numbers in their brass circles blurred. He leaned his elbows on the desktop and rubbed the fog from his eyes. Should have got more sleep last night. Should have thought of a solution.

Instead, he'd paced all night trying to find a way to keep the Simmonses in the house they'd rented for almost three decades. Mrs. Simmons understood why they had to leave. She'd listened patiently as he explained the terms of the sale his father had negotiated, but her quiet resolve only made him feel worse. He had to help them.

First, he would try to persuade the new owner to extend the deadline.

"MacKenzie here." The brusque voice of his father's longtime attorney and executor came on the other end. "What can I do for you, Brandon?"

He hated the attorney's familiar tone, as if he were part of the family. Perhaps he had wiggled his fingers into Father's business. Maybe that's where the money had disappeared. His purchase of the Simmons property was certainly suspicious. He'd said it was just a business venture, that he wanted to open an automobile dealership, that Brandon's father had made the deal before he'd died, but the man was Father's attorney and executor. The whole thing smelled rotten. Unfortunately, Brandon had no proof of wrongdoing.

"I need an extension on the Pearlman property on Main and First." He took a deep breath.

A pause followed. "What sort of extension?"

After weeks of dealing with the attorney, Brandon knew he couldn't push much. But any little bit would help. "The tenants need more time."

"You know the contract terms."

Brandon choked back his impatience. "It's an elderly woman and her daughter. You can't put them out at Christmas."

MacKenzie barely paused. "Your father insisted on those terms."

Brandon didn't believe that for a minute. "Why? It doesn't make any sense. Not only was he keeping the rent unbelievably low, but he sent frequent payments to the family, so why would he sell under such unreasonable terms?"

"Only your father knows."

"Perfect. And he's dead." Once again Brandon choked back his impatience with the slick attorney. "Suppose you make an educated guess."

"I'm not in the business of speculation, nor would it have been appropriate for him to confide in the buyer."

Brandon dug the nib of his pen into the blotter. A trace of ink bled into the fibers, making an ugly black mark. "But I can't force Anna—that is, the tenants—from their home."

"Then refund the purchase price."

Brandon growled, "From what you've told me, that money was spent. Or did my father have you hide it somewhere?"

"I object to your inference," MacKenzie retorted. "The contract is ironclad. Fulfill the terms or don't. The option is yours."

"But I don't have the money."

A pregnant silence followed. "My offer stands. Sign over the deed to your house, and I'll hand you the property on Main and First."

Brandon suspected that's what MacKenzie wanted all along. "This was never a business venture. You want my house. Well, you won't get it. A Landers built this house, and a Landers will always own it."

A click on the line signaled an end to the conversation. Brandon hung the receiver on the cradle and buried his head in his hands. He'd let temper get the better of him and solved nothing.

Lifting his head, he stared dully at the room, hoping for

an answer. The library had always been his favorite place in the family's summer home. The paneled walls and floor-to-ceiling bookcases had fueled his imagination. He'd spent hours dreaming of secret passages and hidden rooms and poking into every nook and corner without success.

It would be nice if those walls did hide a fortune in gold, but of course the house held no secrets and offered no money.

He slipped the sales contract back into its folder. MacKenzie had mentioned the only possible solution, but Brandon couldn't give up this house. It and the bookstore were his future.

Brandon ran a hand through his hair. Somehow he had to help Anna and her mother. He pulled the ledger close and stared at the gloomy figures. He had the house, and his brother had been provided for in an untouchable trust, but the rest of the money was gone. With no income and insufficient savings, the best he could do was find Anna and her mother a decent house to rent.

Too bad they couldn't live here. The house was certainly big enough for two more people. Originally built in the late 1840s, it had undergone so many additions and reconstructions that few people could find the original rooms. Years of neglect had left the heavy velvet drapes white with dust. The dark walnut furniture could use a good oiling to restore the wood's sheen. At least the sage green wool carpet was in good condition. A relatively recent addition, it had seen no activity after the year he turned eighteen, when the family stopped coming here.

Even before that, the long summers of his youth had trickled to a week or two each year, but after the summer his mother died, no one came back. Now this musty old house was his. No money to keep it up, nothing but dust and cobwebs. He'd have to hire a housekeeper; one who wouldn't charge too much, considering his cash had sunk to a pitiful low. Anna's waves of light brown hair floated to mind, and with it came a thought. She cleaned houses. As quickly as he thought of it, he set the idea aside. It wouldn't work. A young woman and a bachelor? Tongues would wag.

If not Anna, then perhaps her mother would take the position. That minister had said her hours had just been reduced. It was the perfect solution. They could live here.

The idea took root and flowered as he imagined Anna sitting by the fireplace, her blue eyes dancing with excitement as he told her about the latest discoveries in the Valley of the Kings. She'd turn toward him, smile and ask his opinion.

He shook his head. What nonsense! The girl couldn't possibly find him attractive. What's more, she'd never agree to live in this house. Even with her mother here, it was too scandalous.

He stared bleakly out the window. Trees lifted their bony limbs to the sky, anxious for the first coat of white. Brown leaves scurried across the brown lawn. The colorless, lifeless landscape sucked any fragments of hope from his soul.

Then a single ray of sunshine highlighted the answer.

The carriage house. Of course.

He shot to his feet. It just might work.

Without bothering to put the ledger back in the desk, he hurried to the front entry and donned his coat, hat and gloves. He could help Anna and her mother after all.

Chapter Three

"Don't worry," Ma said with a pat to Anna's arm. "The Lord will provide."

Anna bit back a growl of frustration and rose from the kitchen table, the eviction letter in her hand. She'd spent yesterday evening and all morning trying to get her mother to commit to leasing a room at either Terchie's Boarding-house or above the drugstore, but Ma would not settle for less than a house.

"For the hundredth time, we can't afford a house. If you won't decide, then I will. We're moving to Terchie's, and that's that."

She crumpled the vile letter, and tossed it into the stove's firebox.

Ma looked up from her grocery list. "Should you have done that, dearest?"

Though Ma had explained that Brandon's father was the one who'd sold the house, Anna couldn't forgive Brandon. He could have renegotiated or done something to change the outcome. After all, he was rich. Instead, he was forcing them from their home at Christmastime.

"We only have twelve days." Anna laughed bitterly at

the irony. "The twelve days of Christmas, only instead of receiving gifts, we'll sell our belongings."

"Why on earth would we do that?"

"Because they'll never fit into a boardinghouse room."

Pans and dishes filled the kitchen cupboards. Every closet contained linens and clothes and coats and galoshes. And that didn't even include the attic. Ma had never thrown out Papa's things. She'd packed them into trunks, which then went into the attic. None of it would fetch more than pennies, but they couldn't take it with them.

"We'll hold a sale this Saturday," Anna stated. "It will be a lot of work, but we can use the money. We'll put everything we can lift into the living room, and Hendrick and Peter can move the rest."

"Slow down, dearest. There's no need to get rid of anything. We have plenty of time to find a house. Besides, this coming Saturday is just two days before Christmas. We can't hold a sale then."

"Yes, we can. It's the perfect time."

"But you can't mean to sell your father's gifts."

Anna choked back tears at the thought of parting with the dolls Papa had given her, but they didn't have room for sentimental treasures. "Maybe someone who can't afford new toys this year can get something from us." She wiped a tear from her eye. "It's time a little girl used my old dolls. I won't be having children anytime soon."

"Oh, my darling girl. All things in good time. There's no need to sacrifice your dolls just yet. If we don't find a house right away, perhaps Mariah and Hendrick will keep them for us at the orphanage."

"Maybe," Anna mumbled, ashamed she hadn't thought of that solution. "The girls there could enjoy them." She wiped her tears on her sleeve. "But there are still the rest of our things. They won't fit into a single room."

"Have patience. There's no need to lease a room just yet," Ma insisted. "The Lord will provide exactly what we need."

"What and how? Tell me exactly, because I don't see it."

"Through faith."

"Faith?" Anna pressed a hand to her throbbing forehead. "Faith is fine, Ma, but God expects us to act. We need to leave this house in twelve days. That's a fact. We haven't leased another place to stay. That's another fact. I don't see a grand house out there with our name on the signpost, and even if there was, we couldn't afford it. No, we have to rent a room. Terchie's Boardinghouse is the best option. If something comes up later, we can move again."

Ma's shoulders slumped. "Can't we wait a bit?"

"No, we can't. Nor can we expect Hendrick and Mariah to house all our belongings. The orphanage is overfull as it is, and the factory is still under construction. Neither has room for old pots and pans. We'll hold a sale."

Ma's hand shook as she lifted a tin soldier from the shelf above the table. From Anna's favorite doll to Papa's anniversary gifts to Ma, this shelf traced a lifetime of memories. The toy soldier's paint had flecked off long ago. "Your father gave this to your brother on his seventh birthday—before you were born," Ma mused. "He saved every penny so he could buy it. Hendrick loved this soldier. He should have it." She cupped the toy in the palm of her hand. "Your brother wanted to join the war, but I was so grateful they wouldn't let him enlist." Tears misted her eyes.

Now she'd done it. Anna hadn't meant to make her mother cry.

"I'm sorry, Ma." Anna wrapped her arms around her mother's shoulders.

"Good memories." Ma kissed the top of her head. "I pray you find as wonderful a man as I did."

Ma still missed Papa terribly, even after so many years. "I don't think there's anyone as wonderful as Papa."

"I'm sure there is. He'd be good and caring. He'd value honor and integrity, and he'd love you above all but God."

For a moment, Anna allowed herself to sink into girlish dreams. "And he'd be handsome."

Ma stroked her hair. "Of course he would be. Take Mr. Brandon, for example. He's quite handsome."

Anna pulled out of her mother's arms. "No, he's not." Though she could hardly take her eyes from him, she wouldn't admit it to anyone, especially since he'd proven heartless and cruel. "His nose is too large."

"It's perfectly proportioned."

"His eyes are too close together."

"I found them quite nicely spaced. Deep blue too."

"Not blue. They're gray."

"Ah," Ma said softly, "I must have been mistaken. But you can't deny he carries himself well. So strong and commanding."

"He limps and has to use a cane."

Ma clucked her tongue. "Anna Marie, that's unkind. He suffered an injury. Why, as a boy he ran around like any other child. He must have been hurt in the Great War. That's something to respect, not turn your nose up at."

"But he doesn't respect us." An angry tear rolled down her cheek. She could forgive his infirmities but not his actions. "If he really cared, he wouldn't evict us from our home."

"Hush, dear. He is simply doing what he must. We are tenants and have no claim on this house. I always knew this day might come."

"You did?"

Ma looked off into space, lost in the past. "Your father sold this property and his portion of the business to Brandon's father years ago. I'm afraid your papa wasn't a very good businessman." Ma smiled softly. "But I loved him still. He had a heart of gold, would give to anyone who asked for help, even if they didn't deserve it. I'm afraid some took advantage of him."

"Like Mr. Landers."

Ma shook her head. "Mr. Landers was simply doing what any businessman would do. Don't blame others for our own faults." She ran a finger down Anna's cheek, wiping dry the track of a tear. "Your father knew that riches in this life did not matter."

Anna wasn't so sure. A decent income would get them out of this predicament. "What about Mr. Thompson? Maybe he can help us. Didn't he own part of the business?"

Ma shook her head. "When your father and Mr. Thompson started the garage, your papa took out the loan for both properties. Mr. Thompson worked for him. He never owned a share of the business, even though your father called him a partner."

Anna's heart sank. Was there no way they could keep the house?

"Sales weren't too brisk that first year. Before long your father began to miss loan payments. The bank held off foreclosing until your father could find investors. The only man willing to invest was Percival Landers, Brandon's father. If not for him, we wouldn't have had this house and the garage for all these years."

"Brandon's father owned the garage too? Did he sell that? Is Hendrick out of work?"

"Both properties sold," Ma said, "but the new owner wants to keep the garage open."

At least her brother would have an income until the factory turned a profit. "I still don't understand why we have to leave. You would think the new owner would want the rental income."

Ma sighed. "Percival Landers charged a very low rent."

"Are you saying he gave us charity?"

"Mr. Landers treated us with Christian kindness, especially after your father's death. I can't count the times he helped Hendrick keep the garage going. You can't blame him for selling the property."

Anna could. Ma might call it Christian kindness, but it didn't sound like it to her. No wonder Hendrick wanted to strike out on his own. No wonder he wanted to make a go of it with his factory. At least he could call it his.

"We're poor." Though she'd always known it, saying the word stung.

"No, dearest. We're richer than the wealthiest man alive, for we have each other and we have God's love."

Anna did not point out that the richest man on earth might also have a family and love God.

Ma offered a gentle smile. Despite losing the love of her life when Papa died, she'd never spoken a word of regret. She gave to all who needed consoling and spent many hours at bedsides and baking for the bereaved.

How blessed Anna was to have her for a mother. She bit her lip to stem the tears, but a sniffle escaped nonetheless. If Ma could stay positive, so could she. "Then we'll be the richest people at Terchie's."

Ma laughed, her cheeks rounding, and Anna couldn't help but smile. Somehow, some way, they'd survive.

"I love you, Ma, and I'm sorry for getting upset."

"I know, dearest, and I'm sorry I—" A sharp rap on the front door interrupted her midsentence. "Are you expecting someone?"

"No." Anna pulled herself to her feet. A hundred worries bounced through her head, but this time she wouldn't let them take root. "I'll see who it is."

She opened the front door. There stood Brandon Landers, his gray eyes dark and his expression unreadable. She flushed at the sight of his perfectly proportioned nose and nicely spaced eyes.

"Miss Simmons."

"Mr. Landers." She ducked her head to hide her reddening cheeks. Why was she reacting this way? He was the *enemy*.

"Is your mother here?"

He looked into her eyes just for a second, but that single glance did her in. Every thought fled her mind.

"Mr. Brandon," Ma said as she wiggled beside Anna. "It's so good to see you again. Would you like to come in?"

"No. I think not." He cleared his throat. "I have a proposition for you." Again he glanced at Anna. Again her pulse raced. "The Landers property includes a carriage house. Perhaps you're acquainted with it?"

Anna nodded dumbly. She'd passed by the Landers estate many a time and as a child dreamed of stepping inside the house that looked like a castle. The gray stone walls and verdigris roof could have graced an English country house. A fence of stone shrouded the property from view, but she'd climbed that fence as a child and had walked its length, dreaming of one day exploring the pretty little carriage house with its dusty windows and the big old house that simply had to contain secret passages.

Brandon cleared his throat, pulling Anna back to the present. "Good, good. Perhaps you aren't aware that it contains a small apartment, quite small, smaller than this bungalow and much older, but it might suffice."

Anna blinked. "Suffice for what?"

"For you. Both of you. You said your brother lives elsewhere."

"As does Peter, my foster son," said Ma. "They both live at Constance House."

He nodded solemnly. "Good. It's only large enough for two. One bedchamber, a small sitting room and a washroom. Would that be adequate?"

"More than adequate," Ma bubbled. "We don't need much space now that my boys are gone."

Anna stared at her mother. Hadn't she just claimed the opposite? "Where would we cook our meals?"

"You may use the kitchen in the house. It has a separate entrance."

"Perfect." Ma clapped her hands together. "We accept."

"Good," he said. "Then it's settled."

Anna shook her head, trying to grapple with what he was saying. "You're offering to lease us your carriage house?"

"Just the apartment and it wouldn't be a lease."

Anna dropped her gaze. "We can't afford to buy."

"No, you misunderstand me." He shuffled slightly, placing his weight on the stronger leg. "It seems we each have a need. You need a place to live, and I need a housekeeper. If you are agreeable to the arrangement, I would like to offer you the use of the apartment in exchange for housekeeping services. Two or three times a week should be sufficient."

Housekeeping? He wanted her to clean his house? When he'd taken her side against Sally, she'd thought he understood how demeaning it was to be a servant. Apparently not. He was just like the rest of the rich people who lived on the hill.

"You want me to clean your house?" Anna sputtered.

He flushed. "Certainly not. That would be highly inappropriate. I was hoping Mrs. Simmons would take the position. You should be able to fit it in around your other work."

Ma wasted no time agreeing to the plan. "That would be wonderful. Oh, Mr. Brandon, how can we ever thank you? Of course we'll take it. It's perfect, isn't it, Anna?"

Perfect? Living on Brandon Landers's charity? Living in what must be servants' quarters? It wasn't perfect; it was humiliating.

"No, thank you," Anna said stiffly. "We can't accept. It's quite out of the question."

"But Anna," Ma said.

She couldn't stand to even look at the man. First he had forced Ma and her from their home, and now he wanted to make them his servants. How dare he?

Without a word more, she slammed the door in his face.

Ma gasped, but Anna couldn't let her mother's desire for a larger home put them into servitude.

"I'm sorry, Ma. But we can't live there. It's not right."

"Why not? It's the answer to my prayers."

Anna cringed. Prayer had not brought Brandon Landers into their lives. He only cared about money. Any man with an ounce of compassion would not first evict them and then make them his servants.

She stormed into the kitchen. "I'm done discussing this, Ma. I will never live in Brandon Landers's carriage house, and I certainly won't have you cleaning his house."

"But it's a place to live at no cost."

Anna saw the pain in Ma's eyes, but she couldn't subjugate herself, not even for Ma. "We'll find something else."

She angrily pulled pans from the cupboard. They all had to be sold. Moreover, the clatter overwhelmed Ma's soft voice. After frequent attempts to speak, her mother gave up and left the room.

Fine. Let Ma stew about it. It wouldn't change her mind. Yes, she did feel a bit guilty that she'd upset Ma. After all, she was supposed to honor her mother, but Ma couldn't seriously expect her to accept charity from the man who'd evicted them. She pulled another pan from the cupboard.

The front door slammed shut.

"Ma?"

No answer.

Where was she going?

Anna set the pan on the table and walked to the front window where she spotted her mother hurrying down the sidewalk toward Brandon's car. Judging by the way she was waving, she was about to accept the deal that Anna had just rejected. Brandon didn't seem to notice her, for he got into his sleek black Cadillac.

That didn't stop Ma. She ran out into the street.

Anna raced out onto the stoop. A light mist was freezing on the trees and bushes. She started to call out to her mother, but the words caught in her throat when she saw Brandon drive forward.

In horrible slowness, like individual frames in a film, Ma slipped and fell—directly in front of Brandon's car.

Brandon didn't see Mrs. Simmons until it was too late. He was still steaming over Anna's blunt refusal. No one had ever slammed a door in his face, especially not when he'd just made a generous offer. He was trying to help thcm. Couldn't she see that?

He'd stormed to the car, and, after several misfires, finally got it started. To be honest, he hadn't even looked for traffic before inching forward. Then he pressed hard on the accelerator, anxious to leave this debacle behind.

Out of the corner of his eye, he saw movement. At first, it didn't register. Then he realized Mrs. Simmons was waving at him. She stepped into the street, and her feet shot out from under her. Down she fell, directly in front of his car.

He swerved and applied the brake, but the road was icy, and the tires skidded.

Please, no. Not again.

Every detail of the war came back. The acrid smell, the dull thud of artillery in the distance, the sharp fear. He'd led his men into the shelled town as directed. Nothing lived there, not even grass. Mud had swallowed the streets. Artillery had demolished the buildings. It had looked like hell, felt like hell, and would surely be his hell for all eternity.

A slight movement to the right had caught his attention. He'd turned, expecting to see the commander he was supposed to meet. Instead, shells rained down. His men scattered. He yelled for them to retreat, but they either could not or would not hear. Helpless, he watched as one by one they fell.

Just like Mrs. Simmons.

Anna screamed, unable to move.

Her mother was going to die, just like Papa had died all those years ago. She'd watched him working on a truck from her hiding place in the pile of tires. Only his legs showed. He lay under a truck that was up on a jack, its wheels off on that side. He yelled for Mr. Thompson, but his fellow mechanic wasn't there, and for a second Anna almost went to him. But she was supposed to be in school, and if she helped him, he'd know she'd skipped class, so she stayed in the tires.

He banged again, and the jack collapsed. The truck fell to the ground. Papa cried out. Once. Then silence. Just a pool of red running out from under the vehicle.

Not again.

The car's brakes squealed. The wheels locked and the vehicle skidded. Closer and closer it came until Anna knew Ma would die.

She closed her eyes and turned away. She couldn't watch.

But then, just like when Papa died, she looked back. She had to look. She had to know.

This time, she didn't see the pool of red blood. The car shuddered to a stop mere feet from Ma.

Thank God. Anna breathed out in relief. Then she noticed her mother wasn't moving.

Brandon flung open his door and clambered out. He lost his balance and grabbed the car for support. Spotting Anna, he yelled, "Call for a doctor."

A doctor? Anna's heart stuck in her throat. Ma must be hurt. Or worse. Fear froze her to the stoop as Brandon inched forward on the icy road. She couldn't move and couldn't stop watching.

At last he reached Ma. While holding onto the car's hood, he leaned over and extended a hand. When she reached up, Anna breathed again. Ma hadn't died. She was just hurt.

Brandon took Ma's hand and attempted to help her to her feet, but they both fell. At last, Anna found her legs.

"Ma!" She hurried across the yard and onto the street. "Are you hurt?"

Her mother's face was pale as snow, but she still managed a smile. "I'm so sorry. I didn't mean to make more trouble for you."

Anna could have wept. She was the one making trouble. If not for her foolish pride, Ma would never have run after Brandon.

He took command. "Let's get her into the house. You take the right side, and I'll take the left. I believe your mother hurt her leg."

Though Ma fussed that she was fine, she winced when Brandon started to lift her. He stopped, but she urged them on. "It's nothing. Just an old woman's aches and pains."

Anna hated to hear her mother call herself old. "You can make it, Ma."

Together, she and Brandon managed to get Ma to her feet.

"Use my cane to steady yourself." Brandon pushed the walking stick into her hand. "Don't put any weight on your injured leg."

Anna held her mother around the waist while Brandon propped her up with an arm under her shoulders. As they moved toward the house, his hand accidentally brushed Anna's neck, and she shivered, but not from the cold.

By the time they reached the stoop, the neighbors had arrived, and Peter hurried over from the garage. He took over Anna's position, and the two men got Ma into the house.

"Miss Simmons, I suggest you call a doctor," Brandon repeated as they settled Ma on the living-room sofa.

He'd asked her to do that earlier, when she froze. But she couldn't call. They had no telephone.

He mistook her lack of response. "If it's a matter of cost, I'll pay the bill."

She shook her head and asked Peter to make the call from the garage. He hurried off while Anna fetched a blanket and a cup of hot tea.

"Stop fussing, dear," Ma chided as Anna wrapped the blanket around her. "I'm quite all right."

"You haven't moved your left leg," Anna said. "Does it hurt?"

Ma sighed and leaned her head back. "Not much at all. Just give me a moment to collect myself."

Brandon motioned for Anna to join him at the front door, within sight of her mother yet beyond earshot. "I believe she may have sprained or broken her ankle."

Anna's heart still thudded wildly after all the excitement, but it practically stopped at his words. She glanced back at her mother, whose face was still pale and drawn. Broken bones were not good for a woman Ma's age. What if they never healed?

She felt a touch to her shoulder and looked up.

Brandon gazed at her with deep concern. "Don't worry. Your mother will be fine. She's a strong woman."

"I hope you're right."

A knock on the door signaled Doc Stevens's arrival. After a quick recounting of what had happened, he tended to Ma while Anna hovered anxiously. Ma flinched slightly when he examined her. Others might not notice, but Anna could tell she was in pain.

"No broken bones that I can discern," the doctor said as he closed his bag. "We could get an X-ray in Grand Rapids. Are you able to make the train trip?"

"I can drive her there," Brandon offered.

Anna shook her head. There was no money for X-rays, and she wouldn't be beholden to Brandon Landers any more than she already was. "Will she heal if we don't?"

The doctor nodded as Brandon quietly slipped out of the room. "Nothing's displaced. Keep her in bed and off her feet. If she must go somewhere, use a crutch to keep all weight off the leg. No work or housework for at least a month."

"A month?" Anna gasped. They had to move in only twelve days. How would she manage on her own? She gnawed her fingernails. Hendrick and Peter would have to help.

"It's a good thing your house is single-story," the doctor said. "I don't want your mother climbing stairs."

But Terchie's Boardinghouse only had upstairs rooms. How could they move there if Ma couldn't climb stairs?

"I've given her a sedative," Doc Stevens continued. "If the pain gets worse, I'll prescribe tincture of opium. Call if she develops a fever or if the swelling doesn't go down in a few days."

After thanking him and sending Peter back to the garage, Anna looked in on her mother, who had fallen asleep, and was surprised to find Brandon in the room. He'd closed the drapes and tucked a pillow beneath Ma's head. Anna's throat constricted. Why was he being so nice? Guilt? That must be it. After all, he was the one who'd precipitated all of this with his impossible offer.

He rose and walked softly from the room, joining her at the front entry.

"You stayed." She whispered the words as an accusation, but part of her was also glad. How could this man both tempt and frustrate her at the same time?

Sadness swept across his features, and he gazed far beyond her into the distant past. "My mother died when I was younger than you. I know how frightening it can be to think you might lose a parent." He swallowed and returned to the present. "I'm sorry, so sorry."

Her wall of anger cracked. He did know how she felt. In fact, he'd suffered more, for both his mother and father were gone. She'd called him insensitive but she was the one who hadn't given him a chance.

"No, I'm sorry." She nipped her lip to stem the sudden swell of emotion. "I shouldn't have reacted so strongly. You meant well by offering us your apartment."

His gaze dropped again. "The fault is mine. I should have realized the offer would insult you."

She shook her head. "I was acting childishly, thinking only of myself." A little sob escaped. "I should have considered Ma. She wants to stay in the carriage house. She believes God ordained it."

He stiffened slightly. "I doubt divine intervention, but the offer still stands."

"But Ma can't work, and I won't accept charity."

"I know." The faintest smile briefly lifted his lips. "Perhaps you would be willing to clean until she recovers."

Anna shook her head. "It's not proper."

"I've been considering that. There's an old wheelchair in the attic. Perhaps if your mother came to the house with you..."

Anna paused, trying to regain control of her senses. His plan made sense, but he stood too close, the raw scent of him muddling her mind. She stepped back and was relieved when he didn't follow. At this moment, she needed to think clearly.

Ma had to live somewhere without stairs. The carriage house was a single-story building. It didn't have any stairs. Presumably the house could also be entered without climbing steps or he wouldn't have suggested Ma supervise from the wheelchair. She had to put her mother's needs first.

"You said you required housekeeping just two or three days a week?"

He nodded. "And prepare breakfast and supper."

That wasn't part of the original agreement, but she couldn't quibble over details when Ma needed a warm single-story place to live. He'd regret that addition when he tasted her cooking. "Then thank you. I accept."

For a month. Then she and Ma would move as far as possible from the man who sent her nerves fluttering every time he drew near.

Chapter Four

"It's perfect," Ma exclaimed as Brandon pushed her wheelchair into the tiny carriage-house apartment.

Anna could think of many other ways to describe the cramped rooms. Musty, cool and damp came readily to mind, but for Ma's sake she held her tongue and walked into the sitting room. Two windows faced the house. Under one sat a small wooden table and chairs.

She pushed open the dusty curtain and a cobweb drifted onto her face. She swatted away the sticky threads. If this apartment was any indication, she'd be working full-time getting the house in order.

"It *is* lovely." Ma patted Brandon's hand. "Thank you for the use of the wheelchair. I can manage from here."

"Not on my watch, ma'am." Brandon hastened to help Ma out of the cane wheelchair and into one of the two armchairs by the fireplace. A cloud of dust motes rose when she sat.

"Here's a cane to help you get around." Brandon placed a stout walnut cane against the side of the chair, within ready reach should Ma need to walk. "I apologize again for the privy."

Ma waved a hand. "I've used privies and chamber pots my entire life."

"Still, with your injury," he murmured, "it's an inconvenience. Please consider staying in the house. It has indoor plumbing."

"I'll be just fine." Ma clucked her tongue softly. "This is so cozy. We're looking forward to settling in here, aren't we, Anna?"

Anna poked at the embers in the fireplace and added another log. "Is this the only source of heat?"

Brandon looked pained. "There are only the two rooms. The fire should be sufficient to heat both."

"Of course it will," Ma seconded.

"Too bad there's not a kitchen," Anna said.

Brandon cleared his throat. "This apartment was built at the same time as the house, in the 1840s. No one thought to put a kitchen in an apartment in those days."

Probably because the apartment was intended for servants. Anna pushed the bedroom door open. This room was even smaller than the sitting room, with the back left corner walled off into a closet. She stepped around the bed that she and Ma would have to share and opened the closet door. None of the rooms had electrical lighting. That made it difficult to see the small iron sink in the back corner. It had a pump to draw water. She tested the squeaky handle and with a few pumps cold, clear water gushed into the sink. Across from the sink, a rack had been nailed to the wall. Perhaps ten or twelve garments could be squeezed onto it.

"I hope it will suffice." Brandon stood anxiously between the bed and the heavy chest of drawers. "I wish I could fit two beds into the room, but the man I hired to open up the place assured me the space was too small."

"Yet someone added a sink."

He nervously swiped at his face. "Sometime before the turn of the century. It was probably the height of luxury at the time."

Anna couldn't do more than nod at his attempted levity. She rubbed her arms. "It's cold in here. I hope the pipe doesn't freeze."

Brandon reached around her and pushed the closet door completely open. The brush of his arm sent an unbidden yet pleasant sensation down her back.

"If it does," he said, "let me know. I'll hire someone to fix it. In fact, if anything breaks or doesn't work—any problem at all—tell me."

Though she kept her gaze locked on the clothes rack, she could feel him near.

He tipped her chin so she looked up into those stormy gray eyes. "I mean it, Anna. If you need anything, tell me. Anything at all."

His touch stole her breath. They were alone. Ma faced the fire in the other room and could hear but not see them. Anna's heart pounded wildly. Was he going to kiss her? Impossible. They'd barely been civil to each other these past two days. Yet he'd just touched her, and that touch made her knees tremble. What would it feel like to be kissed? What if she did it wrong? She'd read about it in novels, but no man had ever kissed her.

She let her lids drift almost shut, terribly conscious of how close his lips were to hers. Mere inches. And he smelled…well…masculine.

"Good." He cleared his throat and stepped away. "I'm glad that's cleared up."

What had happened? Why hadn't he kissed her? Her chin still burned where he'd touched it. She unconsciously rubbed the spot as she followed him into the sitting room. He stooped to talk to Ma in tones Anna couldn't hear.

"Hendrick will bring our things over this afternoon," Ma answered, her voice honey smooth.

Clearly she adored Brandon. Every gesture, every concession told Anna so. For whatever reason, this was where Ma wanted to settle, and she would apparently put up with a great deal of deprivation and discomfort to do so.

"Now give me a hug before you go," Ma commanded.

"Ma," Anna chided. "Mr. Landers is practically a stranger."

"You know the saying: strangers are just friends we've yet to meet. Mr. Brandon and I have met, therefore we're friends."

A smile softened Brandon's stern expression. Clearly he had a soft spot for Ma too. Most people did.

He bent obediently and gave her the required hug. "Please call me Brandon. Mister is a bit formal for friends, don't you think?"

Ma laughed as she patted him on the back. "I'll try. I hope you visit here often." She winked at Anna. "Though I'm sure you'll have plenty of time to chat with my Anna while she cleans your house."

Anna stared at her mother. "You'll be there too."

"Now, I don't see why that's necessary. Mr. Brandon is a gentleman."

So, that was it. Ma was matchmaking. Had her mother seen how close he'd come to kissing her? Heat rose into her cheeks, and Brandon couldn't possibly mistake the redness for anything but a blush.

His stiff response left no doubt how he felt. "I'll be busy with the bookstore. I'll leave the house early and return late." His glance flitted past her. "I suggest you finish your work by six o'clock. Set breakfast in the dining room. Supper can be left in the warming oven." His tone made it perfectly clear that he saw her as his housekeeper and nothing more.

Then what had happened in the closet? Or had she been the only one to feel it? Apparently so. It was the same old story. She always fell for the wrong man, and she'd done it again.

Brandon donned his coat and hat. "You may start tomorrow, Miss Simmons."

Anna nodded curtly. "Yes, sir, *Mr.* Landers."

She'd never again make the mistake of liking him.

Brandon should never have brought Anna to the carriage house. She smelled of cinnamon, sweet yet sharp. Try as he might, he couldn't get that scent out of his mind. That little episode in the closet washroom had only confirmed what he already knew.

He was attracted to her.

Add the very real complication that he'd also hired her to clean his house, and he'd have to work hard to avoid her.

He opened the door to the Cadillac and settled behind the wheel. The solution was clear. Hard labor would erase this ridiculous emotion, and he did have plenty of work to do. The storefront needed an overhaul before he could sell one book.

He put the automobile in gear and pulled away from the source of discomfort. A few hours in the shop would cast away this confusion.

Early to work and late returning home. If he kept to that schedule, their paths would seldom cross.

With a smile of satisfaction, he parked in front of his shop. First order of business would be finding a carpenter. He got out of the car and crossed the boardwalk to the front door. With a turn of the key and a push of the latch, the door opened.

The room looked no better today, but in the soft morning light, he could envision shelves of books and a sales counter of polished oak.

A carpenter could make that happen. Unfortunately, the

man who'd outfitted the carriage-house apartment didn't work with wood. He'd suggested a Mr. Lyle Hammond, who might be coaxed out of retirement at the right price. Unfortunately, money was the one thing Brandon lacked. He needed an inexpensive carpenter, such as a youth.

That pastor had said he could pass the word. No one knew a town's inhabitants more than a minister. Maybe Brandon would take the man up on his offer—as long as the pastor steered clear of anyone named Simmons.

Brandon glanced across the street at the cheery little church. Its oak door and railing had been festooned with evergreens and bright red ribbons that fluttered in the icy breeze. No pretentious stained glass graced the front. Instead, an ordinary window looked out on the street. Brandon liked that homey feeling. A church that didn't put on airs matched the minister who walked through town in a mackinaw coat. If Brandon wasn't on such bad terms with God, he might be tempted to try the service one Sunday.

As if on cue, the easygoing pastor exited the church and headed directly across the street toward him. The man whistled, hands in pockets, until a Model T passed. Then he waved to the driver, calling out a cheery greeting. With a skip, he hopped up onto the boardwalk and strode toward Brandon's shop. After another wave at a passerby, he bounded inside.

"Good morning," Pastor Gabe said as he closed the door. "What a gorgeous day. Perfect for moving."

Brandon stared. Did the man know everything that happened in this town?

"I wanted to thank you in person," the pastor continued. "Ma Simmons is delighted that they can stay in your carriage house. She went on and on about how perfect it was."

"Ma?" Brandon had to ask. "Are you married to one of her daughters?"

Gabe chuckled. "Anna's her only daughter, but in a roundabout way I am related to Mrs. Simmons. My sister married her son Hendrick. We're all one extended family. In fact, we offered the guest bedroom at the parsonage and my sister offered a room at the orphanage, but Ma insisted the Lord wanted them to live at your carriage house. She couldn't be persuaded otherwise. That's the way Ma is. Once she sets her mind on something, no one can talk her out of it."

Brandon's head spun. Sisters and brothers, parsonage and orphanage. It all muddled together. "How many family members are there?"

Gabe laughed. "I can see how confusing it would be. Why don't you join us for dinner after Sunday worship? Then you can meet the whole clan."

After worship? God wouldn't want him in His house, not after what Brandon had done. "I'm busy."

"Heading home for Christmas?"

Though agreeing would end the conversation, Brandon couldn't lie. "This is home." At least it was now.

"Then your family is coming here. Please, invite them too. The more the merrier." The pastor chuckled and added as an afterthought, "Though I suppose I should give my wife, Felicity, an idea how many to expect."

"I doubt my brother will visit."

The minister's brows drew together in puzzlement. "But Sunday is Christmas Eve. Surely you'll get together for Christmas."

The little hole in Brandon's heart that had started to open when Gabe first mentioned family now expanded into a painful gap. "I haven't celebrated Christmas since the war."

His leg had begun to ache after so much standing, and he shifted to place more of his weight on the cane. Though Brandon thought he'd moved discreetly, the pastor noticed.

"Then I insist you join us. We would be honored to include a war hero at our table."

Brandon's composure wavered for a second before he regained control. The pastor didn't know what had happened, and Brandon intended to keep it that way. "Thank you, no. I prefer to dine at home."

After a moment of surprise, the pastor nodded. "Too bad. Ma Simmons will be disappointed. She talks of you constantly, like you're family. And we could use help getting her into the house."

That did not make sense. By Brandon's count, at least two able-bodied men would be in attendance. "Isn't her son coming?"

"Yes, but the parsonage has a lot of steps to climb. Many hands make light work. Won't you reconsider?"

Brandon knew when he was being cajoled. Brutal honesty was the only way out. "I don't attend church services."

Pastor Gabe didn't even flinch, as if he knew that Brandon had strayed from the straight and narrow. "Church attendance isn't required, though you're always welcome. We're a family, sharing our joys and troubles, and our arms are always open. Come to worship if you wish. If not, you're still invited to dinner."

The pastor had effectively trapped Brandon. He fought his way out. "Christmas Eve is a time for family. You'll be exchanging gifts."

"Any gifts or tokens would be exchanged privately on Christmas Day. Sunday is for family."

"I'm not part of your family," Brandon pointed out.

"We're all part of God's family. You too." Gabe grabbed the door handle. "We'd love to have you. Two o'clock."

The man would not relent, but Brandon could be just as stubborn. Work came first, regardless of the day of the week or year. "I'll be busy getting this shop ready. It has to open early in January, the sooner the better. You said you knew someone who could do some carpentry. Perhaps a youth who's good with his hands?"

Gabe mused for a moment. "I think I know the perfect person. Come to dinner on Sunday, and I'll introduce you."

Brandon had been outmaneuvered. If he wanted help, he had to endure Sunday dinner. "Very well."

"Wonderful. We'll have a real celebration then." After a parting grin, Pastor Gabe took off down the sidewalk whistling "Blest Be the Tie That Binds."

Brandon shut the door on the hymn and the wily minister. He had no intention of celebrating on Christmas or ever. He didn't deserve to be happy, not when his men had died.

Unfortunately, the main house had fared little better than the carriage house. First thing the next morning, Anna stood alone at the entrance to the imposing parlor and surveyed the massive task ahead of her. The brass and silver had tarnished to such an extent that she doubted she could bring back the shine even if she polished for a month. Dust coated everything. Dampness had seeped into the very fibers of the wool carpets, leaving the place with the moldy smell of a cellar.

"It's impossible," she murmured.

"What's impossible?" Brandon's question made her jump. He stood in the hallway leading toward the back of the house, impeccably dressed in a dark gray suit, overcoat already on and cane in hand.

She backed into the doorway. The solid plaster walls gave her a sense of protection. "I'm sorry. I thought you'd left for the day. I didn't see your car." At least he hadn't mentioned the fact that she didn't make him breakfast this morning. The car had been gone by the time she'd dressed.

"I returned to fetch a book." He withdrew a slim volume

from his coat pocket to prove the point. "Which reminds me, I promised to lend you Davis's book. Follow me."

Clearly he was accustomed to commanding people. As she hurried after him, she recalled Ma's speculation about where he suffered his injury. "Were you an officer in the war?"

He stopped in his tracks. "My past is no concern of yours."

His glare sent icy shivers down her back. "I'm sorry. I didn't mean anything by it. I was just curious."

As quickly as it had come, his anger dissipated. "Apology accepted. However, I would appreciate it if in the future you could contain your curiosity about my personal life."

Anna swallowed hard. What had she said to set him off? She'd only asked if he was an officer. Maybe Ma was right about the injury. Maybe that's why he didn't want to talk about it.

"I will," she promised.

"Thank you. Now let's fetch Mr. Davis's report from the library."

His house had a library? Anna's pulse quickened. Libraries contained hidden passages and secret rooms. Everything interesting happened in libraries.

He strode down the hallway, his steps strong and confident with barely a hint of the limp. She followed, eager to see the room. The library. The word alone invited intrigue.

Brandon stopped at the third closed door on the right. "Wait here."

He ducked inside, and she barely saw the floor-to-ceiling books before the door shut behind him. Seconds later, he reappeared.

"Here it is." He handed her the slender volume. It had less than a hundred and fifty pages, and a lot of those were illustrations.

The Tombs of Harmhabi and Touatânkhamanou. She read the title, no doubt incorrectly pronouncing the unfamiliar words. "I thought this was about King Tutankhamun."

"It is." He pointed to the last word in the title. "Mr. Davis simply spelled it differently than the reporters do."

"Oh." Somehow the volume wasn't as exciting as the newspaper stories. She flipped to the title page and noticed the date of publication. "1912? Mr. Davis found the tomb ten years ago?"

"Actually, that's when the report was published. His work came earlier."

She couldn't hide her bewilderment. "Then why didn't he take the treasure?"

"Read it," Brandon urged.

He was deliberately holding back, and she could tell by the teasing smile on his lips that he had a surprise in store for her.

"We can discuss it when you're finished," he added. "We'll set aside an evening when you and your mother can come to the house for supper."

It sounded almost like a date, with Ma as chaperone.

She clutched the book tightly. "I'd like that. Maybe next week?"

His smile faded. "Perhaps. If the store's ready. Speaking of which, I'd best get back so you can work." Without further comment, he nodded farewell and departed into the wintry day.

Disappointed, she fingered the book. What had she said? One moment he wanted to talk over supper. The next he couldn't make time.

She turned toward the desolate house and the hard work that awaited her. Only then did the realization hit. He only saw her as a housekeeper. The offer to talk was meant to appease her and nothing more.

Anger flushed through her. He didn't care what she thought about the Egyptian excavations. If she wanted to gain his respect, she needed to make something of herself.

Tomorrow she'd take the train to Belvidere and apply at the cannery.

Chapter Five

Anna never took the train to Belvidere. Ma insisted they decorate the apartment for Christmas instead. Since her mother could barely walk, that left the work to Anna. She gathered pinecones and evergreen boughs, while Ma strung corn she'd popped over the fire. Branches of money plant added pearly white disks to the display. She stuck cloves into apples and hung them from old ribbons. Considering the decorations cost so little, Anna thought it looked pretty good.

"It's not as nice as home, though," she mused.

Ma looked up from her needlework. "This is home now."

"Are you sure no one will mind that I cut off some pine branches?" *No one* of course referred to Brandon, on whose property they'd gathered the boughs and cones and dried flowers.

"Mr. Brandon gave his permission. He even unlocked the garage doors so you could get a saw."

No matter how many times Ma reassured her, Anna still felt like a thief. They might live here, but only as guests.

Just walking into the garage portion of the carriage house had felt like an invasion of his privacy. As a child she'd often wondered what lay inside the thick stone walls. How disappointing to discover it contained the same things as every other outbuilding. In former days carriages must have been parked where he now kept his automobile. Along one wall stood a tool bench with dozens of old tools hanging from nails that had been pounded into a board attached to the plastered stone wall.

The plaster had been a surprise. It was to be expected in the apartment, but why would anyone plaster a garage? Yet someone in the past had done just that. Judging by the dingy film of dirt, dust and cobwebs, the plastering had been done years ago.

Anna had found a rusty old handsaw that managed to cut through thick boughs after jerking the teeth back and forth against the wood.

"I'm sorry I couldn't cut a tree for us," she apologized again to her mother.

"We don't need a big old tree in this little room. We'd never be able to walk around it. If you ask me, the branches are perfect. Smell the pine."

Anna inhaled deeply. The warmth of the fireplace had released the piney scent from the needles.

"It's wonderful," Ma said from her perch before the fireplace, her head back and eyes closed. "That smell always makes me think of Christmas." She chuckled, eyes still shut. "Remember when your father cut down that ten-foot-tall tree? He insisted on stuffing the thing into the living room. We had needles everywhere. I was still finding them in August."

"That must have been before I was born."

"I'm sure you were there, but maybe you were too little to remember." Ma sighed. "Such good memories."

Anna hoped her mother didn't get misty-eyed. "We'll start new memories."

"Yes, we will. And keep some of the old. That reminds me. I promised we'd bring plum duff for dinner tomorrow."

"Plum duff?" Anna couldn't hide her surprise. She loved the traditional steamed Christmas pudding, but Ma spent days preparing it. "There's not enough time. The fruit has to be ripened."

Ma waved a hand. "Mariah mixed the fruit and nuts with the suet a week ago. She dropped it off this afternoon."

Anna looked around and saw nothing.

"I had her take it to the kitchen. You'll have plenty of time to mix the ingredients and steam it."

"Me?" Anna tried not to panic. "You want me to make it?"

"It's not that difficult. I wrote down the recipe. It's on the table."

Anna glanced over to see that indeed Ma had jotted down her recipe. But knowing which ingredients to use wouldn't ensure it turned out. Ma always said plum duff was temperamental.

"It's Saturday afternoon," she pleaded, "and Brandon probably doesn't have the ingredients."

Ma smiled sleepily. "I had him call in an order this morning. The mercantile should have delivered everything by now."

Anna's jaw dropped. Ma had not only ordered items they couldn't afford, she'd somehow managed to suck Brandon into her scheme. "How will we pay for this?"

"Don't fret. Mr. Brandon put it on his account."

"He did?" Anna choked. "Why would he do that? We'll pay him back."

"Now don't you go doing that. He insisted, wished us a merry Christmas. What a fine gentleman. He stopped by while you were cutting the boughs. He wanted to make sure you found everything you needed."

Anna struggled to piece together this very different picture of Brandon Landers. "He always seems so…gruff, like he's angry with me."

Ma smiled softly. "The Lord puts people in our lives for a reason."

"Well, I can't imagine why he put Brandon in ours."

"I'm sure you'll find out one day. He's such a nice man…" She yawned.

Anna glanced outdoors. It must be nearly four o'clock. If they weren't going to be up all night, they had to start the plum duff soon.

"Ma, don't fall asleep. I need your help."

Ma answered with a soft snore.

Oh, dear. Baking had never been Anna's strong suit. Making the plum duff without Ma's help would be difficult. What if she burned it? Or got it too dry? What if… Her mind bounced through a hundred calamities. Worst of all, Brandon would come home in two hours and expect supper.

"I can't do it myself," she pleaded. "Why did you tell everyone we'd bring plum duff?"

Ma just snored.

Hands shaking, Anna picked up the recipe. She'd have to try or there'd be no plum duff for Christmas Eve dinner.

Brandon heard the clatter the moment he stepped into the house. Something metal, he guessed. Pots and pans, most likely, considering the racket came from the direction of the kitchen.

"Get out of there," commanded a very tired and very upset female voice. Anna's voice. "Get out!"

His pulse quickened. Someone had broken into the house and was threatening her. Brandon raised his ebony cane to use as a weapon and headed for the kitchen. The room had a swinging door to assist with dinner service. He now realized this could be used to advantage. He pushed it open a crack to get the bearings of the intruder and prepared to whack the man over the head.

He pressed his face close to the opening and peered into the well-lit room. From this vantage point, he could see only cupboards.

Bang!

"You horrible, stupid thing," Anna exclaimed. "Why won't you come out?"

Come out? That didn't sound like an intruder. Brandon let the door close and lowered the cane. Maybe she'd found a mouse. It was entirely possible, given the age and dilapidation of the house. At least she wasn't screaming at the top of her lungs. He admired that in a woman. It would be more difficult to play the hero, though, since a mouse could easily outmaneuver a man with a bad foot.

A thundering crash came from inside the kitchen, followed by Anna's cry of despair. "I give up."

He thought he heard a sob. He definitely smelled something acrid. Smoke wafted out of the kitchen. That had better not be supper, or he'd be eating crackers tonight. Annoyed, he pushed on the door, intending to have a word with her, but before he got it halfway open, Anna gave out a little sob.

"Why do I have to ruin everything?"

Her plea wrenched his heart. Poor girl. The oil stove must have overheated. It hadn't been used regularly in years. The oil lines might have gummed up or the valves stuck. He could do without supper for one night.

He opened the door to see what could only be described as an explosion. Flour and bits of dark brown goo covered the stove and worktable. Anna sat at the table, dejected, head buried in her hands.

"What happened?" he asked.

Her head jerked up, and she stumbled to her feet. "Bran—

Mr. Landers. I, uh, I—I—I'm sorry for the mess." She swiped at her cheeks.

Not tears. Nothing made him feel more inept than a woman in tears. Should he try to comfort her, or would she only lash out at him? He'd never chosen correctly in the past. Moreover, an employer shouldn't comfort a young female employee. Except Anna wasn't exactly an employee. She was a vibrant young woman who lived on his property.

He flexed his hands, unsure what to do. Deep down he longed to take her in his arms, but he shouldn't. In fact, they shouldn't be alone together in his house. Youth might be ignoring convention these days, but he would not. Yet he couldn't turn her out in this state. Where was Mrs. Simmons when he needed her? It was after six o'clock. Anna wasn't supposed to be here.

What should he do? He couldn't stand to hear her sob.

He absently picked up a glob of the brown gooey stuff. It smelled rather good as a matter of fact, rich with cloves and spices. He tasted it. The moist cakelike substance melted on his tongue.

"Whatever this is, it's delicious." He tasted another bit and then another. "Quite excellent," he mumbled, mouth full.

She hiccuped and lifted her head. "It is?"

"It is," he said between bites. "What is it?"

"Plum duff," she sniffled, wiping her red swollen eyes on her dress sleeve.

Didn't she even have a handkerchief? Brandon pulled out his and handed it to her.

She promptly wiped her eyes and blew her nose. "Thank you." She then offered back the handkerchief.

He grimaced. "You keep it."

She withdrew her hand and tucked his handkerchief into her apron pocket, her eyes downcast. "I'm sorry I made a mess of things."

He hated to see her spirit crushed. She had stood up to the Neideckers. Why would a little cooking disaster set her spirits so low?

"No problem." He cleared his throat. "None at all."

That didn't appear to appease her, for she continued to stare at the black-and-white linoleum floor.

"Well, then," he tried again, "whenever I'm faced with a problem, I assess the situation, figure out what went wrong and determine a new course of action."

At last she lifted her gaze. Though her lashes were dewy, her expression had narrowed in puzzlement. "Even if I understood what you just said, what does it have to do with my problem?"

He'd done it again. Without thinking, he'd taken charge as if he was still in the army.

"Pardon me," he apologized with a flourish. "I meant, let's figure out how to solve the problem."

"Oh." Her full pink lips made him want to think of something much more interesting than cooking. "I don't suppose you know how to make plum duff in a few hours rather than a week."

He had to acknowledge he didn't.

"Or how to get it out of the mold."

Again his knowledge fell short.

"Then you must know how to clean burned sugar out of an oven."

It wasn't a question, and he hated to admit he had no idea. "Hot water?"

Her hands went to her hips. "Just what I suspected. All thought and no action. If you can't cook or clean, how exactly did you plan to help me?"

That was the Anna Simmons he'd liked so much that day at the mercantile, though he had to admit he wasn't quite as keen that she'd directed her biting comments at him.

"I could help you clean if you tell me what to do," he of-fered weakly.

She rolled her eyes. "In your business suit and coat?"

He looked down at his fine attire. Father would have been shocked to hear what Brandon had just offered. No Land-ers had ever done servants' work. When Brandon was no more than five, he'd made the mistake of helping the house-keeper wipe down walls. After shaking him violently, Fa-ther had made Brandon say over and over that he would never do that again.

Brandon eyed the cobwebs in the corners of the old kitchen. Look where that thinking had got Father.

"I'll change," he said.

She filled a pail with hot water and grabbed the bicar-bonate of soda from the cupboard. After hefting the pail from the sink, she set it on the floor in front of the oven with a heavy clunk.

"You'll leave me alone," she said, hands back on those lovely hips. "I have work to do."

That was a command. A wise man would obey. Brandon had always thought himself wise. Until now.

After changing into clothes that were better than most people's Sunday best, the man helped her clean the kitchen. He was worse than useless, but then Anna had to remind herself that she'd been a lousy housekeeper when she'd first started cleaning for Mariah at the orphanage. Still, when she told Brandon to scrub the table, he'd worked and worked at it until she thought he'd rub right through the varnish.

Before scrubbing he'd eaten the bits of her demolished plum pudding. At first she'd taken it as a compliment, but then she realized the poor man was hungry. She'd stuck his beef cutlet in the warming oven and forgot about it. By now it must be as dry as shoe leather. To his credit, he'd never once asked what had happened to his meal. Her boiling temper died to a simmer and then cooled.

She pulled the cutlet from the warming oven and set it on the table. "I'm afraid I ruined it."

"Nonsense." He sat down with knife and fork and attempted to hack off a bite.

"I'll make something else." She reached for a match, but he hopped to his feet and stilled her hand.

"I'll cook something later."

"You know how to use a stove?" She could not imagine Brandon cooking. Ever.

"I'm a bachelor. I have to do many things for myself."

She doubted he had ever cooked or cleaned. Men of his social class hired housekeepers or ate at a club or restaurant. They did not cook.

Still, she kept her doubts to herself. It was pleasant working beside him. She kept glancing over to make sure he wasn't making a bigger mess, and occasionally she found him looking at her. Their glances didn't meet for more than a second, but each time it sent an unexpected thrill through her.

When he worked near her, she could smell that sagelike scent that was all his. She closed her eyes to drink it in, and jumped when he touched her.

"Are you all right?" He looked concerned.

Oh, yes, she was more than all right, though if she had to admit it, his nearness both excited and terrified her. And when she stuck her hand in her apron pocket and felt his handkerchief with his monogrammed initials, she ran her fingers over the embroidery and imagined what it would be like to be Mrs. B.L.

"Can we make another duff?"

Anna shook her head. "The fruit and nuts have to sit for a week."

"A week? Why would you make such a difficult dish?"

"For Christmas. It's like plum pudding."

His gray eyes twinkled in the electric lights. "Like in Dickens's *Christmas Carol?*"

She nodded.

"I'm sorry. Perhaps there's something else you can make." He stood and mopped his forehead.

She noticed he'd stopped using his cane a while ago, and though he balanced against the table when moving about, he could stand perfectly well without the aid of his cane.

"What happened to your leg?" she blurted out, and then, when she saw his expression tighten, instantly regretted the question. "I'm sorry."

"No, no. It's an honest question. It happened in the war." He offered no further explanation.

"It's not much, hardly noticeable."

If anything, his scowl deepened.

Anna tried again. "The cane is so distinguished. Don't all rich men carry them?"

His eyebrows lifted. "You think I'm rich?"

The way he said it sent shivers down her spine, as if she'd just accused him of the worst thing possible. "W-w-well, you have a nice house, one of the biggest on the hill."

At last his expression eased, though it didn't return to the pleasant conviviality of moments before. "I suppose it would seem big to you."

The words cut deeply. Yes, she was poor, and he was rich, but he didn't need to be rude about it.

"It was meant as a compliment. I counted seven bedrooms, two parlors, a formal dining room, this large kitchen and two washrooms. You even have running water."

After a moment, he apologized. "I appreciate your powers of observation and your curiosity." He took a deep breath. "I'm afraid I'm not accustomed to personal questions."

"I won't do it again," she said, fingering the handkerchief.

His mouth quirked up at one corner, making him look younger and even a bit mischievous. "Don't make promises you can't keep."

Anna fought an answering grin. "I'll *try* not to pry."

His laughter rumbled with surprising warmth. "Stay curious. If not for curiosity, Mr. Carter would never have found King Tutankhamun's tomb."

A thrill ran through her. Brandon had just compared her to Howard Carter. Maybe he would help her follow in the man's footsteps.

"I want to do that, to find a lost tomb like he did," she gushed, the words coming out so quickly that they jumbled together.

He smiled, and a dimple appeared in his chin. "Maybe someday you will."

Anna caught her breath. He'd practically promised to help her.

Chapter Six

Brandon got out of his automobile and peered at the unimposing two-story house that served as a parsonage. The place looked strangely quiet, considering Sunday dinner was about to take place. The pastor had indicated the entire extended family would be attending. True, Hendrick Simmons's automobile was still parked at the carriage house, but Brandon expected to see one or two other cars here.

Not so.

Brandon hesitated at the foot of the steps, wondering if Pastor Gabe had taken ill or was called away on emergency.

"There you are," called out the youthful minister from the front door. "Come on in."

Despite the icy December day, Pastor Gabe dressed in shirtsleeves, rolled up to the elbow, much more informal than Brandon expected for Sunday dinner.

He mounted the steps with care, using the handrail to ensure he didn't lose his balance. "I expected to see a car or two in front of the house."

Gabe held the door open for him. "You're the first to arrive."

"I am? It's almost two o'clock."

"The others will be here soon."

Brandon stepped over the threshold and into a Christmas fantasy. Every wall, shelf and table was decorated with greenery, ribbons and bows. The parlor contained some of the finest mahogany furniture that money could buy. A large tree graced the far corner, covered with garlands and crystal ornaments that looked like they'd come from Tiffany. The overpowering scent of cloves must be coming from the apple-shaped golden pomanders. The room reflected high society on a small scale. That certainly did not fit the minister's casual dress and manner. The church must be doing very well indeed.

"Mr. Landers." An elegantly dressed, willowy woman approached with a radiant smile. "It's such a pleasure to finally meet you. Gabe has told me so much—all good. May I take your coat?"

"Pardon my manners," said the pastor. "Brandon Landers, this is my wife, Felicity, the joy of my life."

The man's tender smile made Brandon's heart ache. His mother and father had once shared that tenderness, before Father let business consume his life.

A baby's wail sent Felicity upstairs with an apology. "Little Genie—that's our daughter, Eugenia Louise—must be hungry."

That left Brandon alone with the minister and a lad of perhaps ten or eleven who watched solemnly from the sofa, a storybook on his lap. He was dressed in the finest boy's suit New York could offer.

"This is my son, Luke," Gabe said. "Luke, meet Mr. Landers. He's opening a bookstore in town."

The boy closed his book, carefully set it on the end table and stood to shake his hand. "Pleased to meet you, sir."

Brandon was charmed by Luke's manners. Too many parents these days let their children run wild, without the slightest attempt to teach discipline and good behavior.

The boy had his father's dark curls but otherwise didn't resemble either parent. The dark skin couldn't have come from that porcelain-complexioned wife. And Pastor Gabe looked to be in his late twenties. His wife was even younger, too young to be the boy's mother.

"May I help Minnie set the table?" Luke asked his father.

"Miss Fox," Gabe corrected. "Yes, you may."

After Luke scurried away, Brandon inquired, "Miss Fox?"

"She helps with the housekeeping and cooking on weekends," Gabe said as they sat. "It took Felicity a long time to convince me to hire help, but I gave in when the doctor insisted she rest or risk losing the baby. A man can't deny his wife anything when she's carrying his child."

"I suppose not," Brandon said, though he would never know the joys of marriage and family. "Obviously she's good help, though, if she's been with you so long."

Gabe's brow creased. "Minnie only started here this past summer."

"But you said she'd begun before your son was born."

Gabe laughed. "No, no, my daughter. She was born last July. Luke is adopted. At least, we're in the process of adopting and expect everything to be finalized soon now that his parents' deaths have been verified."

That explained a lot. Except why no one else had yet arrived. The tantalizing aroma of roast turkey hung in the air, making Brandon's mouth water.

Gabe leaned forward, elbows on his knees. "While we have a moment alone, there is something I wanted to talk to you about."

Brandon held his breath, certain this was going to be a request for funding. Surely the man could have approached his parishioners first.

"It's about Anna."

The gravity on the preacher's face made Brandon choke. "Anna?" That was the last thing he'd expected the man to say. "What's wrong?"

Gabe sighed and rubbed his chin. "This is tough to say, because I know she'd be angry if she knew I talked to you, but I feel I have to set things straight." He looked Brandon in the eye. "Anna Simmons is surprisingly strong-willed."

"I've noticed."

The corner of Gabe's lips twitched. "She also has a lot of…pride."

That also hadn't escaped his notice.

Gabe continued, "It runs in the family. The Simmonses are givers. They'll give anything you could possibly need, but they don't receive so well."

Brandon recalled Anna's resistance to his offer of the carriage-house apartment. "I can see that."

"My sister married Anna's brother Hendrick. He manages the garage that I believe your father invested in."

Brandon nodded. It would be too complicated to explain the peculiar relationship his father had with the Simmons garage, that he owned it and inexplicably supported the business and the family for years. The children might not be good at taking, but apparently their parents had no such qualms.

"Hendrick is also starting up an aeroplane-motor factory," Gabe continued. "That requires a lot of capital, yet he won't take a cent from my parents except as investment. That means he doesn't have the money to support his mother."

Brandon was beginning to see where this was leading.

"Anna quit her last job over hurt feelings," the pastor said. "She can take offense at things the rest of us would brush aside."

"I noticed."

Again Gabe's lips twitched. "Then you understand their

dire situation and why I propose you hire Anna at the book-store."

Brandon steeled himself against the rush of emotion that idea generated. Working alongside Anna would be the worst possible situation. To make the bookstore succeed, he needed to concentrate, but he couldn't think of anything rational when she was around.

"That's not a good idea," he said.

The pastor didn't relent. "Her foster brother, Peter, agreed to help out with the carpentry. He's excellent with his hands. Anna would be a superb clerk. She reads voraciously. She's gone through almost every volume in the library. More-over, she knows everyone in town. She'd be a real asset to the store."

The minister had squeezed him into a very tight spot and now looked at him with every expectation that after hearing such a logical plea, he'd agree to hire Anna. That simply couldn't happen. Yet he also knew the man would never let him be without a promise to hire, and he desper-ately needed a carpenter. Perhaps he could satisfy the man with a different hire.

"This boy Peter. Would he work for fifty cents an hour?"

Gabe grinned. "You could probably get him for thirty."

"And he works fast?"

"Very fast. He'll have the work done in no time."

That's exactly what Brandon needed. "I'll talk to him."

"Good, he's coming to dinner today." Gabe rose and ex-tended a hand, as if sealing an agreement. "But understand, the two come as a team. If you hire Peter, you have to hire Anna. And under no means are you to tell her that I had anything to do with getting her the job."

Brandon stared at the hand. He'd been outmaneuvered again, but he needed that shelving built now. No one else would do the job at a rate he could afford. Yet, it meant taking on Anna. Hopefully, she'd refuse, like she'd initially refused to move into the carriage house.

He shook Gabe's hand. "The difficulty, Pastor, will be convincing *her.*"

To Brandon's surprise, Gabe agreed.

Anna tried to shake off the disappointment that she hadn't seen Brandon in church that morning. After their time together last night, she'd hoped he would attend, but his motorcar never left the carriage house.

"Maybe he's not feeling well," she mused over tea at the little table in the apartment.

Anna, Ma and Hendrick squeezed around the tiny table, their elbows knocking whenever anyone picked up a teacup. Her brother Hendrick had stayed with them after church so he could bring Ma to the parsonage for dinner. He glanced out the window and then cast a knowing look at Ma, who shook her head.

"What is it?" Anna said. "Do you know something I don't?"

Ma set down her teacup. "I think we should put the heavier drapes back up." The thin white cotton curtains Ma had made from their old kitchen ones brightened the room but did little to keep the chill out.

"I don't care about curtains," Anna said. "What's wrong with Brandon?"

Her mother sighed. "Absolutely nothing. He's a kind, dear gentleman."

"Who doesn't attend church," Hendrick pointed out unnecessarily. He'd been peeved from the moment they'd arrived home. He'd never liked the idea of them living here.

"Maybe he's sick," Anna suggested.

Hendrick sat back smugly. "I don't think so."

Anna started to protest, but then she heard the big carriage-house doors creak open. A minute later, Brandon's Cadillac started. She hurried to the window and saw him drive away.

"I'm sorry, dearest," Ma said sympathetically. "I'm sure he has his reasons for not attending church."

Hendrick stood and stretched. "He's like his father."

"You don't know that." Anna faced off against her brother. "You don't know him at all."

"I know that Percy Landers betrayed us."

Ma scolded, "Hendrick, that's not fair."

"He sold the house and garage out from under us," he countered. "Didn't even have the courtesy to let us know."

Anna bit her lip. She couldn't explain that away.

Ma could. "He was dying. We were the least of his concerns."

A shadow of remorse crossed Hendrick's face, and he sat down heavily. "You're right, Ma, but couldn't Brandon have notified me? A gentleman wouldn't spring this on two women."

"That's my fault," Anna admitted, settling back in her chair. "I took the letter. He wanted to give it to you."

"See? He's the best of men," Ma said. "He proved it last night when he called up Lily Mattheson to order a cake for today's dinner."

Anna stared. "He did?"

"It's not plum duff, but it'll be wonderful."

"What happened to the plum duff?" Hendrick asked. "Mariah got the fruit and nuts ready for you."

"I wrecked the first one," Anna admitted.

"But our Mr. Brandon helped her clean up *and* supplied another dessert." Ma practically glowed, as if she knew how closely Anna and Brandon had worked last night.

Anna ducked her head to hide a sudden rush of heat, which Hendrick didn't fail to notice.

"You and Brandon Landers? The man must be ten years older than you."

Anna bit back a retort. Of course he was older, but ten years did sound like a lot.

"Ten years is nothing at all," Ma said. "Why your Mariah is almost four years older than you."

"I still say it's wrong," he muttered. "Anna's my *little* sister."

"I'm almost as old as Felicity was when she got married to Pastor Gabe, and no one thought a thing of it." Anna rattled off more examples of girls who had married at her age and younger.

"Of course you're old enough." Ma patted her hand. "Your brother is just being protective. It's what older brothers do."

Anna crossed her arms. "Well, I don't need it."

"Apparently you do," Hendrick retorted. "Men like Brandon Landers can't be trusted. Keep your distance, sis."

"I'll do no such thing. I'm perfectly capable of making my own decisions." She turned to Ma. "Can't we leave yet?"

"Pastor Gabe said not to arrive a minute before two-thirty. He was quite specific about that."

Anna wrinkled her nose. "Why would he say that? It's not like Felicity is cooking. I know for a fact that she has her mother's cook over for the day, and Minnie Fox is helping." She gasped as realization struck. "Hendrick, is Peter still sweet on Minnie?" Maybe Gabe and Felicity wanted to give the two a little time together. "You said he already left for the parsonage."

Hendrick shrugged. "How would I know?"

"You work with Peter. He lives with you. How can you not know?"

Ma chuckled. "Men aren't in tune with matters of the heart the way we are." She squeezed Anna's hand. "Rest

assured we'll be able to figure out if there's anything between them during dinner. It'll be great fun."

At least it would take Ma's matchmaking efforts and
Hendrick's overprotectiveness away from her and Brandon
for the afternoon.

When Hendrick wheeled Ma up to the parsonage's front
steps, Anna expected Pastor Gabe and Peter to come out to
help. She didn't expect Brandon to pick his way down the
steps, Gabe close behind.

"Take my arm, Mrs. Simmons." Brandon bent down so
she could more easily reach him.

The gesture was kind. In fact, his every move demon-
strated consideration. He treated Ma as if she was his own
mother. What a fine son he must have been, and what a good
father he would make. For a second, Anna allowed herself
to imagine him with children of his own. He would ensure
they treated their elders with respect. No sassing or going
behind their parents' backs.

Anna bit her lip at the rush of memories. She'd gone
against her parents' wishes by letting false friends talk her
into skipping school. Look what had happened. Papa died.
She shook her head to dispel the memory.

Brandon was staring at her. "Will you get the door, Miss
Simmons?"

From the way he said it, he'd apparently repeated it more
than once. Embarrassed, she hurried ahead to open the door.

Brandon and Gabe helped Ma inside and let her settle
in the wingback chair at the head of the long dining-room
table. Anna counted eleven place settings. Felicity's entire
family must be coming.

Ma protested the seating arrangement. "This is your
home, Pastor. You belong at the head of the table."

Gabe would hear none of it. "You're our guest, and we insist."

When Felicity nodded in confirmation, Ma finally accepted the honor.

"But please, stop hovering over me. I have everything I need. Anna, why don't you and Mr. Brandon have a chat in the parlor? I'd like to talk to the pastor alone for a moment."

"Excellent idea," Felicity seconded. "Let's all go to the parlor."

Anna hesitated. Why would Ma need to talk to the minister alone? She wasn't involved with any programs at church. She hadn't attended the Ladies' Aid Society meetings since her fall, and Pastor Gabe wouldn't be the one to talk to about Society business anyway.

A terrible thought crossed her mind. What if Ma was ill? The doctor hadn't told Anna anything, but what if he'd found something that Ma hadn't revealed yet? What if Ma was dying? She'd never regained her color. Anna's throat pinched shut.

"Go," Ma said with a wave of her hand. "It's just a little personal business."

That didn't make Anna feel any better, but she obeyed. Clearly Ma wasn't going to tell her anything in front of the family. Not to mention Brandon. Anna eyed the man. Why exactly had he been invited? He wasn't family. He didn't even attend their church.

"We'll have a nice little chat," Felicity said as she led them into the parlor. Every inch of the room had been decorated for the holiday, including an enormous Christmas tree with crystal ornaments that reflected the light in little rainbows.

The moment they arrived, Felicity doubled back. "I need to check on dinner preparations and make sure Minnie has everything she needs. Peter is going to sit with the children in the kitchen."

Anna lifted an eyebrow. That confirmed Felicity was trying to get Minnie and Peter together as much as possible, since Minnie would be in and out of the kitchen all afternoon.

"Hendrick," Felicity continued, "Mariah is upstairs getting the children ready. Will you make sure she has things under control? Anna, I'm expecting my parents and my brother's family. Will you let them in when they arrive?"

Though Hendrick gave Anna a warning glance, he did go upstairs to help his wife. Within seconds, Anna and Brandon found themselves alone in the room. At first, he said nothing, and she couldn't seem to think of one shred of small talk. It was ridiculous to talk of the weather when they'd both just traveled through it. Mentioning church would drive a wedge deeper than the Grand Canyon. Last night's time together in the kitchen wasn't quite appropriate chatter for a parsonage.

"Um, what a big Christmas tree," she finally said.

He glanced at it but said nothing.

She checked her fingernails. Ragged, as usual. She should stop chewing them. Mariah had mentioned it more than once. Ma had given up trying to get her to stop.

Brandon motioned toward the elegant Chippendale-styled sofa. "Please have a seat."

Excitement skittered up and down her spine. Of all the seating in the room, he'd chosen the sofa. Did that mean he would sit next to her? To optimize that possibility, she sat to one end. Her hopes were dashed when he pulled a wing-back chair opposite her.

"Miss Simmons." He leaned slightly forward, as if delivering bad news.

She gulped.

He cleared his throat, looked over her head out the window. "I understand you're looking for employment."

"Employment?" That's the last thing she'd expected him to say. Confusion muddled her thoughts until she realized what must be bothering him. "You said the housekeeping would only be two or three days a week. I can manage another job and still get the cleaning done. I'll get up early and have it all done before you get out of bed, or I'll clean the house in the evenings. You won't notice a thing."

His gaze had settled back on her, those gray eyes dark. "Regardless of the impropriety of your suggestion, I'm not concerned about your ability to clean the house."

"Then what?"

This time his gaze didn't wander. "I want to offer you a job."

"A job?" She clapped her jaw shut but couldn't stop staring. "What job?"

"At my bookstore."

"Your bookstore."

His eyebrows lifted. "Do you always repeat what's said to you?"

Despite the chill radiating from the front windows, perspiration dotted her face. She fanned herself with her hand. "I was surprised, is all."

His lips twitched just a little, enough to clue her in that he wasn't as stern and solemn as he pretended to be. "It'll be hard work at first. The place needs a good scrubbing."

Anna had no doubt. The former occupant wasn't known for keeping a pristine shop, and the place had sat vacant for a year. "I can do it."

"You would work six days a week, full-time on those days you don't clean the house, afternoons on the days you do. After we open, you will be responsible for handling sales and maintaining inventory. The shelves must be dusted, misplaced books reshelved in the proper location, detailed records kept of all sales…"

Anna listened to his list of duties and began to wonder what would be left for him to do.

"You don't plan to work at the store?" she asked when he finally stopped.

His jaw tightened. "I will be in and out."

That sounded suspiciously as though he would leave her alone to deal with the customers. Though she appreciated his trust in her abilities, she also worried that customers would have questions she couldn't answer. "But you're the owner. Shouldn't you be there, at least at first?"

"I have other business to attend to," he said stiffly, his gaze drifting again to the window.

What other business? Brandon had spent every day this week at that bookstore. Yet suddenly he didn't want to be near it. She swallowed hard. What if it was because of her? But then why hire her? Why offer her the job? She knew a handful of women who would leap at the opportunity.

"The wage is a dollar an hour," he said.

Her jaw dropped. A dollar an hour? That was more than she could get at the cannery, and she wouldn't have to spend part of her wage on the train.

"Do you want the job or not?"

She swallowed. "Yes. I'll take it."

The hint of a smile returned. "You will?"

She nodded, momentarily ecstatic. Then her emotions jumbled into a knot. Working with him could throw her life into turmoil. Hendrick's caution came to mind. Stay clear of Brandon Landers. Rich men like him don't fall in love with poor girls.

She'd have to check her emotions at the door. The spark she'd felt last night meant nothing, which she'd best remember.

Chapter Seven

Brandon knew the moment he was alone with Anna in the parsonage parlor that he couldn't work alongside her. He'd be hard-pressed to get through dinner. Something about her drew him as irresistibly as iron to a magnet.

Oh, he wanted to work with her. He wanted to spend every waking moment with her, but that path could only lead to despair. If she ever discovered what he'd done in the war, she'd hate him.

As it should be. Anna deserved much better than him.

The sooner he could get away from the parsonage, the better. He glanced around the parlor with its oppressive decorations. Every bow and festoon reminded him of the families who wouldn't celebrate Christmas, thanks to him. The scent of pine and cinnamon and cloves gagged him. As soon as dinner ended, he'd make up some excuse and graciously bow out.

When each member of the family arrived, he memorized their names and greeted them with civility, but once the eleven adults sat at the dining-room table and conversation turned to the minutiae of everyday life, he paid only passing attention.

The sprigs of holly with their bright red berries mocked

him. While the others laughed and told stories of Christ-
mases past, he tried to stop his ears. He did not deserve
happiness on this or any Christmas. Why hadn't he made
an excuse or feigned illness? The only reason he'd been invited was to offer Anna a job. He'd done that, and she'd accepted. Business over. He did not have to endure a family's
joyful celebration.

At last the cake was served. Soon he could leave.

Anna gazed at him with gratitude for providing the dessert, and curious warmth stole into his heart, just like it had
last night. She *did* like him, and, try as he might to deny
it, he did care.

At that point, Anna's mother began a direct frontal as-
sault on his bachelorhood. "Doesn't Anna look lovely tonight? Red is particularly good for her coloring."

He had to admit he hadn't paid much attention to her
dress. It was adequate, simple and serviceable. He didn't
care about lace and trim. Not when the woman in question
boasted sky-blue eyes that glittered with excitement. Clothes
didn't make the woman. Her spirit did.

"She's a very hard worker too. Isn't she, Mariah?" Mrs.
Simmons was saying. "Don't listen to anything Evelyn Neidecker says. Anna had good reason to resign, and it has
nothing to do with the quality of her work."

Evelyn Neidecker must be the mother of the snobbish girl
in the mercantile. Mrs. Simmons need not worry that he'd
listen to anything a Neidecker said.

Confident she'd gained sufficient leverage, Mrs. Simmons moved in for the attack. "Naturally, she should have
a position where she can use her talents. Did you know that
she received top grades in literature?"

"Ma," Anna hissed, embarrassment coloring her cheeks
a lovely shade of pink.

Her mother, like every mother before her, seemed determined to convince him that Anna was the finest woman to walk the face of the earth. He didn't need any persuasion. Anna was the finest woman he'd ever met. The trouble lay with him.

Since he couldn't explain the problem, he evaded her attack by diving into the white cake with caramel frosting.

"Her teacher wept when she learned Anna couldn't go to college." Mrs. Simmons paused expectantly.

"She would be a fine student," he mumbled between bites. She'd certainly be better than his kid brother, Reggie, who was wasting his education.

"I plan to go to college," Anna asserted, her cheeks still pink, "as soon as I earn enough for tuition."

Her determination broke his heart. No job in Pearlman paid enough to fund a college education. He wished he could pay her more, but the store's bank account hovered near the bottom. The wage he'd offered her was already double what he'd intended to spend. The bookstore had better turn a profit and soon.

"What would you study?" the pastor's wife asked Anna. Her elegance and fashionable attire would have told him she came from money even if he hadn't met her blustering father and pretentious mother.

"Classics," Anna answered without hesitation.

Nearly everyone chuckled, as if humoring a child, but Brandon respected her passion.

"She should study what excites her," he said. "The world would be a better place if more people pursued education and fewer resorted to war. Classics are the foundation to a solid education."

"And that's how I can study archaeology," she said. "I want to find ancient treasures, like that Egyptian tomb Mr. Carter just unearthed."

"Egypt!" Felicity's father, Mr. Kensington, guffawed.

"You don't have to go to Egypt to find treasure. Rumor has it there's one right here in Pearlman."

Brandon stiffened. Not that ridiculous rumor again.

But Anna leaned forward, eager to hear more. "There is? Where?"

"Nowhere," Brandon said to quell the buzz of excitement that had started around the dinner table. "It's something someone made up years ago."

Kensington thumbed his gold pocket watch. "That so?"

"In my estimation," Brandon said firmly, "the greatest treasure in Pearlman is its citizens."

Kensington laughed. "Well said. But tell me, what is the greatest treasure in your family?"

Brandon stared down the man. He knew the way the wealthy operated. They thought they were entitled to know everything. Well, they weren't.

"Our rare book collection," Brandon stated decisively.

Anna didn't look as though she quite believed a book collection could be valuable, but he had no intention of explaining. He'd thought this rumor had been crushed years ago.

"That reminds me," he said. "I just received a newspaper with the latest news on Mr. Carter's find. There are even photographs."

Her gaze settled on him, sending his fickle heart soaring again. As expected, she forgot about the Pearlman treasure.

"There are?" She clapped her hands together. "I can hardly wait to see them. Are there pictures of the inside of the tomb? The chambers are supposed to be packed with treasures. What does it look like? Can you tell if anything's gold?" She spoke faster and faster, as if trying to grasp a fleeting dream.

"I'll loan you the newspaper the next time you clean the house."

Her smile offered greater payment than he'd ever received for the mere loan of a newspaper, but he stifled a return smile when he realized everyone else had grown silent. The women cast knowing smiles at each other. The men watched their wives then looked to each other to confirm what they'd figured out. Clearly Anna's placement across the table from him was no accident.

Brandon squirmed and glanced at the doorway. With dinner over he could now beg his leave. He opened his mouth, but the words became stuck when he spotted Hendrick Simmons's glare.

Clearly the man hated the idea of Brandon being matched with his sister. Brandon understood. He wouldn't be pleased either, but the truth was that this match could never happen. He gave Hendrick a curt nod to indicate he had no intention of pursuing a relationship with Anna.

Instead of relief, the man's eyes narrowed, and he scooted away from the table. "It's time to take Ma home, Anna."

It wasn't a suggestion.

Anna's smile fell. "Already?"

"I'm quite comfortable," Mrs. Simmons chimed in. "Let's stay for coffee."

Mariah, Hendrick's wife and a woman of quiet command, touched her husband's arm. "It's Christmas Eve." Her throaty voice drew Hendrick back into his chair.

Brandon took that as his cue to excuse himself. The family needed its time together. He would gracefully retire and leave them to their holiday celebration.

He rose. "Thank you for the delightful dinner, ma'am," he said to the pastor's wife, "but I should be returning home. It's growing dark."

"Please stay," she urged with the gracious ease born of wealth. "I'm sure your assistance helping the ladies home would be most welcome."

That delicate wording no doubt referred to Mrs. Simmons, since Anna could easily walk the six or seven blocks.

"I can bring Ma," began Hendrick before stopping abruptly. Judging by his wince of pain, the change of heart had been spurred by a sharp jab of his wife's persuasive elbow.

"That would be lovely," Ma Simmons said over top of her son's objections, "but you and Mariah need to return to the orphanage soon. I'm sure Mr. Brandon won't mind taking me home."

The short, plump woman had an uncanny ability to calm people. She hadn't the grace of the pastor's wife or the command of Mariah, but something else that Brandon couldn't quite define. If he'd been the sentimental type, he'd say she had a glow about her, but seeing as he preferred science to sentiment, he could only say she was amazingly persuasive. She had a knack for getting her way while making the other person glad to do so.

"Now that that's settled, let's take coffee in the parlor," Ma Simmons urged, "where we can enjoy Felicity's beautiful Christmas decorations. Mr. Brandon, will you escort me?" She held out her hand, and he had no choice but to help.

Brandon assisted Ma into the parlor with such tenderness that Anna's heart swelled with gratitude and something much more dangerous. She paused in the arched entry to watch him fawn over Ma, ensuring she was warm enough and situated in the best possible place to both view the sparkling tree and converse with the family. She rewarded him with the smile reserved for family and close friends. If it were up to Ma, Brandon would be her son-in-law by year's end.

Could it happen? Anna bit her lip to contain her roller-coaster emotions. He was simply helping an injured older lady. Any gentleman would do the same. It meant nothing more than that.

A sharp rap sounded on the front door, halting the various conversations.

"I wonder who that could be," Felicity said as she glided to answer the door, her green silk gown rustling softly as she passed.

Anna wished she could move that gracefully. Instead, she'd always jerked along like a wounded bug. Ma said it was because she'd grown too fast, all in one summer when she was fifteen, but that was over five years ago. The countless hours walking with a book atop her head should have done something for her awkward gait.

"Gabriel, you really should hire a butler," Mrs. Kensington called out loudly, as if the pastor couldn't hear her from five feet away. "Felicity is much too busy with the children to answer doors."

Pastor Gabe nodded, though Anna suspected he let his mother-in-law's advice skip right in one ear and out the other. Mrs. Kensington *always* offered suggestions. Anna thanked the Lord above that she didn't have to deal with someone like that, unless...

She glanced at Brandon. Was there a Mrs. Kensington in his family? His mother had passed years ago, and his father had just died, but there might be sisters or aunts or cousins. She shuddered. Judging by the Neideckers and the Kensingtons, wherever there was money, there were people determined to get their way.

Felicity had not yet returned. Though the conversations had resumed, Anna could still hear muffled voices in the hallway. One sounded masculine.

Brandon suddenly stiffened, and his color drained.

Anna looked toward the hall, but Felicity hadn't returned yet. Still, Brandon had risen and was walking slowly toward the parlor doorway. Before he could reach the festooned entry, Felicity appeared, followed by a tall, dark-haired gentleman a few years older than Anna. His suit was styled in the collegiate fashion, and he grinned when he saw Brandon, who had halted a few steps short of the entry.

"Merry Christmas, brother." The man spread wide his arms, revealing a candy-apple-red satin waistcoat.

Anna stared at the garish thing, which was out of place beneath the tweed suit and completely inappropriate during a time of mourning. Brandon must have noticed the same thing, because he didn't move a muscle. No embrace. No word of welcome. To anyone present, it was clear that Brandon had no love for his younger brother.

The brother shrugged and lowered his arms. "No one was home, so I traipsed around town until I saw your car parked out front." He gestured toward the street with a thumb.

Anna looked from Brandon to this man and back again. They had the same nose and chin. They stood about the same height, and their hair was the same shade of brown, but the resemblance ended there. The younger brother carried himself with a jaunty ease that Brandon never had. The bottom button of his waistcoat was undone. His hair was styled rakishly, and no dimple dotted his chin. He grinned quickly and laughed loudly. She suspected most women would consider him the more handsome of the two, but he acted with such reckless disregard for propriety that her guard went up. That man would break hearts without a second thought.

"Reggie," Brandon finally said, clearly pained. "I didn't know you were coming."

"It's Christmas, old man. Of course I'd come home." Again he surveyed the room, his gaze sweeping past the couples and decorations until it landed on her. "I don't suppose you'd care to make introductions."

Brandon's expression got even grimmer when he saw Reggie smiling at her.

"This way." He tugged Reggie toward Pastor Gabe and Felicity before proceeding around the room. Anna couldn't help noticing he'd started as far away from her as possible.

Reggie gallantly kissed the ladies' hands and shook the men's. In every way he acted the gentleman, but Anna had seen similar behavior last summer on her trip to Montana, and that man had turned out to be a criminal. No matter how handsome the face, she had no intention of letting Reggie Landers kiss her hand.

"Little Reggie," Ma cooed when he got to her. "You were just a lad the last time I saw you. I don't suppose you remember stopping by the house with your father."

"Of course I do," he said. "Quaint little place. So sorry to hear Dad sold it."

Anna saw Brandon cringe, his scowl growing deeper. Clearly there was no love between the brothers, at least not on Brandon's side. For whatever reason, he resented Reggie, and that reaction was enough to reinforce Anna's caution.

While Reggie and Ma chatted, Minnie arrived with the coffee service. Just seventeen and still finishing high school, Minnie worked weekends at the parsonage. At least Felicity didn't make her wear a uniform.

"Set it on this table," Felicity directed.

"Yes, ma'am."

At the sound of Minnie's voice, Reggie turned around, and Minnie froze. Her eyes widened, the tray tilted and the whole service—cups, cream, sugar and coffeepot—crashed to the floor.

A collective gasp went up. For a second, Anna wondered why Minnie acted as though she knew Reggie. Impossible. Their paths could never have crossed, yet Minnie had clearly been thrown by his presence.

"Are you all right?" Felicity reached for Minnie, who backed away from the mess, hands covering her mouth and tears in her eyes.

Shards of china littered the wooden floor, and the dark stain of coffee mingled with the cream in a great muddy pool. Flecks of liquid dotted her stockings and apron. Tears threatened to spill, and Anna rushed across the room to help.

"Oh, no." The girl sobbed and tried to pick up broken bits of china. "I'm so sorry, Mrs. Meeks. So sorry."

"Stop," Felicity commanded. "You'll cut yourself. Did the coffee burn you? Is anyone hurt?"

Minnie just kept sobbing and gathering jagged bits of porcelain into her apron.

Anna tugged her to her feet. "Come with me. We'll fetch a mop and broom." She knew how embarrassed Minnie must be with everyone watching her.

She led Minnie into the kitchen and sat her at the table.

Peter, who was helping Luke make something unrecognizable out of his erector set, looked up. "What happened? I heard a crash."

"Just a little accident," Anna said, handing Minnie a towel so she could dab some of the coffee off her clothing.

"Sounded like a big accident," Peter said.

Anna shot him a warning glare. Her foster brother could be such an idiot. He'd never win over Minnie if he didn't show a little more compassion.

"What?" the fool asked.

Anna just rolled her eyes and turned her attention back to Minnie, who'd buried her face in the towel. "Where does Mrs. Meeks keep the broom and mop?"

The girl lifted her face just enough to wail, "I-in the closet. It was an accident, but now Mrs. Meeks will give me a bad recommendation, and I'll never get the job."

Peter snorted. "It's just some spilled coffee."

Anna glared at him again.

"Yeah, just some spilled coffee," Luke echoed.

"Peter, show some manners," Anna reprimanded with a nod toward Luke. "You're old enough to demonstrate good behavior."

He made a face and crossed his arms before his chest, ready to debate, but she didn't have time for Peter's thick-headedness. She walked to the closet for the mop and broom and shot over her shoulder, "You can start by getting a pail of water."

He cocked his head. "How much will you pay me?"

She spun around and braced her hands on her hips. "A kick in the behind if you don't do it. Not to mention telling Hendrick."

That got him moving. Hendrick and Mariah had taken Peter in at the orphanage, and Hendrick was his boss at the garage. Anna's brother would make Peter's life miserable if he knew Peter was sassing Anna. He filled a pail with hot water and carried it across the kitchen. She handed him the mop.

"You can mop up the coffee," she commanded, "and I'll sweep up the broken china."

"I don't see why I have to do it. I'm not the one who dropped the tray."

Honestly, she could swat that boy. "Act like a man." She pushed on the kitchen door but stopped when a thought crossed her mind. "Why would you think I'd pay you?"

He shrugged, suddenly wary. "Everyone else is."

She knew Hendrick paid him at the garage, but the orphanage didn't have much extra funding. "Mariah is paying you?"

He shook his head. "Mr. Landers is giving me fifty cents an hour to build shelves in his new store."

Anna's mouth went dry. Brandon had hired Peter? And

he was paying less for skilled labor than clerical. After the shock died down, a low rumble of anger started building in her gut and grew larger as she swept up the pieces of broken china. Brandon and Reggie, along with the family, watched the cleanup, but she couldn't get her mind off one fact. Brandon hadn't hired her because he needed help. He was giving her charity.

Anna Simmons did not take charity.

Chapter Eight

Anna stewed about Brandon's job offer the rest of the afternoon. Why would he pay her more than Peter? Her initial anger subsided as she watched his tender care for her mother. Rather than leave at once with his brother, he waited until Ma was ready. He assisted every step to and from his car, helped her into the apartment and settled her in her chair by the fireplace. No son could have done more.

"Merry Christmas, Mr. Brandon," Ma said as he buttoned his coat.

"To you also," he barked. Before leaving, his gaze landed on Anna and, for a moment, softened.

She felt her cheeks heat. Why did a simple gaze do this to her?

With a final nod, he darted out the door. The room felt cold and lifeless without him. Anna rubbed her arms to warm them.

"Wasn't that a lovely dinner—" Ma sighed "—and so nice of Mr. Brandon to bring me home when he wanted to spend time with his brother. I told him Hendrick could do it, but he insisted. Such a gentleman."

That wasn't the way Anna remembered it. Hendrick had insisted, even demanded, he bring Ma home until Mariah intervened. She'd pointed out that since Anna and Ma lived on Brandon's property, he wouldn't have to go out of his way.

Yet it was an inconvenience, for Brandon clearly wanted to speak privately with his brother. The delay seemed to gnaw on him and only got worse when Reggie dashed off to the house on their arrival. Ma had suggested Brandon run along after him, but he would not leave until she was settled into her chair. His unceasing generosity tugged at Anna's heart but also troubled her.

"Brandon offered me a job at the bookstore." She sat in the other chair by the fireplace. "I don't know if I should take it."

"Why not?" Ma looked up, concerned. "Isn't he paying a good wage?"

"More than good." She held her cold fingers toward the fire. "That's the problem. He's offering far too much. I couldn't get that wage at the cannery."

Ma blinked. "I thought you said the cannery paid a dollar an hour."

"I was wrong. The cannery only pays men that much." Anna stared at her mother as realization dawned. "How do you know Brandon offered a dollar an hour?"

"Didn't you just say that?" Ma shook out the blanket she kept by her chair and draped it over her legs. "Hmm, I must have heard it somewhere."

"You talked with him about the job, didn't you?"

Ma shrugged. "I might have mentioned the wages at the cannery."

Anna groaned. "That explains it. But it's too much. He is only paying Peter half the rate. I can't accept it." How could she explain that the exorbitant wage made her feel beholden to him?

Ma smiled softly. "Perhaps he values your abilities." She

leaned forward to chuck Anna's chin. "You are gifted with intelligence and a love of literature, after all."

Anna looked away, embarrassed. "I prefer dime novels."

"I imagine even Mr. Brandon likes a good adventure tale from time to time. Take the job. Enjoy it. Give your all. If you still feel the wage is unfair, ask for less or donate the balance to someone in need. If you don't take the job, someone else will."

Anna gnawed on her fingernails. She and Ma could use the money, but Ma's words reminded her of something.

"Minnie Fox said she was looking for more work, but she's still in school. She wouldn't quit, would she?"

Ma heaved a sigh. "Mrs. Fox's dress shop isn't doing as well now that the mercantile carries so many ready-made dresses and people are ordering from the Sears and Montgomery Ward catalogs."

"So Minnie has to leave school to work?"

Ma hesitated a moment. "Promise not to say a word to anyone, but Minnie's father needs treatment for his weak heart. He had rheumatic fever as a child. The poor man has never been very strong, but it's gotten worse this year."

"How bad is it?"

"He's going to the Battle Creek Sanitarium in the hope that their health regimen will improve his weakened heart, but it costs a great deal of money. The Aid Society is hosting a benefit supper after the New Year, but the Foxes will need much more than we can raise."

Anna wrinkled her brow. "But Beatrice Fox married into the Kensington family. Surely they'd help with the expense." But as soon as she said the words, she knew they wouldn't. The rich didn't part with their money easily.

"I understand that they offered to pay the entire cost, but Mr. Fox refused."

"Why would he do that? They still have four girls at home."

Ma patted her hand. "I'm sure you understand how difficult it is for most people to accept charity."

Her words stung. Anna had decried Brandon's lodging and job offers as charity.

"I'm afraid today's festivities tired me," Ma said as she dug around in the basket of knitting and mending that sat beside her chair. "Oh, dear, I forgot to give Mr. Brandon his gift." She came up with a small, book-shaped parcel wrapped in butcher paper and tied with one of Anna's red hair ribbons. "Would you run to the house and give this to him for me?"

The thin package felt light in Anna's hands. It couldn't be one of those first-edition leather-bound books that Brandon valued so highly. Judging by the weight, the book was paperbound and no more than a hundred pages in length. Though it probably didn't cost a great deal, the fact remained that Ma had spent precious money on a gift for Brandon. Anna could guess why. Ma had high hopes for a match, but Anna wasn't that confident. Any time she got close, he pulled away.

"Perhaps you should give it to him tomorrow. I'm sure he'd rather get it from you. Besides, he's probably busy talking to his brother."

Ma refused to take the gift from her. "We'll be busy tomorrow, remember? We're spending the day with your brother and Mariah and the children. Just drop it off. It'll only take a minute, and he'll have something to put under his tree."

Brandon didn't have a Christmas tree or decorations of any kind. She wasn't even sure he'd appreciate the gift. Once Ma set her mind on something, though, she couldn't be dissuaded. "All right, but if he doesn't answer, I'm leaving it inside the kitchen door."

"That's a good girl."

As Anna donned her coat, Ma hummed "We Three Kings of Orient Are." The irony wasn't lost on her. She doubted she'd receive as welcome a reception as the magi. Nor was she offering frankincense, myrrh and gold.

Gold! Anna halted. "What did Mr. Kensington mean when he said there was a treasure buried in Pearlman?"

"It's an old, old rumor. If you ask me, Mr. Brandon is right. Any fortune here would have been unearthed years ago."

Then why hadn't she ever heard about it? And how did Brandon know so much about it, unless… "Here? Do you mean it was buried on this property?"

"So they say. Almost a century ago." Ma clucked her tongue. "Foolishness, if you ask me."

Anna looked out the window, but darkness had fallen and she saw only black. A treasure buried here. What did it matter if everyone thought it had already been discovered? She'd read Mr. Davis's book. He thought he'd found King Tutankhamun's tomb and that it had been pilfered by grave robbers. But Mr. Carter proved him wrong.

"Maybe the treasure is still out there," she said. "Wouldn't it be exciting to find?"

"Exciting, yes, but what would you do with it?"

"Give it to Brandon, of course. Think how happy he'd be." Maybe he'd smile more often. Maybe those lines of worry would leave his brow.

"Money doesn't buy happiness," Ma said softly.

"Well, it couldn't hurt." Anna buttoned her coat, pulled on her gloves and stepped out into the falling snow. Maybe if she found the buried treasure, Brandon would see her differently. Maybe he'd respect her. Maybe he'd see her as an equal.

Fluffy snowflakes floated lazily downward, the perfect picture of Christmas Eve. Anna counted her blessings, from a family who loved her to a warm place to live. Mary and Joseph hadn't been so fortunate that first Christmas. She'd had to give birth in a cold, dirty stable. Ma had sacrificed so much for her.

"I love you, Ma," she whispered back at the carriage house. Through the window, she could see Ma sewing, her head bent down in concentration.

Ma was happy here. To her the carriage house meant a new start, filled with promise. For the first time, Anna felt that too. Maybe God had brought them here for a reason.

She tucked the gift in her coat pocket and walked into the starless night. Atop the gentle rise, Brandon's windows glowed with welcoming warmth, guiding her across the snow-covered lawn.

On that first Christmas, angels and a bright star led shepherds to the poor stable where God gave the world the unexpected and unwarranted gift of His Son. The enormity of that gift sank in as the church bells pealed the six o'clock hour. With each stroke of the bell, the answer to her dilemma became clearer.

Help someone in need. Ma had pointed the way.

With a lightness of step, Anna danced forward, certain of her course.

Brandon scowled at his brother from behind the desk in his library. The grandfather clock ticked off each excruciating second.

"Merry Christmas to you too," Reggie said as he uncorked a bottle of brandy that he'd found somewhere in the cellar. Judging by the mold and dust on the bottle, it had been half-buried for years. He poured himself a glassful and held up the bottle. "Care for some finely aged spirits?"

"I do not drink liquor."

"Nor do you celebrate holidays, apparently." Reggie draped himself across the sofa, his boots resting on the rich brocade and his arm cast over the back while he sipped the brandy. "This place is depressing. Not one pine bough or wreath or sprig of mistletoe. How is a bachelor to claim a kiss?"

"From what I've heard, that's the least of your problems." The biting comment was meant to wake Reggie from his dissolute ways, but his brother ignored him.

"We should have a party. That'll get you in the spirit. First thing in the morning I'll have your manservant cut a tree for us. There are dozens in those little woods there that will do nicely. We can string some cranberries or popcorn or whatever your cook can spare. What do you think?"

"I don't have a manservant." He stopped there, not willing to call Anna a cook.

"No valet or butler? How do you get by?"

"Quite nicely, thank you."

"That's my brother. Tightfisted to the last." Reggie lifted his glass in a mock toast. "Relax a little."

Brandon gritted his teeth. Reggie could play the gentleman in good society, but, left to his own devices, he slipped into the vulgarities of the smart set. "Please remove your muddy boots from my sofa. Anna has enough to do without cleaning up after you."

"Anna?" Reggie jerked to a sitting position. "That plain girl I met at the parsonage that's all elbows and knees? The one with the hand-me-down clothes and outdated hairstyle? She's your housekeeper?"

Brandon fought the urge to strangle his brother. Anna was far from plain, and he liked her long, flowing hair.

Much better than the latest craze for bobbed hair. She also was much more than a housekeeper. "She cleans the house two or three times a week."

Reggie rolled his eyes and flung out his arm with great exaggeration. "My brother, the man of fashion, has only one part-time servant. I suppose you pay her pennies."

Servant? Anna was no servant. Brandon fought the flaring anger. "My finances are not your concern, but your expenses are mine." He slid open the top desk drawer and removed the pile of bills that had been forwarded by the trustee. "Twenty-nine dollars owed at Forsby's." He flipped to the next one. "A hundred and thirty overdue to Brook and Sons, Clothier. Do I need to say more?"

Reggie shrugged. "Necessities for college."

"A dance hall is necessary?" Brandon narrowed his gaze, trying to bore some sense into his brother. "One that undoubtedly has a speakeasy and gaming tables in the back."

Reggie rose and strolled to the fireplace, which was glowing softly with late-day embers. "Why did MacKenzie send the bills to you? They're supposed to come out of the trust."

"Because you've overspent your monthly allotment."

"Then take it out of next month's."

"It doesn't work that way, and you know it." Brandon tapped his pen on the blotter. "You need to accept responsibility for your actions. Father might have paid for your shenanigans, but I won't."

That drew his brother's attention. "Dear brother, generous to the end. The war changed you."

Brandon tightened his fist but managed to keep his seat and his wits. Anger would not resolve the situation or teach his brother to mind his ways. "It's time you learned responsibility," he said through clenched teeth. He pushed the bills to the other side of the desk. "You incurred the expense. You find a way to pay it."

Reggie half choked and half laughed. "How? All I have is the trust money."

"Get a job."

Reggie's eyes bulged. "But I'm in college. That takes all my time."

"Apparently not, considering you had time to run up a bill at a dance hall."

Reggie cast him the boyish grin that had doubtless worked hundreds of times with Father. "You do want me to marry well, don't you?"

Brandon folded his arms. "Frankly, I don't care if you ever marry, and given your current habits, I pity the woman who would depend on you for her welfare."

"She'd be better off than any woman who depended on you for affection."

"That is uncalled for." Shaking, Brandon pulled himself to his feet, using the desk for balance. "I will not fund your vices. It's time you grew up."

Reggie slammed his empty glass onto the end table. "It's time I left. Merry Christmas, brother."

"Where are you going at this hour of the night?"

"To stay with friends, who will no doubt welcome me more than my own brother."

Reggie yanked open the library door and stalked down the hallway. Brandon followed, but he couldn't match his brother's pace.

"This is your home," he called out.

"It's your home." Reggie had already donned his coat and hat. He pulled open the front door, but rather than rush out, he froze.

Brandon hobbled toward him. Maybe the boy had come to his senses and was ready to accept responsibility for his actions.

Within five steps he saw that wasn't the case. In the doorway stood Anna, one hand poised to knock and the other holding a gift tied with red ribbon.

Brandon's brother stared at Anna as if she was a ghost.

"Miss," Reggie finally said. "I'm afraid you arrived just as I was leaving." He stepped aside to allow her to enter and then, with a quick glare at Brandon, stalked out into the night.

Anna had heard the shouting. Brandon had sounded so angry that she'd almost scurried back to the carriage house with the gift. But Ma wouldn't understand. She would say Brandon needed a gift even more. So Anna had knocked. Then Reggie had opened the door.

All the blood had drained from her limbs. Brandon's resolve and Reggie's fury had frozen her in place. Both of them stared at her. She couldn't make out what they thought of her presence, but it wasn't good.

She'd dropped her hand and clutched the gift to her breast.

"I'm sorry," she'd mouthed, barely audibly.

Instead of accepting the apology, Reggie had stepped aside to let her enter. Somehow she managed to get her limbs moving, but she felt as though she was walking into an interrogation chamber. Brandon, leaning heavily on his cane, glared past her into the night.

"I'm sorry," she repeated, this time louder. "Where is your brother going?"

Brandon must not have heard because his gaze was locked on the empty doorway, his jaw taut and his expression hard as flint.

She shut the door to keep the snow out. At the click of the latch, Brandon finally noticed she was there.

"Miss Simmons."

Her heart sank. Somehow she'd been demoted from Anna, their time together in the kitchen forgotten, and it was all Reggie's fault. He must have said or done something to infuriate Brandon, but to squabble on Christmas Eve? Surely they could get along for one day of the year. Instead, Reggie had bolted for a friend's house.

"May I help you with something?" he asked, emotions carefully guarded.

How she wished she could hold him and tell him it would be all right, that she believed in him and with a little effort things could be patched between the brothers. But of course she couldn't do that.

"Your business, Miss Simmons?" Brandon asked for the second time.

"Join us for Christmas dinner tomorrow." The invitation burst out from nowhere. "It's at my brother's house, the orphanage. Mariah always makes plenty of food."

His lips curved into a bitter smile. "I doubt I would be welcome."

"Of course you would," she said, though she knew he was right. Hendrick wouldn't let Brandon in the door.

"Thank you for the offer, but I will be busy."

She hoped that didn't mean he was working at the store. Christmas was on a Monday, but surely he wouldn't work on Christmas Day. "Did you expect me to work? At the store, I mean. I will make breakfast and supper for you."

"No." His gaze focused on her. "No need. Take the day off. Here too. I'll get along fine."

"Are you sure?"

His lips twitched. "Thank you for your concern. Is the invitation the only reason you came here tonight?"

His gaze landed a bit lower than respectable, and she realized she was still clutching Ma's gift to her chest. "Uh, no. This is for you."

She held it out to him. Between being shoved into her

pocket and crushed against her body, the bow had got kinked and lopsided.

He stared at the package but made no move to take it. "You're giving me a gift?"

She shook her head. "It's from Ma. She wanted you to have it tonight." Her hand wavered. "She'll be upset if I go back without delivering it."

"Your mother," he stated dully. "Why would she give me a gift?"

"Because it's Christmas. Because Ma likes you. I don't know." She pushed the gift into his hands.

The paper crinkled at his touch. "I'm… I don't know what to say." His expression softened, and he even blinked, as if choked up. "I didn't get anything for her. Or you." He shifted his weight uncomfortably. "I didn't think…"

"True giving never expects anything in return." Ma's saying rolled easily off her tongue, though, to Anna's shame, it wasn't one that she often practiced.

"Should I open it now or wait until tomorrow?"

Anna was curious what her mother had got him. "I think she'd like you to open it now." Ma wouldn't care.

He motioned toward the parlor, where a sofa and two stuffed chairs were placed in an arc. "Perhaps we should sit."

He slowly hobbled toward the farthest chair, leaning more heavily than normal on his cane. Tonight's argument must have taken a lot out of him.

She followed. The firelight sparkled off the dots of melted snow on her coat like diamonds.

She sat on the sofa, hoping he would join her, but he chose the chair farthest away. In the flickering light, the room looked gloomy, the floor-to-ceiling dark-paneled walls even blacker.

"I should have put up some Christmas decorations," she

said nervously, clutching her knees. "Some pine boughs and pomanders would get that musty smell out of the air."

"Please don't."

He looked so uncomfortable. The way he held the gift, like it was a poison letter, coupled with his stiff posture, made her feel like giggling.

He swallowed hard. "I suppose I'd better get it over with."

She couldn't help herself. A laugh sneaked out, and she couldn't get her hand up quickly enough to do more than turn it into a snort.

He stared at her. "What?"

"It's not going to hurt you."

He stiffened even further, though she'd doubted that was possible. "Of course it won't."

In one motion, he untied the ribbon. The paper slipped off, and he stared at the thin book's title, a puzzled expression on his face.

Anna could barely contain herself. What was it? A book of psalms? Meditations? A sermon? Knowing Ma, she would have given Brandon something to draw him back to Christ.

All she could see was a dull blue paperboard cover with black lettering. He began flipping through the pages.

"Well?" She leaned forward, wishing she could see the title.

He reexamined the title page and read aloud, "*A History of Pearlman, Michigan, from Its Founding until 1900* by Mrs. E. S. Neidecker."

"Mrs. Neidecker wrote a book?" Anna had no idea. The woman had always seemed grasping and pretentious, her vaunted education a smoke screen for ignorance. Write a book? "Impossible. Maybe Mr. Neidecker's mother wrote it. When was it published?"

"1903."

"Oh, dear, maybe she did write it, but no wonder I never knew. I was only one at the time."

He looked up, an eyebrow arched, and she realized she probably shouldn't have said that. Now he knew she was a mere child.

"Well, I might be young, but I'm well-read," she said, trying to impress him with something other than her age.

"Apparently not in local history." Though his mouth had twisted into a grin.

She knotted her fingers in her lap, wishing she could gnaw on a fingernail but knowing she shouldn't. A lady did not chew her nails.

"I, uh, I didn't know the book existed." That much was true.

He set the book aside. "Please thank your mother. It was a thoughtful gift. She must have learned how much I enjoy history."

Anna wished she'd read more history instead of all those dime novels. "I like literature. Hawthorne and Kipling and Poe." She named every important author she could remember reading.

His lips twitched, almost into a smile. "Quite admirable. That reminds me." He rose and walked over to a table near the window.

She wasn't sure if she was supposed to follow him or wait, so she compromised and stood. He picked up a newspaper, leafed through it and then folded it back to expose one page.

"I promised to give you the latest newspaper story on Mr. Carter." He limped back and handed her the precious paper.

"Thank you." She couldn't help glancing at the photographs. "That's the burial chamber?"

"The antechamber. They haven't opened the burial chamber yet."

She wanted to read it right that minute.

He must have noticed. "Take it with you. I've already read it."

She pressed the newspaper to her chest, feeling the excitement build. She'd be up late tonight reading and rereading. "Thank you," she said again. Oh, she could just kiss the man. He'd given her dreams hope. Between his knowledge of archaeology and hiring her at the bookstore…

Oh, dear. She'd intended to talk to him about the job after hearing Minnie's predicament. But if she asked him to give the job to Minnie, she might not get another job. She certainly wouldn't find one that paid so well. Her throat constricted.

"It's late. Perhaps you should be going," he finally said. "Your mother will worry."

She swallowed hard, knowing what she ought to do but not wanting to do it. "Maybe I should." She tucked the paper into her coat pocket and walked slowly toward the front door, debating in her head whether or not speaking up for Minnie was the right thing to do.

As he opened the door, she looked down at the carriage house. The window was still lit, but Ma must have gone to bed. Ma always knew best.

Ignoring the snow falling on her hair, she turned back to Brandon. "The bookstore job. What if there's someone more deserving? Someone who needs the income more?"

He smiled, admiration softening his gaze. "There may be others more in need, but no one is more qualified."

Her heart skipped a beat. Perhaps Ma was right. Perhaps God had brought Brandon into her life for a reason. Perhaps He meant her to take that job.

She returned his smile. "Merry Christmas."

He nodded. "Merry Christmas to you, Anna."

He'd called her by her first name. She was Anna to him

again. Laughing, she skipped to the carriage house like a little girl, twirling and holding her mittens out to catch the snowflakes.

Chapter Nine

Anna needn't have worried about avoiding Brandon. After he unlocked the bookstore each morning, he returned home. When she cleaned the house, he went to the store.

Peter worked after school and on Saturday. In two weeks, he'd constructed all the shelving for the store. Anna's ears rang from all the sawing and hammering. Next they varnished, and Anna battled headaches from the fumes. The woodstove barely put out enough heat for the varnish to dry, so they didn't dare open the door or windows to ventilate. She was always eager to go home.

"I'll be glad when the shelves are done." She plopped into one of the chairs at the table and rubbed her aching temples.

Ma handed her two aspirin and a glass of water before sitting opposite her. Her leg had improved to the point that she could get around in the apartment using a cane, but Doc Stevens didn't want her going outdoors alone just yet.

"What comes next?" Ma asked as Anna downed the tablets.

"The books." She stretched her aching limbs. "We get to put them on the shelves once the varnish dries."

"You'll have fun opening the boxes to see what Mr. Brandon ordered."

"That's the odd thing. Only two cartons have arrived. That won't fill one set of shelves, least of all the whole store."

"Maybe he's storing them at the house until the store is ready."

Anna shook her head. "I haven't seen any there either."

"Then they'll arrive soon. Mr. Brandon is the kind of man who has everything in order."

Ma's optimism was ordinarily contagious, but Anna's headache put a damper on her spirits. "I wish he'd stop by more. I'd like to ask him if he's heard more about the excavations in Egypt. I wonder if they've gotten into the burial chamber yet. According to the last article I read, that's where they expect the most spectacular finds."

Ma patted her hand. "I'm sure Mr. Brandon will spend a lot more time at the store once you start shelving the books. You can have a good chat then."

"Maybe." Considering Brandon was avoiding her, she doubted he'd suddenly spend all his time at the store. "I don't think he wants to talk to me."

"Of course he does. He simply has a lot on his mind right now. Why, every day his frown grows deeper, and he won't tell me what's troubling him."

"You talk to Brandon every day?"

Ma traced the pattern on the gingham tablecloth. "He brings me lunch."

"But I leave you a sandwich every morning."

"He claims hot soup will make me feel better, and I think he's right. I've gained so much strength in the last couple weeks."

Anna stared at her mother. "He makes you soup?" The man didn't know the first thing about a kitchen.

Ma looked sheepish. "I think he gets it from Lily's Restaurant."

Anna processed the fact that Brandon was going to all this trouble without her knowledge. "What else are you hiding from me?"

"Hiding? I'm not hiding anything."

"Then why didn't you tell me that Brandon visited?"

Ma's eyes twinkled. "Because it's not important."

Brandon, who avoided people whenever possible, chatted with Ma every day, and she thought it was nothing? "What do you talk about?"

"Oh, the weather, people in town, nothing much."

It sounded innocuous enough, but Anna suspected one more topic came up. "I don't suppose you mention me?"

Ma smiled. "Of course, dearest. How could I not boast about my wonderful daughter?"

Anna wondered what Brandon said in return, but she couldn't bring herself to ask. Why was he avoiding her? He'd changed since Christmas, and the only reason she could come up with was his brother, who had returned to college without seeing Brandon again.

"Does he ever talk about Reggie?"

"That's a sore subject." Ma shook her head and sighed. "Sometimes that's the way it is between siblings. I'm so glad you and Hendrick are close."

Close was not the word Anna would have used to describe their relationship. Hendrick treated her like a kid, always telling her what to do. On their trip west this past summer, he'd tried to lord over her, and at Christmastime…

She still got angry when she recalled his warning. Why, he'd practically forbidden her from seeing Brandon. Well, she was a grown woman now, and he couldn't tell her what to do.

Frustrated and with her head splitting, she rose from the table and walked over to the window. Frost fringed the glass, but she could still make out the house. The verdigris copper roof was covered in snow now, making the gray house blend into the bleak winter landscape. Gray and white. Not one speck of color, not even a cardinal. Winter had barely begun, but she already longed for spring.

"You two should do something together," Ma suggested. "Go ice skating."

"Me and Hendrick?" Her brother hadn't skated since childhood.

Ma chuckled. "No, you and Mr. Brandon."

"Brandon?" Anna shook her head. "He wouldn't want to skate. His leg."

"Oh, I suppose you're right. Perhaps you could go to the Valentine's Ball."

"That's not possible." Anna had forgotten about the social event of the season. Brandon might be invited but not her. The Neideckers hosted the ball, which only doubled the certainty she would not be welcome.

"We're never invited," she pointed out, just like she did every year. "It's only for people who live on the hill." In other words, the wealthy, for they owned the houses dotting what everyone referred to as "the hill."

"We live on the hill now."

Anna rolled her eyes. "That hardly makes us one of them." She tossed her head. "Besides, I wouldn't set foot in the Neideckers' house if you paid me. They're too high-and-mighty for me."

"Miss Sally might be a touch spoiled—"

"A touch? You're not around her enough to know what she's really like. And her mother's just the same."

Ma clucked her tongue. "You should only say nice things about people."

Anna huffed but kept her thoughts to herself. Sometimes Ma sounded like that Mrs. Post's etiquette book.

"I pray you'll be able to attend this year," Ma said, resuming her optimism. "Invitations should arrive soon. Maybe Mr. Brandon will ask you to join him."

This time the heat started at the tip of Anna's toes and raced upward. She pressed her hot forehead to the frosty glass.

"No, Ma. He won't." She could think of nothing Brandon would like less than a dance, but her imagination had a mind of its own, generating images of him sweeping her across the dance floor. Her silk dress flowed. Her necklace glittered. The tiara, the jeweled shoes. Sally would gawk as Anna claimed the most handsome man in the room. He would look down at her, his gray eyes soft as spring rain, and his lips would touch her forehead as his hand cradled her waist.

"Ack!" She started when melted frost ran down her forehead and into her eyes.

"What's wrong?"

Anna wiped off the moisture with her dress sleeve. "Nothing. Nothing at all."

If Brandon Landers could be considered nothing.

The new bookshelves gleamed in the late-afternoon sunlight streaming through the front windows. Brandon had to admit Peter and Anna had done a good job. Not one trace of the old harness shop could be detected, not even the smell. He reveled in the scent of fresh varnish and sawdust. As soon as his books graced the shelves, he'd be ready to open. That would be a welcome reward after the difficulty with Reggie. At least his brother had returned to college.

Peter appeared from the back with the first carton of books.

"Set it there." Brandon pointed to a shelf along the wall across the room from the sales counter. Bowing to economic necessity, he'd purchased a selection of the better contemporary authors, such as Fitzgerald and T. S. Eliot. "The other box can go there too."

Peter nodded and headed to the back room.

Brandon counted out the lad's wages. Considering the fine carpentry, he'd felt guilty paying Peter so little and ended up matching Anna's wage. It would set him behind, but the sale of a few books would make up the difference.

"That all, Mr. Landers?" Peter asked as he set down the second box.

"All except for your pay."

The boy's eyes lit up when he saw how much Brandon had given him.

"For a job well done," Brandon said. "Will you be able to help me move books here from the house tomorrow?"

"Yes, sir, after school lets out."

"You must be what—seventeen? Will you be graduating this spring?"

"Wish I was done now, but Hendrick insists I get my diploma."

"Smart man." Brandon opened the door to let Peter out and paused when he saw one very familiar person heading his way.

"Thanks again, Mr. Landers," Peter said, tipping a finger to his cap. "Hey, Anna. What are you doing here? Place is all clean."

Anna shrugged, her hands buried in her coat pockets. A proper felt hat topped her hair, which looked short, as if she'd got it bobbed. Brandon stifled a surge of displeasure. He liked long hair, but every woman seemed to be cutting hers. Even Hendrick's wife wore her hair short. Not Anna. Please, not Anna.

"I wanted to see the books on the shelves," she said a bit too brightly.

"Ain't none there yet," Peter informed her.

"Aren't any," she corrected.

The boy rolled his eyes and took off for home.

Brandon smiled at Anna, especially now that he could see she'd just put her hair up, not cut it. "You have a bit of schoolteacher in you."

"I just know what's correct and what isn't." She stepped into the store. "Peter's right. You don't have any books on the shelves."

Naturally she went to the two boxes Peter had just brought from the back room. Then she slowly turned, surveying the entire store.

"Is that all?" Her voice echoed in the nearly empty storefront.

"The rest are at the house. Peter will help me move them tomorrow." As if he owed her an explanation.

"Ah. Shall we shelve these?" She opened the box and pulled out the first book. "*The Ambassador* by Henry James. Interesting, if a bit dated." One by one she pulled out the books and set them on the shelf in alphabetical order by author. With each one, the frown on her face grew deeper.

"You don't have to do this now," he protested, uncomfortable at her disapproval of his literary selection. "It must be time to fix supper. Past time, actually."

"Supper is already done and in the warming oven. More Henry James." She sighed. "Most of these were published decades ago. You should have consulted me before ordering."

"Why?" He bristled. "I might have lost time fighting in the war, but those months of recovery gave me plenty of time to read."

"And this is what you read?"

"Naturally. I appreciate quality literature."

She shook her head. "Pearlman is not Detroit."

"I wasn't in Detroit."

Her gaze riveted on his face, making him even more un-comfortable. "Where were you, then? I thought you'd come home to recover. It's been four years since the war ended."

He did not care to explain those painful years, but her expression told him she would not let it go until he gave her a satisfactory explanation. He gripped the head of his cane tighter.

"I wrote for the *Boston Herald* before the war. When it began, I pestered the editor to let me correspond from the front. He refused, saying the paper couldn't afford to send another correspondent to Europe, but I know my father was behind it. He wanted me to take over the family business." At her look of puzzlement, he added, "Automobile-related products."

"Ah." She looked unimpressed. "I'd want to be a jour-nalist too."

He had to smile. Of course she would. Her eyes lit up whenever travel or adventure was mentioned.

"But that doesn't explain what happened in the four years after the war," she persisted. "Were you an archaeologist? Did you join excavations in Greece or Rome?"

He could have laughed. Even if he hadn't been injured, postwar Europe was not the place to conduct archaeological excavations. "I did tour Rome after I learned to walk again."

"What was it like?" Her eyes sparkled, the book absently clutched to her chest. "Did you see the Forum? What about the Coliseum? And the Pantheon and St. Peter's?"

She named so many sites so quickly that he couldn't get an answer in. When she finally paused for breath, he sim-ply replied in the affirmative.

"All?" she cried. "Which was your favorite?"

He could hardly suppress a smile. "I couldn't name a favorite."

"I have to go someday." She gripped the book with such

fierce longing that he wished he could make her dream come true. Alas, it wasn't possible.

"It's busy and dirty," he said to let her down a bit, for the odds of Anna Simmons going to Europe were long indeed. "And the influenza epidemic left so many sick and dead."

"Oh, I forgot about that. Did you get sick?"

He was touched that she thought of him. "Yes, but I recovered, unlike others."

"I never got sick," she said softly, as if embarrassed she hadn't suffered. "How long did you stay there?"

"I returned to the States in October of 1919."

"A whole year." She said it dreamily, as if imagining he'd toured the Alps and the great cities that hadn't been shelled to dust, when in fact he'd spent most of that time in the hospital and then a rented room.

"It wasn't glamorous."

She averted her eyes, and that glorious touch of pink dusted her cheeks. "I know." She lifted her gaze. "But you were *there*. I want to go somewhere exciting just once in my life."

Brandon reached into his inner jacket pocket and pulled out her pay. "Perhaps if you save a portion of your wages, you will."

She stared at the twenty dollar bills he held out to her. "For me?"

"You earned it."

For a second he could see the dream animate her features, but the moment quickly passed, replaced by calm resignation. She took the money, folded it and carefully tucked it into her coat pocket.

"Thank you," she murmured.

He couldn't bear to see her dream vanish the way his had. "I went back to the paper," he said.

She looked up. "The newspaper in Boston?"

He nodded.

"Why didn't you stay?"

The truth was bitter. "They would only let me report city-council meetings."

She nodded, as if she knew what he hadn't said, that his bum leg meant he could never again be a foreign correspondent or much of a reporter at all. The war had stolen his dream. He'd learned to adjust and now looked into the past to find his future. Now he read about antiquities rather than discover them. Anna, though, still had a chance.

"Don't let go of what you want," he urged. "Go to college. Meet a professor who will take you to an excavation. See everything you've always wanted to see."

Resignation curved her lips. "I have an errand to run. Your supper is in the warming oven."

That's not the response he'd hoped to hear.

Anna found Pastor Gabe still at the church. That made her task a lot easier. She didn't want to discuss the subject in front of Felicity, who would ask about Ma and Brandon and her job.

"Good night, Mrs. Williams." Anna nodded at the church secretary, who was donning her coat and hat when she walked in.

"Office is closed," Florabelle Williams huffed. "It's past five o'clock. I shoulda been home already makin' supper for my Henry."

"Then you'd better hurry," said Gabe. "I'll close up."

Mrs. Williams cast Anna a suspicious look before acquiescing. "Well, you are family of sorts," she muttered as she left the office.

Both Anna and Gabe waited until the front door closed behind the secretary and notorious gossip.

"Please sit," Gabe said, motioning to one of the chairs in the center of the small office. During Reverend Jacobsen's tenure, anyone seeing him had to sit across the desk from the minister, with Florabelle Williams watching them both. Pastor Gabe had positioned two chairs beneath the window and asked Florabelle to step out whenever someone met with him. Mrs. Williams doubtless protested, but it certainly made people more comfortable.

Anna sat in one of the chairs, situated at an angle to Pastor Gabe so they could converse comfortably.

"What can I do for you?" he said.

She fingered the money in her pocket, suddenly doubting. Taking this step meant setting her dreams back again, but then she thought of Minnie not finishing high school. What dreams would she lose? And Mr. Fox was so ill. What if Minnie lost her papa just like Anna? She took a deep breath and pulled out the money.

"I want you to make sure the Foxes get this." She counted out half her wages, a full forty dollars. "I heard Minnie might have to leave school to work."

Pastor Gabe refused the offering. "That's generous of you, Anna, but are you certain you don't need it?"

"Ma and I still have plenty."

His dark eyes bored into her, searching her soul, but not unkindly. "I understand Minnie has already taken a position at the Neideckers."

"The Neideckers? My old job?" Poor Minnie would have to wear that short dress and endure Joe's ogling. Worse, Minnie wasn't strong enough to tell Joe to keep his eyes where they belonged. "She can't work there."

Gabe's brow furrowed. "Why not?"

Anna sucked in her breath. Did she dare tell him her misgivings? Ma's voice popped into her head, telling her that if she couldn't say something nice, not to say anything at all. Maybe Anna was wrong. If so, telling Pastor Gabe would be just like Mrs. Williams spreading gossip. Better to warn Minnie.

"She needs to finish high school," she finally said. At his expression of puzzlement, she added, "Ma said she was quitting school to work. She only has this semester. It's not fair that she'd have to leave school to work when she's so close to finishing."

Pastor Gabe finally accepted her money. "I will make sure the Foxes get this. I'll also ask about Minnie's schooling." He smiled and rose. "I'm sure we can work something out with Evelyn Neidecker to ensure Minnie gets her diploma."

Anna breathed out in relief. "Thank you, Pastor." It still felt awkward calling him pastor when two years ago she'd had a terrible crush on him. That was before he married, before he even courted Felicity. He'd been kind to her but never romantically inclined. That's the way it always went for her. None of the men she liked were ever interested. Including Brandon.

She shook Gabe's hand, pleased that the old embarrassment was finally gone. Maybe one day she'd even be able to call him pastor without wincing.

They stepped out into the icy wind. Anna lifted the collar on her coat and dug her hands into her pockets. She should get home to bring Ma her supper.

"Good night, Anna," Pastor Gabe called out as he headed toward the shoveled path that led behind the church to the parsonage.

A screeching roar, like the sound of something enormous collapsing, echoed through the air and stopped both Gabe and Anna in their tracks. She stared down Main Street, trying to find the source of the noise and spotted a plume of dust or smoke rising at the far end of town in the direction of…the garage.

"Hendrick. Peter," she cried and set off at a dead run.

The garage had exploded.

Chapter Ten

Anna's feet pounded the board sidewalk, each step reverberating against her skull. Her side ached. She couldn't breathe. Hendrick. Peter. They could be hurt or…worse. She saw again that pool of blood under Papa.

Her brothers. And she and Hendrick fought the last time she saw him.

Tears stung her lids. Her lungs burned.

"Anna! Anna, slow down."

She heard Pastor Gabe call out to her, but she paid him no heed. This was her brother. Eight years older, he'd been like a father to her. He'd left school to support her and Ma. And how had she rewarded him? By fighting him every step of the way.

By the time she reached the mercantile, she couldn't draw in enough air and had to stop to gasp for more. Only then did she realize that others headed toward the garage. By car or on foot, all of Pearlman streamed toward what she could now see was a cloud of dust. No fire. No fire engine. Hendrick's reengineered pumping motor wouldn't be needed.

Hendrick. Her throat constricted.

"Are you all right?" Pastor Gabe had caught up to her.

She didn't want to talk, not when Hendrick might be

hurt. She raced down the final block, oblivious to everything except that cloud of dust. Crowds had gathered, and she couldn't see the building.

"Hendrick," she called, trying to push around the throngs.

Then she saw him. He stood in the middle of the intersection, arms crossed, pure anger etched onto his face. Beyond him, a tractor pulled down the last wall of the house with a crash, and the plaster disintegrated.

"My house," Anna gasped. "Our house."

The house she'd grown up in, the only home she'd ever known, lay in ruins.

She angrily brushed aside the tears that formed. "How could they?"

Hendrick swept an arm toward the scene. The motor garage still stood untouched by the wreckers, but the house was gone. "Look what your Mr. Brandon has done."

He was right. She couldn't deny it. Brandon had evicted them so he could demolish their home. He knew this would happen, yet he'd said nothing to her. Just like when he evicted them. Hendrick had been right about him all along.

A sob hiccuped to the surface. She pressed a hand to her mouth, unable to look away. Her bedroom, Ma's room, the kitchen where they'd shared every dream and worry... all gone.

"Don't watch." The strong hand beneath her elbow didn't belong to her brother or Pastor Gabe.

It was Brandon.

Anna shook off his touch. "You knew."

The accusation hung between them on the steam from her breath, yet Brandon didn't flinch or waver. If possible, he looked even more distressed than her brother.

"I'm sorry," he said. "I should have warned you this might happen, but I didn't know for certain that they were going to do this, and I certainly didn't know they were doing it today."

Anna could almost accept his apology. "Yes, you should have told me." She wrapped her arms around her body, suddenly chilled.

If she'd known the house was going to be demolished, she wouldn't have been caught by surprise. Instead, she stood on the street corner, drawing looks of pity from everyone gathered to watch the spectacle. Well, she didn't want to be pitied. She didn't want people staring at her.

"The new owner is building a Cadillac dealership," Brandon said, more to Hendrick. "It'll benefit the garage's business."

Her brother's sour expression didn't change. "Cadillac? Just like your car. I suppose that's why you sold the place. You had an arrangement with the new owner."

Brandon looked stricken. "I didn't sell the prop—" He halted and left the declaration of innocence on his tongue.

Though Anna knew Brandon was right, she couldn't bring herself to tell Hendrick that, not when her home lay in ruins and her brother glared at Brandon.

Just moments before, her course had seemed clear. She would work in the bookstore and help Minnie stay in school. Ma adored the carriage-house apartment. Most of all, Brandon had finally begun talking about himself. She had seen a narrow path into the future.

Now that certainty lay shattered.

"Let me take you home," Brandon offered.

"That's my responsibility." Hendrick moved between Brandon and her, his hands fisted. He looked as though he would punch Brandon at any moment, and Brandon showed no sign of backing down.

Brandon nodded agreement but didn't give an inch. If Hendrick threw a punch, he looked ready to not only take it but to return the favor. She couldn't let them fight in the middle of the street.

"I'll walk," she said loudly enough to get through their thick skulls. "I'm sick of looking at this anyway."

Then she turned her back and left.

Considering Brandon didn't intend to marry anyone, including Anna, he shouldn't care what Hendrick Simmons thought of him. Yet he'd nearly told the man that Father had sold the house, not him. That would have been futile. Hendrick didn't differentiate between father and son. He held Brandon responsible, and no argument could change that.

Nor should it. With Father gone, he *was* responsible. Just like with his men. The old sickening dread filled him, beginning with his stomach and spreading outward like ice flowing through his veins.

"Are you all right?" It was the minister, Pastor Gabe.

"I'm fine. Should be getting home." He looked around for his car and realized he'd left it at the bookstore. His only escape was on foot, and he took it.

Alas, the minister came with him. Despite his shorter stature, he kept pace with Brandon. "Hendrick will get over it."

Brandon let the comment pass.

"So will Anna," Gabe said. "She's resilient, strong. Did you know she was in a fire this past summer?"

That brought Brandon to a stop. "A fire?" He glanced back at the house. The dust probably looked like smoke. No wonder she'd been so frightened.

"Not here," the minister said, mistaking Brandon's glance. "It happened in Montana. Mariah took Anna and Hendrick west with her. She had to prove the man who'd claimed our Luke wasn't really his father."

Brandon struggled to piece together what the minister

was saying. This man who'd claimed to be Luke's father must have been in Montana.

Gabe chuckled. "Judging from your expression, you're surprised to learn Anna made such a long trip."

"Long? It couldn't have taken more than a few days by train."

"Oh, no. They drove."

Brandon had to blink. Several times. "A car?"

The man's grin got wider. "That's what I said when Mariah proposed it, but my sister has a mind of her own, and no one—man or woman—will stop her once she sets her mind on something. The best I could do was convince her to take Hendrick and Anna along."

"Then Anna has traveled." That explained her hunger for adventure.

"From what I hear, she loved every minute of the trip."

"Except the fire, I assume."

Gabe and Brandon began slowly walking toward the bookstore. "Lightning sparked a wildfire near a school." Gabe shook his head. "Mariah told me Anna stayed calm and helped bring the children to safety. That sort of experience can either drive fear deep into a person or make them stronger."

"I gather you think it made Anna stronger."

The pastor didn't answer at first. "When I first met Anna, she was a shy, awkward girl of seventeen. I'm guessing she never had a beau. I hardly ever heard her speak in public. She talked a little around family but barely said a word to me. When she returned from Montana, she chattered away to everyone."

Brandon had a difficult time imagining Anna acting shy. She didn't hesitate to tell him what she thought.

"Don't worry about Hendrick," Pastor Gabe said as they

reached the bookstore and Brandon's car. "He's just a lit-tle protective of his kid sister. She was only seven when their father died, so he ended up being more a father than a brother to her."

That explained a great deal. If Brandon had had a sister, he would have scrutinized each suitor. A daughter? Any man who approached her would find the Spanish Inquisi-tion easier than dealing with him.

"If he doesn't come around," the pastor continued, "I'll have Mariah speak to him."

The pastor's words came as a jolt. Apparently he'd al-ready matched Brandon with Anna.

"That won't be necessary," Brandon said quickly. If Pas-tor Gabe approached Hendrick, it would only second the man's fear that Brandon wanted to marry his sister.

"If you say so." Gabe bade him farewell before loping across the snow-covered street.

As Brandon opened the door to his car, he wondered how many people in town had paired him with Anna. Probably everyone. It was a small town, after all. He settled behind the wheel. By offering her a place to live, he'd opened him-self to such speculation. No doubt the entire town knew she cleaned his house. Rumors would swirl, some unkind.

He clenched the icy cold steering wheel. He'd never meant to hurt Anna's reputation and prospects. How would she find a husband with those rumors in the air? Now he'd offered her the bookstore job, which would only make things worse.

"Small towns," he muttered as he started the car and put it in gear.

He'd hoped to escape the past here. Instead, the trouble had followed him here, and this time a beautiful young woman would suffer.

For her sake, he must cut the ties between them.

* * *

"They demolished our home," Anna cried as she burst through the carriage-house door.

Ma looked around the room from her perch in the fire-side chair. "Whatever do you mean? It looks fine to me."

"Not here." Anna tugged off her gloves. "Our old house."

"You know that house wasn't ours. We simply rented it."

Anna unbuttoned her coat and flung it over the back of the other chair. "But I grew up in it. It was home." She fought through the lump clogging her throat. "They knocked it down. My bedroom." A little sob escaped. "The kitchen."

"Hush, child. A home is where your family lives, not bricks and mortar." She extended her arms, and Anna gratefully fell into her embrace.

"Dearest, this is home now." She cupped Anna's face and gave her a smile.

"It's just an old, musty carriage house."

"It's warm and dry, and I count my blessings every day. If not for Mr. Brandon, we would be living in the boarding-house. You must admit that in comparison, we have much to be grateful for."

Anna bit her lip, not quite willing to let go of the hurt of seeing her childhood home demolished. "It's just that…" She drew a breath. What was it that brought such ache? "It's that we'll never be able to go back."

Ma smiled softly. "Why ever would you want to go back? It's the future you need to seek, dearest, not the past."

Anna knew she was right, but what future could she look forward to? Her dreams seemed out of reach, hopeless.

A knock sounded on the door.

"Who could that be at this hour?" Ma said. "It's nearly suppertime."

Anna wiped her damp eyes. "Supper. I forgot." She should have brought their meals down from the house.

A second knock sounded.

"I'll get it." She rose, composed herself and opened the door.

Brandon stood on the other side, his coat and hat dusted with snow, which was now falling steadily. In his free hand he held the basket she used to bring their meals down from the house.

"Your supper." He held out the basket, covered with a thick towel.

She was touched that he'd taken such care to keep their meals hot. "You shouldn't have gone to so much trouble. I was on my way to fetch them."

But instead of leaving, he nodded toward the interior of the apartment, "May I step inside a moment? I need to discuss something with you."

His grave expression worried her. After seeing the house tumble, she wasn't sure she could handle more disappointment.

"What's wrong?" she asked as she took the basket from him.

He stepped inside, and she closed the door behind him.

"Please have a seat," Ma said, rising.

"You're walking well, I see." But he didn't take the offered chair.

"Doc Stevens says I'll be able to walk outdoors in a week or so, but I won't be able to work for some time yet."

Anna couldn't mistake the look of distress that furrowed his brow. Ma apparently didn't notice, because she rambled on cheerfully.

"I'm afraid that means Anna will have to continue cleaning the house. But she does such a good job. You couldn't get a better worker. I understand she's doing a fine job at the store too." Ma grasped his hand. "I can't thank you enough. You're a godsend, an absolute godsend."

Instead of appreciating her gratitude, he looked even more distressed.

"Yes, thank you." Anna said no more when she saw the haunted look in his eyes. What was wrong?

"Yes, well, I can't stay," he said, looking everywhere but at her. "I hope…" He never finished the sentence. Instead he twitched, as if coming out of a nightmare. "I did want to give you the latest news on the excavation."

He withdrew a newspaper from his coat pocket. A small envelope peeked from between its folds.

She reached to take it from him, but he pulled it back and removed the envelope before handing the paper to her. The envelope vanished inside his coat.

Though curious about the envelope, she couldn't help scanning the headline. It didn't mention the burial chamber, but the photographs depicted amazing artifacts.

"Thank you," she breathed.

Looking up, she saw him already at the door. This time he did meet her gaze, but his eyes were filled with bottomless sorrow. Why? Because of the house? What had Hendrick said to him? If her brother did anything to hurt Brandon, she'd have words for him.

"You're welcome," he said before leaving.

But the words carried no warmth and no hope.

Chapter Eleven

The visit had proven a fiasco. The second Brandon saw Anna's tear-swollen eyes, he'd been unable to sever the connection to her. Then her mother poured on the gratitude. He couldn't dismiss Anna, even for her own good.

What a fine mess he'd created.

Then he'd almost given Anna the invitation. That little envelope from Mrs. Evelyn Neidecker had slipped between the pages of the newspaper, and he'd nearly handed it to the only woman he'd consider taking.

Valentine's Day Ball?

He hated balls.

Brandon did not dance. He avoided any possibility of dancing.

After stewing about it that night and the next day, he decided to send his regrets.

He pulled a sheet of paper from the desk in the bookstore's workroom. The stationery was stamped with the business's name, The Antiquarian, and address. He poised the fountain pen over the sheet and hesitated.

Personal correspondence should not be written on business letterhead.

When the doorbell tinkled, he shoved the stationery back

into the drawer, grabbed his cane and walked to the front of the store.

"I'm here," said Anna, her cheeks delightfully rosy from the hike down the hill. She scanned the crates of books that Peter had carted to the store yesterday. "Where should I begin?"

He pulled himself away from admiring her complexion. "I had Peter set the boxes near the shelves where the books belong. Put them in alphabetical order by author."

"And subject," she added as she stripped off her gloves and hat. Strands of hair pulled out of the coil at the nape of her neck and floated around her face. "People will want all the biographies in one place and the adventure books in another."

"Naturally," he said, though he could hardly keep his attention on business. What would she look like on a dance floor, all sparkling and lively? Years ago he would have whirled her around the ballroom.

She opened a carton. "Are these in any order?"

"Uh, yes." He cleared his throat and his fickle imagination. "I sorted them by subject before packing them in the crates. You simply need to put them on the proper shelves."

She peered into another crate. "They're old books."

"That's why it's an antiquarian bookstore."

She looked again. "You're not selling your archaeology books, are you?"

Her panic made him smile. "No. Not yet. At least not until you've read them. There are some fine books on Michigan history and the state's progressive stand on abolition and the Underground Railroad."

Anna shrugged off her coat and looked around for a place to hang it. Brandon had never thought to install a coat hook, even in the back room.

"Give it to me," he said. "I'll find a place for your coat in back."

"Thank you." Her gaze swept over him quickly and then returned, as if she'd summoned the courage to address him. "Do you think Mr. Carter is telling the newspaper everything?"

It took him a moment to leapfrog to the new subject of conversation. "About the excavation in the Valley of the Kings? I'm sure he's very careful what he reports. Antiquities authorities will review every piece removed from the tomb."

She nibbled on her lip, something she did unconsciously when thinking. "Will everything stay in Egypt?" Her uplifted eyes placed total trust in his knowledge. It had been years since anyone gave him such a look.

"That remains to be seen." He tried to focus on archaeology, which suddenly seemed quite dull. "Historically, Egyptian authorities allow a division of finds, with duplicates given to the excavators, but this is the first time an intact tomb has been found. The Egyptians might claim it all."

"Why would Lord Carnarvon and Mr. Carter spend so much on the excavation if they can't take any of the treasure?"

Brandon stifled a smile at her innocence. "Aside from fame and the thrill of discovery, they will earn a lot from lectures and publications."

The bridge of her nose wrinkled, endearing her to him even more. "Will people be able to see what they found? I wish I could be there when they open the sarcophagus." She closed her eyes, the lashes brushing her cheeks. "There must be gold inside. He was a pharaoh, after all. Oh, how glorious to see such splendor."

He didn't have the heart to tell her that only high-ranking

officials and members of the excavation team would be present for that momentous event.

"Perhaps you will one day go to Cairo and see the tomb's contents. From there, it's a short hop to Luxor and the tomb itself."

Her eyelids fluttered open, and her longing was so evident that he wanted more than anything else to give her that glimpse of the past. "Do you think so?"

"Anything is possible." He recalled her trip to Montana. "Especially for someone who traveled west by motorcar."

"My travels last summer." Her lips curved upward. "That was an adventure."

"I'd love to hear about it."

The hours spent unpacking books passed quickly thanks to her tales of the trip west. From prairie dogs to storms, she made every event a highlight.

"You should write those stories down," he urged, wanting her to reach for every possibility.

"Maybe someday."

"Do it. Write them like you just told me, so others can experience what you did. Very few are able to take a trip like that."

She pondered his statement a good while. "I suppose you're right."

He nodded. "They're fine stories."

"I love a good story." She stood and looked around. "Speaking of which, where will the dime novels go?"

Brandon cringed. "The popular-fiction section is to your right."

She stared at the shelves she'd loaded the day before yesterday. "I wouldn't call those popular. You won't sell many books if that's all you're going to have in your fiction section. Where are the mystery and adventure novels? Allan

Pinkerton's detective stories? Zane Grey and Mary Roberts Rinehart?"

"Those are not appropriate for an antiquarian bookstore. Besides, the mercantile already carries a wide selection of bestselling novels."

"You'll never make money if you don't carry what people want to buy. You need popular novels and magazines, like *The Argosy* and *Action Stories*. Oh, and *Detective Story Magazine*. That has some good stories too."

Brandon had to swallow the instinct to vilify the pulp magazines. Clearly Anna loved them, but he wanted to promote literature and learning, not aimless fantasy.

"The drugstore carries those," he stated, returning to his work.

Though he could feel her piercing gaze on his back, he continued to work. If anything, he shelved faster and more noisily.

"You could at least have a children's section," she finally said, the hurt obvious. "Girls like The Bobbsey Twins and boys love Tom Swift."

Brandon hadn't meant to snub her. He was simply running short of cash. "I'll consider it."

"They would sell nicely. I'm sure you'd like to make a profit."

More than she realized. He drew a deep breath. Perhaps he could loosen his standards a bit. "Make a list of popular novels you think we should carry, and I'll order a selection of them."

"You will?" She clapped her hands together. "Oh, thank you, thank you." She danced to the front of the store. "You should place them here, right in front where they'll catch people's attention."

He gritted his teeth. The front-and-center shelving was intended for the most beautiful books in his collection, those with colored plates and photographs. "All fiction will be shelved together."

"Not the children's books." She spun around, looking for a spot, and settled on the nook near the side window. "That would make a cozy corner for the children. We could put a rocker there for the mothers and little chairs or benches for the boys and girls."

Children in his bookstore? Brandon hadn't quite planned on that. Not that he didn't enjoy children, but they were naturally curious and clumsy. He could see them pulling his valuable books off the shelves and ripping pages. "No children's section and no furniture. We don't want people staying here all day. This isn't a library."

She looked at him as if he'd lost his mind. "No children's books? But they're the most important ones of all. We have to encourage the children to read. It's the key to everything."

He was surprised by the passion in her voice. This she truly believed, and, if he thought about it a moment, he did too. Literacy gave a man opportunity. Train him to read while still a boy, and the world opened to him.

"We will have a small selection," he conceded, "but no furniture." Other than a locking bookcase where he could store his most valuable books.

She looked so pleased that he could ignore the hint of worry that niggled at his mind. Surely nothing bad could happen if he took precautions.

"You will be in charge of any children that come in," he said. "There will be no running and no pulling the antique books off the shelves. Understand?"

She laughed and straightened as if to salute. "Yes, sir."

The words sounded obedient, but the truth was far different. That woman had wrapped him around her finger without much effort at all.

* * *

Anna reveled in the added responsibility. By the end of the week, she compiled a list of books Brandon should purchase. When he glanced through the titles without protest, she knew she'd done a good job. Brandon wasn't one to shower unwarranted accolades.

"The grand opening will take place on Saturday," he said, setting aside the list.

"Before my books arrive?"

His eyebrows lifted slightly. "We do have other books to sell."

She supposed some people would be interested in the Fitzgerald and Ferber, but few would leap to purchase the antique books that Brandon spent all his time reading. In fact, he was immersed in one now. It looked like an old ledger, with ruled lines and illegible numbers.

"What's that book?" She wiggled behind the sales counter to get a better look.

He slammed the book shut. "Nothing important."

What an odd reaction. "You mean you're not going to sell it?"

"Definitely not."

"Then why bring it here?"

His brow puckered in a frown. "I mistakenly put it in one of the crates." He drummed his fingers on top of the leatherbound volume, which was stained and starting to peel at the edges. "I'll have to go through every book on the shelves to make sure there aren't any others."

"Does that mean you're not going to open Saturday?"

"The store opens as planned. Just don't sell any of the antique books without my permission. Only sell the popular fiction."

With a grimace, he rose to his feet and grabbed his cane.

Until now, she'd never realized that his injury might still cause him pain.

"Let me help you." She held out a hand.

"I'm not an invalid," he bristled. "Nor do I need mothering."

"There's no reason to fuss at me. I just wanted to help."

After a long pause, he relented. "I'm sorry. Please understand how important it is that I manage on my own."

She heard again that deep sorrow hidden beneath the words, but if he didn't reach out to someone, he'd never find relief. "We all need help sometimes."

"Not me." Ledger tucked under his arm, he limped past her on his way to the back room.

She didn't want their conversation to end this way. Even the Bible said not to go to sleep while still angry...or something to that effect. Maybe what Brandon needed was to get this out in the open.

"How did it happen?"

He halted and slowly swiveled toward her. "How did what happen?"

She remembered then how badly he'd reacted the last time she'd brought up this subject, but she'd incur his wrath if he'd only let her help him. "Your injury. You said it happened in the war."

His mood darkened, and Anna knew she'd erred even more. "I'm sorry. That's none of my business."

He could have berated her, could have made her feel lower than dirt, but instead he answered. "Artillery shattered my foot. I lost the big toe...and my balance."

Anna felt worse than horrible. His injury could not be fixed. Maybe that's why he was so mad at God, why he wouldn't set foot in church.

Seeing as she'd already angered him, she figured she

might as well try to draw him to the Lord. "We can celebrate the store's opening at Sunday worship."

He stared at her as if she'd said the most ridiculous thing ever. "At church?"

"I know it's not the usual place to celebrate, but we're having a potluck dinner afterward. I'd love to have you join us. Ma would love to have you there too." She must have been blathering away because his eyes had glazed over.

"No, thank you," he said curtly. "I will be busy."

Alone in his big old house? Or counting the receipts from the day before? At least this time she had the good sense not to say what she was thinking out loud.

If sheer numbers of people equated to success, the bookstore's opening could be considered successful, but Brandon knew better. The steady stream of the curious didn't account for many sales. Two books sold would not keep the store afloat for long. He needed money from another source. At this point he was willing to believe the rumors of a long lost family fortune.

The quiet of his library offered little relief for his aching head. He stared down at the old family ledger. Surely his ancestors had written something that would confirm or deny the existence of the fortune, but he hadn't come across one word.

He slammed the book shut. Worthless thing. But it was the last place left to look.

His eyes burned, his head ached and his conscience tormented him from the moment the church bells rang this morning. The hopeful look in Anna's eyes when she'd asked him to attend had haunted him every moment since. He should have gone. God might not want him there, but she did.

What was it the Bible said about the Pharisees? That

they'd hardened their hearts? Brandon had put all his trust in God from an early age, following his mother's lead. Mother practically glowed with patience, kindness and love—all the fruits the Bible talked about. Her every touch was gentle, caring, a lot like Mrs. Simmons. What had she ever seen in Father? The crass entrepreneur saw little need for religion except as a tool to form business connections. He attended church services to broker deals, not worship God.

As a youth, Brandon had vowed to cling to God. But God hadn't stuck by him, not when it really counted.

He closed his eyes against the firestorm of memories and yanked on his hair to blot out the pain of what had happened.

It wasn't his fault. It couldn't have been his fault. He obeyed his commanding officer. He'd been a good soldier. Then why had his men died? If only God had heard his pleas, but He'd abandoned him.

The telephone rang, jolting Brandon from the miserable memories. He swiped a hand over his jaw to force himself back to reality and picked up the receiver. The operator informed him that he had a call from Ann Arbor.

His brother. What now?

Reggie's voice came on the line momentarily. "Halloo, brother," he said cheerfully, a bit too cheerfully.

"What's wrong?"

Even with the static, Brandon could hear Reggie's laugh. "That's my big brother, always leaping to the bottom line. No pleasantries. No 'how do you do.' No catching up on what's happened."

"Long distance is expensive. Do you have a point?" Brandon knew his words sounded harsh, but with a pounding head and a guilty conscience, he couldn't muster civility.

"Can't I talk to my only brother?"

"I know you. You only call when there's a problem or you need money."

Reggie laughed again. "Such a jokester. Maybe this time I'm calling to inquire after my beloved brother. How is Anna?"

Brandon tensed. "You didn't call to ask about Anna."

"Aha! I knew you felt something for her."

Brandon had to put a stop to this line of conversation at once. "She is a nice girl. Nothing more."

"So you say. Have you told her what happened in the war?"

Brandon could have crushed the receiver if it hadn't been made of such sturdy materials.

"How much do you need?"

The ensuing pause was so long that Brandon feared the connection had broken. "Hello? Are you there?"

"Yes." Again Reggie paused.

This could not be good.

"Two thousand."

Brandon coughed. "Two...what?"

"I wouldn't ask if I wasn't desperate."

"A year's tuition and board don't come to that, and the trust already paid for those." As Brandon said the words, he knew the expenses had nothing to do with education. Reggie had started gambling again. "I told you no before," he yelled into the receiver. The bookstore's bills were piling up. He couldn't afford the debts he already had. "It's still no."

"But Brandon—"

"No excuses. No exceptions. I'm sorry, Reggie, but it's time you grew up." Without waiting for a response, he broke the connection.

His stomach had knotted, and sweat dripped off his brow despite the chill in the room. Father had begged him to look after Reggie, but he'd just turned away his only brother. It was for Reggie's good. Father and Mother had coddled him.

That couldn't continue if he was ever to become a man. Reggie needed to take responsibility for his actions.

Brandon hoped he'd done the right thing. He stared out the window, deep in anguish, and almost didn't see Anna walking toward the kitchen door carrying the basket she used to transport meals.

She glanced at the library window, as if she knew he was in the room. He quickly looked down at the desktop, where the useless ledger lay. He pushed it aside, uncovering the little ivory envelope with Mrs. Neidecker's invitation. An exclusive ball just for handpicked guests—Pearlman's elite. No event could possibly disgust him more. He'd learned from Pastor Gabe that only the rich were invited. Though Gabe had received an invitation, he and his wife sent their regrets in the hope the Neideckers would open the event to all.

"It's like the man in Luke's gospel who gave a banquet," Pastor Gabe had said. "If none of the invited attends, then the hosts will have to ask the less fortunate."

Brandon doubted it, but he knew another way to rattle the Neideckers, a way that also, he had to admit, would make the event enjoyable for him too.

He rose and walked to the window.

Anna had paused before reaching the house. Snow dusted her handmade knit red hat. She bent to pull an acorn from the snow and held it out to a waiting squirrel. Anna Simmons gave from her heart. He might not be able to attend her church, but he could give her a gift she would never forget.

Chapter Twelve

Anna must not have heard Brandon correctly. Snow melted off her hat and coat and dripped onto the kitchen floor while she considered his invitation.

When she finally spoke, her voice came out in a squeak. "Me? You want to take me? To the Valentine's Ball?"

Thoughts whirled through her head. Mrs. Neidecker would be embarrassed, furious even, to see her there. Sally's eyes would bulge from her head. She'd probably say something nasty, but Anna would arrive on the arm of the handsomest man in town.

"I would be honored if you would join me," Brandon repeated.

The electric light sparkled in his dark eyes, not stormy dark but warmly dark and inviting. Her heart skipped a beat. He would escort her onto the dance floor, take her in his arms and waltz past all those girls who'd been whispering about him since he arrived. Many girls dreamed of catching his attention, but she, Anna Simmons, would be the one dancing with him at the Valentine's Ball.

"I'm afraid I won't be able to dance," he said, crushing her fantasy, "but I promise lively conversation."

Anna tried to mask her disappointment, but judging by

the shadow of distress that crossed Brandon's expression, she'd done a pretty poor job of it.

She swallowed hard, trying to stay calm. "I—I—I'd be honored to join you." The stammer brought a rush of heat to her cheeks. Why couldn't she speak eloquently and maintain her composure like the other girls?

He either didn't notice or didn't care. A rare smile flickered into place. "Thank you."

She nearly swooned. The Valentine's Ball. She was going to the Valentine's Ball.

How many times she'd wished someone would invite her but never as much as she wanted Brandon to. When Ma had suggested the possibility, she pretended not to care, but she did. Brandon somehow meant more to her than anyone she'd ever known, yet he'd always seemed so distant.

Until now. His smile at her acceptance brought a flood of warmth, followed by excitement. She was attending the Valentine's Ball with the most handsome man in Pearlman. She would walk into the house on his arm. Everyone would notice. Everyone would comment. Some would be disappointed. Others would be furious.

A giggle escaped when she imagined the look on Sally's face.

His brow puckered. "Did I do something wrong?"

She shook her head and pressed a hand to her mouth to keep in the laughter. "I'm just happy."

"You are?"

She could only nod, because the way he was looking at her sent the most amazing feelings through her. She could have danced around the kitchen and laughed until dawn. Most of all, she wanted to do every bit of it with him. Brandon Landers. The man she'd once hated.

Why had she ever felt that way? He'd been more than kind to her and Ma. He'd righted every wrong, soothed every hurt. And now he'd chosen her—poor Anna Simmons—as his companion for the biggest social event of the season. He must know what people would say, that they'd pair the two of them and speculate when the engagement would be announced.

Her knees weakened at the thought, and she leaned on the kitchen worktable for support. Her hands were trembling. Her head grew light; the stove began to blur.

"Are you all right?" He reached an arm around her waist and gently led her to a chair.

She didn't want to sit. She didn't want to leave his arms. Such strength. The spicy scent of a man filled her senses and cleared her head. She looked up into those gray eyes, still dark and filled with concern.

"Please sit," he said. "You'll feel better."

"I'm better now," she whispered, making no move to leave his embrace.

His right hand braced her upper back while the left cradled her elbow. How easy it would be to slip her arms around his neck, to close her eyes and feel his lips on hers. Would he? Her heart nearly stopped beating. His eyes had grown darker, reflecting only her. His expression softened, and his lips, oh, his lips. If only he would kiss her.

She let her eyelids drift almost shut, leaving just enough of a slit so she could see if he was leaning toward her. At first he did nothing, and then slowly he drew closer. She stopped breathing and shut her eyes, waiting for the moment she'd dreamed about all her life.

Instead, he cleared his throat. "The chair is right behind you."

Her lids flew open, and she saw a look of bemusement on his face. He didn't laugh at her or call her silly, but she felt the sting anyway.

What a fool she was.

* * *

"It doesn't matter what I wear when I look like a maid," Anna cried as she helped Mariah wash the dishes after putting the orphans to bed. Between cooking and cleaning at Brandon's house, working at the bookstore and helping out occasionally at the orphanage, her hands were raw and chapped. Certainly not the hands of a lady.

The Valentine's Ball was just a week away, and she looked a fright.

"My hair isn't stylish," she moaned at she wiped the last plate dry. "No one wears long hair anymore."

"Mrs. Shea and Mrs. Evans do."

"They're *old*." Anna looked hopefully to her sister-in-law. "Will you cut my hair? I want mine bobbed like yours."

"Are you sure? Bobs might be practical for some of us, but most men prefer long hair."

"Hendrick likes your hair short."

Mariah laughed. "Oh, he'd prefer long hair if he had his way. Keep yours long. It's so beautiful."

"It's dull and drab. Plain old brown, not brunette or blonde." She looked at her reflection in the polished steel of a soup ladle. "Sally Neidecker has a bob."

"I wouldn't put any stock in what Sally thinks or does. I've seen Brandon admiring your hair."

"You have?" The thought sent a flush of heat to her cheeks. "Do you think he likes it?"

"I know he does." Mariah handed her a soapy pot. "He's a traditional kind of man. He'd prefer an elegant chignon over a bob."

Anna dunked the pot in the rinse water. "I don't think I can look elegant."

"Don't fret. I'll help you get ready. Hendrick can watch the children for one night."

Hendrick. The thought of her brother sent a chill down

Anna's spine. "Does he know that Brandon invited me to the ball?"

"Of course."

"He doesn't like Brandon."

"Nonsense." But Mariah didn't look at her when she said it. "He's just cautious. He doesn't want you to get hurt."

"Brandon would never hurt me," Anna said, though doubts immediately followed her words. He did have a habit of pulling away whenever they got close. "Can you convince Hendrick of that?"

Mariah lifted an eyebrow. "Do you think I'm a miracle worker?"

Anna couldn't help but laugh.

Mariah touched her hand. "Seriously, don't worry about your brother. He'll come around. It'll just take time."

Anna hoped she was right.

"While we finish up here, let's plan our preparations." Mariah handed her another pot. "If you come here to dress, I'll style your hair."

"Dress?" Anna lost hold of the pot, and it clattered to the floor. "I don't have a dress. What will I wear? My Sunday best isn't good enough for a ball, and I can't afford to buy a gown." She picked up the pot and handed it to Mariah, who wiped it clean again.

"You can borrow one of mine."

Anna eyed her sister-in-law skeptically. They couldn't possibly fit the same dress. Mariah was shorter and had a somewhat larger build, still trim but not rail-thin like Anna. "Your dresses would have to be altered."

"Hmm." Mariah stepped back from the sink, hands soapy, and assessed Anna from head to toe. "Perhaps you're right. I know what we'll do. We'll ask Felicity. I'm sure she would lend you one of hers since she's not attending this year."

Anna blanched. Felicity Kensington Meeks lend her a

dress? They'd never really been friends. And then there was the embarrassing matter of Anna having a crush on Pastor Gabriel three years ago. It had all worked out for Gabe and Felicity, but Anna was still embarrassed by the way she'd acted at the time.

"I don't think she'd lend me a dress."

"Sure she would. I'll call her right now." Mariah wiped her hands dry and headed for the wall telephone.

"No, don't." Anna ran past her and plastered herself against the telephone.

Mariah looked amused by Anna's panicked reaction, but she didn't comment or try to get to the telephone. Instead, she quite reasonably asked, "Why not? You do want to look your best for Brandon, don't you?"

Of course she did, but ask Felicity? Anna would die of embarrassment. "I—I think it's better if I ask in person."

"I think we'd do better together. Let's walk to the parsonage after finishing the dishes. Hendrick is here in case any of the children wake."

Anna scrambled to dissuade her from this course. Felicity would never lend her a ball gown, and Anna couldn't bring herself to ask. "I doubt it would fit anyway."

"Nonsense. You're almost exactly the same size. She might be a touch taller, but that won't matter one bit with a ball gown."

"She might not want to part with her gown. Or maybe she doesn't have any."

Mariah set the last pan in the rinse water. "I happen to know she has several, and she will lend you one."

"But—" Anna had run out of excuses.

Mariah always saw through to the heart of the issue. "Trust me, the past is long forgotten. Felicity bears you no ill will. Surely you know that by now, after all the Sunday dinners and family gatherings."

"I know," she said glumly. Felicity did treat her kindly, but Anna couldn't forget the way she'd behaved, chasing after Pastor Gabe when he liked Felicity. If someone did that to her and Brandon, she'd be furious.

Mariah held out her coat. "Best to face your fears or they'll control you for the rest of your life."

Resigned, Anna donned her coat and followed Mariah out the door.

Mariah was right.

Anna gaped at the row of ball gowns hanging in Felicity's closet. Every one must have cost a fortune—more than Hendrick earned in a year—and each came with matching hat and bag.

"Pick the one you like best," Felicity said breezily as she plucked one gown after the other out of the closet and threw them on the bed. "Do you have shoes? You must have ivory pumps for anything other than black, but black is so drab. You'll want to turn heads, especially a certain someone's."

Anna couldn't hide the heat that rushed to her cheeks. She grabbed the black gown tucked far in the back of the closet. "This one will do."

Felicity ripped it away from her and tossed it aside. "Nonsense. That's for matrons. You're young and smart. You'll want a dress that highlights your coloring. Blue or blush, I'd say, wouldn't you?" She looked to Mariah.

Mariah agreed. "Blush would bring out her fair skin and the reddish highlights in her hair."

Anna covered her head with both hands. Red? She had red in her hair?

"And blue will accent her eyes," said Felicity, surveying Anna from head to toe. "Mother always insisted green best brought out my eye coloring."

"Blue would be lovely for her eyes," countered Mariah, "but its coolness won't help her fair skin."

"I don't have fair skin," Anna protested. "Freckled is more accurate."

The two women ignored her.

Felicity headed for the closet. "I think I have just the gown."

Anna couldn't move, couldn't breathe, couldn't imagine wearing any of Felicity's dresses. What if she spilled something? What if she caught a sleeve or the hem and ripped it?

Felicity emerged from the closet with a large pasteboard box and set it on the bed, right on top of the expensive dresses. "This will be perfect." She untied the ribbon and lifted the box lid to reveal a glittery dress in the most exquisite shade of blush.

"Perfect," agreed Mariah.

Felicity brushed aside the tissue paper and lifted the gown from the box. She held it up to Anna's shoulders. "A bit long in the arms, but Mrs. Fox could fix that in no time."

Anna didn't have the heart to tell her that she couldn't afford alterations.

"If you ask me," Mariah said, "it will fit perfectly. No one would notice a half inch at the wrist."

"Some would."

Anna knew Felicity meant Sally Neidecker. The two had butted heads in the past. Apparently nothing had changed. "I don't care what anyone says. I like it just the way it is. But it looks new. The tissue isn't even crinkled."

Felicity shrugged. "I was going to wear it to the ball until Gabe and I decided not to attend. I couldn't bear to leave Genie alone at night."

Though Anna knew Pastor Gabe had other reasons for skipping the ball, she was relieved to see that Felicity didn't harbor any resentment over missing the social event of the season.

"Understandable," Mariah tactfully murmured.

Anna ran her fingers over the silk. It was styled in the very latest fashion, if *Vanity Fair* was to be believed. The filmy fabric had been gathered at the hip in a bow that featured a sequined circular ornament in the colors of the rainbow. Its handkerchief hemline accentuated Anna's height while hiding her knobby knees. A turban, complete with a short peacock feather, and jeweled bag completed the outfit.

"It's beautiful." Anna sighed. "Too beautiful. I can't wear it."

"Of course you can," said Felicity, tossing the dress into the box without bothering to fold it. "I insist. Someone needs to wear the gown, and it might as well be someone looking to catch a certain man's attention."

Anna felt the heat again. Why did she blush every time someone mentioned Brandon? "I think he just invited me to thank me for helping with the bookstore."

Mariah and Felicity glanced at each other, and then Mariah burst into a deep, throaty laugh. Felicity soon followed, and the two of them roared until tears came to their eyes.

"What's so funny?" Anna asked.

Mariah wiped her eyes. "I've never seen a man more interested in a woman."

"You haven't?" Anna sank onto the edge of the bed. "You can't mean that. He's always so standoffish with me."

Mariah and Felicity exchanged another meaningful glance. Both had married recently, Mariah just last September.

"Exactly," Mariah said.

Felicity nodded. "That's the way they are."

"I remember Gabe pretending he wasn't interested in you," Mariah said to Felicity.

"Those were awful days, but it all came out in the end." Felicity sat beside Anna and took her hand. "It'll work out fine for you too."

Anna wasn't so sure. Felicity had married an open, caring man. As for Mariah, well, Hendrick had been in love with her from the moment they'd met. Neither one had experienced anything like what she was going through.

Felicity hugged her. "Trust me, Brandon Landers likes you. He might be a little confused right now, but he'll come to his senses. You just need to show him how invaluable you are and how much he'll miss if he doesn't marry you."

That sounded impossible. "How?"

"Discover his needs and fulfill them."

Mariah nodded her agreement.

Anna panicked. "But how do I do that?"

"You both like archaeology, right?" Felicity said. "Find something that you can do together. I know. Maybe you can search for that lost fortune that Daddy is always talking about."

"But Brandon says there is no fortune."

Again Felicity and Mariah exchanged a glance.

"Do you believe him?" Felicity asked.

Anna thought back to the odd way Brandon had acted in recent days—the hours spent in the library, the old ledger he wouldn't let her see, his adamant denunciation of the rumor.

"Do you think…?" she asked breathlessly. "Is it possible?"

Felicity shrugged. "I have no idea, but it certainly wouldn't hurt to try. You'd have such fun together. It would be like a treasure hunt, like that Mr. Carter's find in Egypt."

Anna's pulse raced. "A real treasure. Right here in Pearlman."

Mariah frowned. "Just remember, the best treasure in life isn't money. Fortunes can divide people."

Mariah might have a point. After all, she'd given up comparative wealth to marry Hendrick. But if Anna helped Brandon find the lost fortune, he *had* to respect her. Maybe he'd even love her.

"Money can cause problems," Felicity agreed, "but if two people have their hearts in the right place, they'll use it for good. I'm sure Anna's focused on what's important." She tossed the hat and bag on top of the dress and closed the box. "Until then, my dear, dazzle him at the ball."

Anna caressed the beaded gown. Maybe with such a dress, she could.

Chapter Thirteen

Dressed in Felicity's finery, Anna felt like Cinderella going to the ball. Mariah and Felicity had come to the carriage house to assist her. Felicity supplied every last detail of clothing, down to the elbow-length gloves. When Mariah finished with Anna's hair, she didn't recognize herself. An elegant woman gazed back at her in the scratched old hand mirror.

Felicity lifted the turban hat from the hatbox and held it up to Anna, surveying the effect. "I'm not sure you need a hat."

Anna was afraid to even touch her hair, lest the beautiful coil come tumbling down. The hat would require hatpins to stay fixed in place since it ran a bit small on her. "Do I have to leave it on the entire time?"

Felicity smiled indulgently. "Of course."

"What if it slips off? It doesn't fit quite right."

"That settles it. No hat." Felicity put it back in the hatbox. "Not everyone wears them at formal balls anymore."

"Are you sure? What if I'm the only woman not wearing one? I don't want to look out of place."

"You won't," Felicity assured her, but Anna still worried that people would laugh.

At that moment, Brandon knocked on the carriage-house door, and all thought of hats vanished from her mind.

"He's here," she hissed, frantic. "Do I look all right?" She smoothed the skirt and checked that it was straight.

"You look lovely," Ma said with a smile. "My beautiful daughter." Tears misted her eyes. "Your father would be so proud."

Mariah and Felicity nodded, pleased with their handiwork, but the moment Ma let Brandon in the door, Anna only had eyes for him. How dashing he was in his black evening suit. He'd chosen the short suit rather than tails, which Felicity confided was now the fashion, but Anna could not have cared less. His crisp white shirt and black bow tie made him look regal. A black wool overcoat and trilby hat completed the portrait of a gentleman.

His stunned yet pleased expression made her thoughts whirl.

She smoothed her skirt. "I hope I look all right."

His gaze softened. "You're beautiful." But then he shook his head. "No, beautiful isn't adequate. Exquisite can only come close. Anna…" His voice deepened. "I'm honored you would join me tonight."

She lingered on his words. Beautiful? Exquisite? Never had anyone used those words to describe her. She was Anna Simmons, the poor mechanic's daughter.

Was this truly happening? Was she really attending the Valentine's Ball? All her life she'd wondered and wished, and now she would arrive on the arm of the most handsome and wealthy bachelor in Pearlman. Not only that, he thought her beautiful. She clutched at the pearls she'd borrowed from Felicity, unable to speak or move.

"Shall we?" He extended an arm.

Felicity held up an elegant black cape that she'd brought

for Anna. It hung a touch too long, but Brandon didn't appear to notice.

Anna took Brandon's arm with her ivory-gloved hand. He helped her to the car, which he'd parked very close to the carriage house so she wouldn't have to walk far in the snow with Felicity's pumps.

"Thank you," she murmured as he opened the passenger door and ensured she was properly seated.

While Brandon assisted Felicity and Mariah into the rear seat, Ma watched from the window. Anna waved at her as the women in the back giggled like schoolgirls.

"Are you excited?" Felicity said while Brandon opened the driver's door.

Anna could barely breathe. She certainly couldn't express herself with any degree of calm, so she nodded.

Brandon took his seat and started the car.

"You'll be fine," Mariah whispered with a squeeze of Anna's shoulder. Her voice rose. "Remember to follow the lead."

Anna's mouth went dry as Brandon gave her a sharp glance. She hadn't exactly told Mariah and Felicity that Brandon wouldn't dance. But then she supposed that didn't mean *she* couldn't dance. Someone might ask her.

"I haven't seen your mother this excited since my wedding," Mariah said.

Anna watched Ma in the apartment window as Brandon drove down the driveway. Only when they neared the stone fence did she lose sight of her mother. Too bad Ma couldn't attend also. She would have loved to see all the gorgeous gowns and handsome gentlemen. Anna would have to remember everything and tell her afterward. Knowing Ma, she'd stay up waiting for her return.

First, they dropped off Felicity at the parsonage and then bade good-night to Mariah at the orphanage. That left Anna alone with Brandon in the automobile. His spicy masculine scent made her both nervous and excited. This was truly happening!

They'd got a late start as it was. When they'd passed the Neidecker house on the way to the parsonage, Anna had seen a dozen cars parked in their yard. Stopping at the parsonage and orphanage had taken precious time. They would be terribly late.

"Please hurry," she urged Brandon as he inched the car up the hill to the Neideckers' house.

She didn't want to miss one minute of the evening, for surely, like Cinderella, something terrible would happen at midnight, and the glorious dream would end.

"The street is icy," he said, not accelerating the car one bit.

She knit her gloved fingers together, decided that wasn't ladylike, and moments later reknit them. The satin slipped so easily against itself, not like wool or cotton.

"We're going to be late," she finally said when she couldn't bear waiting any longer.

A brief smile flitted across Brandon's lips. "I thought ladies preferred to arrive fashionably late."

Anna had no idea what was fashionable or not. Had she already made a gaffe by urging him to hurry? Thankfully Brandon knew what they should and shouldn't do. She would try to follow his lead, like Mariah suggested.

Moments later, Brandon pulled the car to the Neideckers' front door. A valet opened her door, and she wondered if she was supposed to get out right away or wait for Brandon. She edged a foot out of the car, but when he hopped out and walked around the car, she pulled it back in. Apparently, she was supposed to wait.

When Brandon reached her, he extended his hand and

helped her from the vehicle. He then walked her up the steps to the door, which was opened by yet another servant.

"What do you do with your car?" she whispered, worried he would leave her here while he parked.

"The valet will take care of that."

She breathed a sigh of relief, and then caught her breath as they stepped into the entry hall. For three months she'd cleaned this house, but it had never looked like this. She barely recognized the hall with all the shimmering decorations. Ribbons and swags and glittery glass-heart ornaments left no doubt this was a romantic affair.

The butler, Graves, took a second look at her before taking their coats and hats. Anna had to smile. He'd barely recognized her. Graves was too well trained to show his surprise, but she knew he was shocked. The Neideckers would be even more so.

"The guests are in the parlor, Mr. Landers," Graves said before whisking off with their outerwear.

Brandon walked her to the formal parlor, a large, high-ceilinged room. All but a few chairs had been removed, and a string quartet played in the opposite corner. Several couples were already dancing.

Anna felt Brandon tense and noticed he gripped his cane tighter. Of course he would feel awkward in a ballroom, but that's where everyone was gathered.

"I see two open chairs across the room," she whispered and was delighted when he relaxed a bit.

All who entered must first greet the host and hostess. Anna steeled herself for the confrontation with her former employer. What would Mrs. Neidecker think? What would she say?

Mr. Neidecker came first. He greeted them both warmly, clapping Brandon on the back and remarking that Anna looked lovely. Mrs. Neidecker was chatting with Flora-

LOVE INSPIRED® BOOKS,
a leading publisher of inspirational
romance fiction, presents...

Love Inspired **HISTORICAL**

A SERIES OF HISTORICAL
LOVE STORIES THAT WILL LIFT YOUR
SPIRITS AND WARM YOUR SOUL!

GET 2 FREE BOOKS!

2 FREE BOOKS

TO GET YOUR **2 FREE**
BOOKS, AFFIX THIS
PEEL-OFF STICKER TO
THE REPLY CARD AND
MAIL IT TODAY!

Plus, receive two
FREE BONUS GIFTS!

HURRY!

Return this card today to get

2 FREE Books and **2 FREE Bonus Gifts!**

GET 2 FREE BOOKS!

Love Inspired HISTORICAL

YES! *Please send me the 2 FREE Love Inspired® Historical books and 2 FREE gifts for which I qualify. I understand that I am under no obligation to purchase anything further, as explained on the back of this card.*

affix free books sticker here

102/302 IDL FNR5

FIRST NAME

LAST NAME

ADDRESS

APT.#

CITY

STATE/PROV.

ZIP/POSTAL CODE

BUSINESS REPLY MAIL

FIRST-CLASS MAIL   PERMIT NO. 717   BUFFALO, NY

POSTAGE WILL BE PAID BY ADDRESSEE

THE READER SERVICE
PO BOX 1867
BUFFALO NY 14240-9952

NO POSTAGE
NECESSARY
IF MAILED
IN THE
UNITED STATES

belle Williams, the biggest gossip in Pearlman. Brandon and Anna waited until they finished. At last Evelyn Neidecker turned to greet them.

"Mr. Landers," the woman cooed as Brandon took her hand. "I'm so delighted you're here at our little party." Only the way she said it left no doubt that she considered the party to be nothing short of spectacular.

"I'm pleased to meet you," he said curtly.

Anna had to smile at his abrupt manner. Brandon didn't warm easily, but he was always civil.

"Likewise. Why, we're practically family."

He frowned, clearly puzzled by her statement.

Mrs. Neidecker then turned to Anna. "And who is your lovely lady?" Even before the words finished coming out of her mouth, she must have recognized Anna because shock flashed across her face. "Anna Simmons?" She surveyed Anna's gown. "What a surprise." Her gaze flitted back to Brandon. "I had no idea."

The words ripped through Anna. Clearly, Mrs. Neidecker didn't think Anna was good enough for Brandon. Her tone hinted that any relationship Anna might have with Brandon would be improper. Instead of triumph, Anna felt even less like she belonged here.

Though her limbs trembled, she would not let Evelyn Neidecker spoil this night. She struggled to regain her composure by straightening her back and nodding with what she believed to be elegance. "I'm pleased to be here."

"As am I." Brandon's crisp reply gave her strength.

He would let no one slight her. No one dare see her as anything but a lady tonight, and for that she could kiss him.

"Shall we?" he asked, pointing toward the ballroom with his cane.

She nodded and let him lead her forward, but they didn't get two steps before Mr. Kensington stopped Brandon.

"How's the bookstore doing?" Kensington asked.

"Well enough considering the snowstorm we had this week."

Soon the two of them were deep in discussion, debating the effects of weather on business. Bored, Anna looked around the room to see who had been invited.

The Vanderloos waltzed near the band, every step sure and elegant. When Mr. Vanderloo swept his wife into a turn, Anna imagined the thrill of having a man do the same with her, but of course Brandon couldn't dance.

She looked to the far side of the room. Florabelle Williams had joined Mrs. Kensington and Mrs. Evans in the corner. Her back was to Anna, but the other two were looking directly at her. Mrs. Williams leaned close to whisper something. Then they all turned to stare at Anna, leaving no doubt that she was the topic of conversation.

Anna looked away and met the unfettered glare of Eloise Grattan. At twenty-seven, the plump girl was considered a spinster by most. Anna hadn't failed to notice Eloise's interest in Brandon. She wanted to yank him to the other side of the room, but that would look desperate, so she slipped toward the punch bowl, hoping to meet someone friendly.

She didn't expect to see Minnie. The girl stood behind the table ladling punch into tiny crystal cups. Naturally she wore that disgusting uniform with its ruffled apron and starched cap. The skirt rose above the knees, which Minnie could more or less hide by staying behind the table.

Anna felt a wave of guilt. She'd intended to warn Minnie about working for the Neideckers but forgot. "Minnie?"

The girl looked up, startled. "Anna. I didn't expect to see you." She looked around the room. "You're a guest?"

Anna knew how improbable that was. "Brandon invited me."

Minnie's eyes grew round. "Mr. Landers? Is...that is, do

you know if his brother is planning to be here?" Her gaze dropped at the last, and Anna detected a flush in her cheeks.

Oh, dear. That must be why Minnie dropped the coffee service at the parsonage on Christmas Eve. She had a crush on Reggie Landers. That would never come to anything, not from what she'd seen of the younger brother. He was part of the smart set. Someone like Minnie wouldn't even register as more than a servant. Speaking of which…

"I'm surprised to see you working here." Anna stopped just short of spilling the secret that she was the one who'd sent the Foxes the extra funds. "I thought you were in school and helped out at the parsonage."

Minnie looked around nervously. "I just work a few hours a week and for special occasions."

"Then you are continuing school?"

"Of course." Minnie acted offended, as if the thought of leaving high school had never crossed her mind.

"Good. Getting a diploma is important."

Minnie tossed her head. "Not for girls. We just have to marry well, like Beattie."

Anna winced. Minnie's older sister had married the Kensington heir, but Beattie Fox was the beauty in the family. Minnie was more like Anna, the quiet, plain little sister. Minnie didn't have Beatrice's pale blond hair or brilliant blue eyes. She hadn't the grace or elegance of her older sister. She couldn't expect to marry as well.

"I'd rather be able to support myself," Anna said, trying to point out that education was important.

"You clean houses just like me."

This time Anna's hackles rose. "Yes, but I intend to go to college. As soon as I earn enough at the bookstore, I'll apply to the University of Michigan."

Minnie looked skeptical. If she knew Anna was giving half her wage to her family, she'd have just cause, but Minnie couldn't possibly know. Pastor Gabe had promised to keep the source of the gift secret.

"Don't look now," Minnie hissed, "but here come Mrs. Kensington and Mrs. Neidecker."

Anna looked up and, sure enough, the two women were headed her way. Under no circumstances did she want to face their interrogation, so she drifted toward the band, which chose that moment to take a break. As the din settled into relative quiet, one shrill voice rose above everyone else's.

"She's nothing more than a mechanic's daughter."

Eloise Grattan. Though Anna knew the icy slur was spoken from envy, it still hurt. Her hope that no one had heard evaporated as every eye turned toward her. Not only did they hear; they knew Eloise was speaking of her.

Anna tried to swallow, but her mouth had gone dry. She tried to smile, but it looked false. She tried to let the barb bounce off by straightening her back, but it had struck home, mortally wounding her pride. She stood, alone, in the middle of the room.

Then, from the midst of the faceless crowd strode Brandon, fire in his eyes. His cane tapped across the polished wood floor, but he didn't lean on it. He wielded it like a weapon and walked faster than she'd ever seen him move.

When he reached her side, he extended his arm. "I believe I promised your mother to get you home early."

Anna knew what he was trying to do, but she could not leave now. It would confirm what those bullies were saying and imprint her humiliation in their minds forever.

She lifted her chin. "Ma told me to stay as long as I wanted." She glared at Eloise, who turned away and pretended to check her necklace to make sure the clasp was still in the back. "I want to stay."

Admiration shone in Brandon's eyes. As people returned

to their conversations and the band resumed playing, he leaned close. "Then I believe I owe you a dance."

Anna's heart leaped as he set aside his cane and took her in his arms. All the snobbery in the world could not ruin this night, not when Brandon held her close.

She sank into his arms, trying to remember the steps that Mariah had taught her. Brandon was patient when she hesitated and held her at a proper distance. Some of the young couples danced horrifyingly close to each other. Lydia Renfrew, her lips stained red, actually leaned her face on Joe Neidecker's shoulder. Anna shuddered.

"Are you cold?" Brandon asked.

She drew her attention back to him. "Not when I'm with you." That was true. He sent warmth surging to her very toes. His touch burned. His gaze...oh, my. She could swoon at the way he looked at her.

The straight nose, strong jaw and dimple in his chin. The spicy smell that dizzied her. Oh, he was fully a man. The feel of his hand on her back, the way they spun across the floor without the hint of a limp. She saw nothing but him, heard nothing but his words, felt nothing but his touch. She could stay in this dream forever.

It took all of Brandon's skill not to wobble when he landed on his lame foot. He hadn't danced since before the injury, but for Anna he would do anything. Her eyes shone. Her face glowed. Truly she was the most beautiful woman in the room. The others faded away beside her.

He spread his fingers against the small of her back, feeling again that jolt of pleasure. Perfume clouded the room, but he could still smell her soapy clean scent. He greatly preferred it.

Midway through the second dance, she closed her eyes and breathed deeply.

"Are you tired?" He hadn't considered that she might grow fatigued.

Her perfect lashes fluttered open. "I could dance all night."

So could he, as long as he was with her. That thought caught him by surprise This had truly been a night for surprises, all of them delightful. Anna's stunning beauty. The way she looked at him. Feeling her hand on his arm and now holding her close. Every bit of it felt like a dream, as if it belonged to some other man.

He didn't deserve such happiness.

Yet she gazed at him with such warmth that even that painful thought melted away. He saw only her. Sparkling eyes. Upturned nose. Rosy lips curved into a smile. He had the terrible urge to kiss her right there and then, but of course that would set the gossips afire. So he looked over her shoulder and saw...

Anna stumbled when Brandon halted in midstride. He steadied her by reflex, but his attention was focused on something over her shoulder.

"What is it?" She twisted to see what he was looking at, but Eloise Grattan blocked her view.

Instead of answering her, he dropped her hand and swayed on his feet, his expression turned to stone.

"Brandon," she cried, afraid she'd overexerted him.

She looked around for his cane but couldn't see it, so she offered him her arm.

He brushed it aside and stepped past her.

She turned and this time saw Brandon's brother standing in the doorway, a foolish grin fixed on his face. The lights glittered off droplets of melted snow on his coat. He must have just arrived.

"Brother," Reggie said, stepping toward them. "I never expected to see you at a ball."

Brandon snapped, "Shouldn't you be in college?"

Anna cringed, praying the brothers wouldn't argue in front of all these people. Sally Neidecker slithered up beside Reggie and wrapped her arm around his. "We couldn't miss Daddy's party." She shot a look of triumph at Anna. "We drove all day to get here."

Brandon looked as though he would explode. "Reginald, we need to talk." He spotted the cane that Anna couldn't find and limped toward it. "At the house. Now."

Anna reached for the cane, but Eloise Grattan got there first. She snatched the cane away from Anna and gave it to Brandon, who mumbled his thanks before turning back to his brother. Anna felt sick.

What had happened? In an instant, the evening had been ruined. Everyone watched the brothers.

Even the band stopped playing. Minnie looked horrified. Eloise smirked. After a moment of feeling abandoned, Anna felt her anger build. Why had Reggie shown up today? He'd ruined everything and acted as though he didn't care.

Brandon abruptly left Reggie and limped toward her. His jaw ticked, and she spotted distress in his eyes. Her anger evaporated, replaced with the deep desire to help and comfort him.

"I'm sorry," he said with genuine regret, "but I must return home. I can fetch you later if you wish to stay."

She shook her head. Without Brandon, the ball held no appeal. "Please take me home."

Chapter Fourteen

"How bad is it?" Brandon sat at the desk in his library, steeling himself for the news.

His stomach had churned from the moment Reggie told him he was in trouble. Nothing less would have pulled him from Anna's arms. Those few moments on the dance floor had made him feel whole again. He'd believed that anything was possible.

Reggie examined the books on the half-full shelves. "Where did the rest of these things go? You didn't sell them, did you?"

"They're at the store," Brandon growled, impatient that his brother was trying to evade the question at hand.

Reggie, book in hand, whirled around. "You're selling the family collection? You, who loves these musty old things more than life itself?"

"I have an antiquarian bookstore. In case you happened to miss your classics courses, that means the books are old."

Reggie fanned the pages of a book. "There's no need for sarcasm." He replaced it on the shelf and pulled off the next one.

He gripped a pencil in both hands. "You didn't answer my question. How bad is your situation?"

"If the lenders have their way, I'll soon be on my way to becoming one of your precious antiquities."

Brandon snapped the pencil in half. "Are you saying that they threatened to beat you?"

"No." After fanning the pages of the book, Reggie replaced it. "They promised to kill me."

Brandon sucked in his breath. Reggie had a gift for hyperbole, but this time felt different despite his brother's affected nonchalance. Brandon had seen a trace of fear behind that carefully crafted exterior. "Who are they?"

"Some bootlegging thugs from Detroit."

"Bootleggers?" Brandon slammed his fist on the desktop, making the fountain pen jump off the blotter. "Why would you get involved with criminals like that? Don't answer." He waved away his foolish question. "The point is, all we need to do is contact the authorities."

Reggie's derisive laugh grated on his nerves. "The authorities are in on it."

"What do you mean?"

"A little money goes a long way toward police protection."

Brandon felt ill. "Why would you get involved with people like that?"

Reggie abandoned the books and peered into a vase on the fireplace mantel. "I needed cash, and you weren't willing to loan me any."

Brandon exploded to his feet. "Because your debts came from gaming and womanizing." He would shake some sense into this brother of his if it took all he had. "You're supposed to be studying. Do you have any idea what people have sacrificed for your sake?"

Reggie appeared unmoved by Brandon's appeal or threatening stance. "Father? He never sacrificed anything for either of us. You know that."

"You're wrong." Brandon couldn't believe he was about to defend Father, but he'd learned a few things these past months. "He sold the Simmons house and garage to pay your debts."

Reggie shrugged. "Father had a lot of property. What's one house more or less? Or are you upset he didn't leave you more?"

Brandon could have throttled the fool. "Those were the last properties he had left."

"There's this house."

Brandon bulled past Reggie's insensitivity to make his point. "In order to pay your debts, Father sold a widow's house and forced her to move."

At last his brother looked the slightest bit distressed. It was good to see a tiny flicker of human decency still dwelled in the man.

"Yes," Brandon repeated for emphasis, "a poor widow and her daughter had to leave the only house they've known."

Reggie's insipid grin finally disappeared. "I didn't realize… Wait a minute. Did you say Simmons? As in the girl who keeps house for you? The one living in the carriage house? The one you were waltzing around the dance floor tonight despite your bum leg?"

"If you say one word against Anna or her mother…" He let the threat hang unfinished.

"Fine, fine." Reggie backed away, hands up in surrender. "I had no idea she meant that much to you."

Did she mean something to him? Brandon liked Anna, certainly. He wanted the best for her. He enjoyed her company, but he wasn't in love with her. He couldn't be. She deserved a good man, an honorable man, not one stained with the blood of innocents.

He struggled to explain himself and wipe the simpering

grin off Reggie's face. "I simply meant you shouldn't slander an innocent woman, especially one you don't know."

"And one you do."

Brandon would not see Anna's reputation sullied. "Unlike you, I have never acted less than the gentleman with any woman, and that includes Miss Simmons."

Reggie plopped onto the sofa. "I'm sure of that. You haven't done one wild thing in your life. Never take a risk. Never try for anything really important."

Brandon could have slapped him. Instead, he settled for slipping back behind his desk. His leg ached, and his emotions were frayed. Neither lent to calm decision making, but Reggie was his brother and his responsibility. If his life was at stake—and he believed Reggie was telling the truth about that, at least—then he must help.

He pulled the checkbook from the drawer. "How much do you need and when do you need it?"

Reggie sat up, the smirk gone, and made his way to the desk. "Thank you, brother. I knew I could count on you."

"How much?" He poised the pen over the check. "Two thousand? That's what you told me during the last telephone call."

Reggie licked his lips. "Three, more or less."

"Three thousand?" Brandon dropped the pen.

Reggie backed away. "I knew you'd react this way. It's just money, and what's money anyway?"

"It's what feeds and clothes you," Brandon growled, "and what keeps you in college, which apparently is an unwise investment."

"The trust pays for college," Reggie pointed out, sounding a bit panicky. "You can't touch my trust."

"Apparently it's not enough. Father put two women out of their home to fund your trust, and you waste it."

At last his words seemed to sink in, for Reggie dropped

to the chair opposite Brandon and slumped forward. "You're not just saying that?" He scrubbed his chin, which Brandon noticed wasn't as clean-shaven as normal. In fact, Reggie's attire didn't come to his usual high standard.

"I found the transaction in Father's account books. Would you like to see it?" He hauled his father's final ledger from the desk drawer.

"No. No." Reggie shuddered. "I believe you." He looked up, and Brandon noticed he'd paled and his lips trembled. "What do we do?"

In all Brandon's days, Reggie had never come to him for advice. As a child, he'd run to Father, always to Father, who gave him whatever he wanted. Now that this security was gone, Reggie had nowhere else to turn.

Brandon sighed. "What is the exact amount you need to pay off this debt?"

"Three thousand three hundred and eighteen dollars."

Brandon stared at his checkbook balance. Thirty-four hundred dollars. And that was his personal account. The bookstore account contained less than a hundred dollars, not enough to cover the mounting pile of bills. He'd planned to pay them from his personal account. If he gave Reggie the full amount, there wouldn't be enough left in both accounts combined to settle the debt he already had, not to mention ordering the popular novels and paying Anna's wages.

"Do you have any money?" he asked, more hopeful than expectant.

"I already gave them everything, even sold my best suit, but they increase the interest every day."

Brandon squeezed his eyes shut. He had to do it. "Then you'll need three thousand four hundred." The entire balance in his account.

Reggie's hands shook. "If you can spare it."

Brandon turned the checkbook around so Reggie could see that he was giving him a check for the entire balance.

His brother blanched. "I'm sorry. I'll find some way to repay you."

Brandon numbly wrote the check. Reggie wouldn't repay him. His brother couldn't hold on to a dime. "Where are you staying tonight?"

"With the Neideckers." Reggie did not lift his eyes to look at Brandon. "Sally promised to drive me to Detroit tomorrow if I got the money."

Brandon tore the check from the checkbook and handed it to his brother. "You'll stay here." He wasn't about to offer his brother an option.

Reggie held the check as if it were gold. "Thank you, brother."

"As you can see, there's no more where that came from."

Reggie nodded as he stood. "I'll pay you back."

Another idle promise. Brandon waved him away. He needed time alone to consider how to get out of this financial mess. He'd just given all he had to help someone in need, exactly what the Bible preached.

He looked at the window, blackened by night. *Does this repay the debt, Lord?*

He hoped for an affirmative reply, but deep down he knew it would never come.

Anna could hardly wait to see Brandon the next morning. His brother left early, while she was walking toward the house to make breakfast. He'd seen her but looked away at once and hurried on his way by foot. She feared the brothers had quarreled. Brandon certainly hadn't been pleased with Reggie when they'd left the party. The two men hadn't said a word during the drive home.

She wondered if it was because Reggie appeared at the

ball with Sally. Or maybe he was angry that Reggie missed his Friday classes. Though the Neideckers held the event on Friday evening rather than on Valentine's Day, the drive from Ann Arbor would have taken all day.

For the first time, she served breakfast in the dining room. Ma had walked to the house using the cane Brandon had loaned her, and, after Anna got her seated, she called upstairs that breakfast was served.

Brandon descended moments later, but instead of joining them, donned his coat. "I have business at the bookstore."

"But Ma's here today. She'd love to see you."

The tightness of his jaw told her he would not budge. "Give my regrets to your mother." He did not wait for her reply.

The cold air and slam of the door smashed her joy. Last night they'd been so happy together. He had set aside his cane and danced with her. His limp had vanished. Today, he leaned more than ever on the cane. Worry scoured his brow. His shoulders slumped. Something terrible must have happened.

"Brothers often fight," Ma said over breakfast. "I'm sure they'll work it out in the end."

Anna looked at Brandon's empty chair. "Maybe I can help."

Ma shook her head. "It's between them, dearest. The best we can do is to pray for them."

Anna couldn't just pray. God had given people hands and feet so they could act. She would root out the problem and fix it.

Later, while cleaning the house, she pondered the situation. No doubt Reggie had done something foolish that irritated Brandon. Perhaps a little commiseration would do the trick. Unless it was more serious. Then Brandon would need more than cheering.

Perhaps a distraction would help. Anna always found that she thought more clearly when she wasn't staring at the problem up close. Maybe he would go to the cinema with her. A Buster Keaton short was playing. No, he'd say that would set the gossips' tongues wagging.

She propped her chin on the broom handle, thinking. At last an idea popped into her head, a brilliant idea. Between the excavation in Egypt and the rumors of a lost fortune in Pearlman, the town had been abuzz. Everyone was talking about treasure hunting. She could follow through on Felicity's suggestion to search for the lost fortune with Brandon. Of course he'd denied such a fortune existed, but maybe he'd tell her the truth now, after their dance last night.

Even if he refused to hunt for treasure, she could talk him into adding a section on Egyptian antiquities to the bookstore. That would attract customers.

She whistled as she worked, delighted with her ideas. The housecleaning took less time than ever, and by eleven o'clock, she was on her way to rescue Brandon from his doldrums.

The bookstore was dark and silent when Anna arrived.

She pushed the button to turn on the new electric lights and looked around for Brandon. The front door was unlocked. He should be here. Yet there was no sign of anyone.

What if something had happened to him? What if the store had been robbed and he'd been hit over the head? What if the thief was still here? A robbery hadn't happened in Pearlman in years, but that didn't mean it couldn't.

"Brandon?" She crept between the shelves, looking left and right, alert to any sound.

He didn't answer.

"Brandon?" she said a bit louder, hoping to scare off any thief. "I'll get Hendrick and Peter. They're nearby." That wasn't exactly true, but hopefully a thief wouldn't know the difference. Unless the thief came from Pearlman. Then he'd know that Peter was four blocks away and Hendrick a good quarter-mile distant.

Still no reply.

The door to the back room was closed. Brandon usually kept it shut when someone was at the sales counter, but he never shut it when he was here alone. Hand trembling, she turned the knob and pushed the door open.

A solitary lamp lit the room. Brandon stared vacantly at a pile of paper on his desk. He didn't move. He didn't look at her. He appeared comatose, frozen in place.

"Brandon?" she whispered, half afraid he wouldn't answer and half afraid he would.

The man looked like death, with dark rings under his eyes. The tiff with his brother must be worse than she thought.

Slowly, achingly, he looked up, and his eyes gradually fixed on her. His jaw worked. He swallowed. Then he looked again at the papers, as if the bright light behind her was too much to bear.

"I'm sorry," he croaked.

She rushed to him, knelt beside him at the desk. She wanted to comfort him, to wipe away the anguish, but how? She couldn't find the words and was afraid to touch him. In such a state, he might lash out. So she asked what he was sorry about.

He dropped his head into his hands. "I had to cancel the popular-novel section."

"Why?" This made no sense. What on earth could a fight with Reggie have to do with her popular-novel section?

He pushed aside the papers and shut the ledger. "I can't make it work."

He was giving up. He couldn't give up.

"You haven't even tried," she cried. "I'm positive the popular novels will bring in more business than ever."

Earlier that week he'd agreed to do this. What had changed his mind? Had Reggie said something about her, something that turned Brandon's opinion? Reggie had come to the ball with Sally. She might have told him a terrible lie. She had been furious with Brandon that day in the mercantile when he'd cut her to size.

Anna swallowed hard. "Whatever your brother said, it can't be true."

Brandon didn't even look at her. This was worse than she thought.

Trembling, she rose. "Don't you trust me?"

"Trust has nothing to do with this." His voice sounded flat, dull, tired. "I made a decision. I'm sorry."

She stared, slowly moving her head from side to side in disbelief. "Is that all? Aren't I entitled to some explanation?"

He rubbed his eyes. "I've said enough."

"But—"

"Please. I don't want to talk about this now."

He was dismissing her, sending her off like a child. Well, she wasn't a baby. She was entitled to know why he was doing this, why he'd changed overnight. She worked here. She had helped put this store together. Her ideas would work; they would, but not if refused to try them.

"Don't I deserve to know what's going on?"

He sighed. "Please, Anna, the store is closed. I need to be alone."

But he'd left the front door open. He was in no condition to be left alone. "I won't leave you."

"I don't want to fight." He pushed aside the ledger and stood. "Please lock the door when you leave."

"B-but I came here to work."

He lifted dull, vacant eyes. "I'm sorry, but I can't afford to keep you on."

"What?" Had she heard correctly? She staggered back a step. He was firing her? Whatever Reggie had told him must have been awful. "It's not true." A little sob rose in her throat. "Whatever you heard, it's not true."

"You're making this harder." He turned from her. "Please do me this last favor and leave me alone."

Last favor? Dear Lord, he despised her. The sob raced up her throat, and her hand couldn't keep it from coming out. He hated her. He couldn't stand to look at her.

Tears blurred her vision, but somehow she found the doorway, stumbled through and made her way past the book stacks and out the front door into the cold. Sleet pelted her cheeks, but it could not cool her distress.

"Why, Anna, whatever's wrong?" asked Eloise Grattan, her bulk blocking the sidewalk. "Did you quarrel with Mr. Landers? He is rather a cold fish."

Cold fish? Her words snapped some sense into Anna. She turned on Eloise. "Brandon is the most giving and honorable man I know."

Eloise tossed her head in a poor imitation of Sally. "Then why won't he help his brother?"

"That's between them and none of our business."

"Don't you mean *your* business?" Eloise lifted her nose. "I know why you're chasing him, but don't think for a moment that he's going to give you a dime of that lost fortune."

"He said there is no fortune."

Eloise laughed unkindly. "Of course he'd say that. But I have it on good authority that they're looking for it."

"No, he's not," she said, but was she sure? "Who told you this?"

Eloise gave her a knowing look. "You know who. They're practically engaged."

Engaged? Surely Eloise didn't mean Brandon. He hadn't spoken of any other woman. She must mean Sally and Reggie. They'd attended the ball together last night. Given that Eloise was a friend of Sally, it was the only logical explanation.

With a parting grin, Eloise said, "Don't think a cent of it will come to you. Money always marries money."

A lump formed in Anna's throat but not because of the treasure. It was never hers to begin with. No, she ached for Brandon. What if the quarrel between Brandon and Reggie had been over the lost fortune? What if Reggie and Sally had found it and took all the money for themselves? That would explain Brandon's distress. That would explain everything.

She stumbled backward and leaned against the front window for support. Poor Brandon.

And she'd just run out when he needed her most.

Chapter Fifteen

After collecting her wits, Anna walked back into the book-store. He'd said he couldn't afford to keep her on. Well, she'd offer to work without pay. If he still needed money, she'd tell him she knew about the family's lost fortune and offer to help find it. If Reggie had already found the money, she'd turn to her second idea and propose the archaeology section. Maybe he'd like that better than the popular fiction.

Her heart pounded wildly as she made her way between the shelves to the back room. It nearly beat through her rib cage when she knocked on the closed door.

She waited, listened.

Nothing.

Another knock brought the same lack of response. What if something had happened? What if he'd tripped and cracked his head on the corner of the desk? What if he was lying unconscious on the floor?

She pushed open the door and found the room…empty.

"Brandon?" she asked tentatively.

He wasn't anywhere near the desk. The pile of paper, ledger and old books sat exactly where they'd been a moment before. He wasn't at the shelving or in the washroom. Its door stood wide open. He was simply gone.

Brandon wouldn't have left the store without checking that she'd locked the front door, which of course she'd forgotten to do. Nor would he leave the lights on. Where had he gone?

She scoured the room again, this time more carefully. When she reached the desk, she noticed something had changed. This time the ledger lay open. A glance at the figures made her gasp. She settled into the chair for a closer look.

The bookstore had laid out a great deal of money to get up and running, and the balance had dwindled to almost nothing. Beside the ledger sat a pile of bills—unpaid bills. They had to total almost four hundred dollars. Maybe Brandon was a poor businessman, like her father. A career in journalism didn't prepare a man to run a business.

A lump formed in her throat. Brandon was in trouble.

No wonder he'd closed the store today. No wonder he'd let her go. No wonder he'd canceled the popular-novels section. He couldn't afford them. That meant he couldn't afford an archaeology section either.

If he didn't supplement the store with his own money, it was going to fail. Before today, she would have assumed he'd do just that. The Landerses were wealthy. At least everyone thought they were. She suspected that wealth was only a mirage. Why else would the brothers be looking for the lost fortune?

She rubbed her temples. What could she do? How could she help? The wage he'd paid her was far beyond his means. He'd given Ma and her a place to live. They ate his food, enjoyed his hospitality.

Her lips quivered, flavored by salt. She brushed away a tear. He'd given her so much, and how had she repaid him? By fighting him, taking from him and asking for more.

From now on, she would work with him. Somehow, together, they'd find a way out of this mess.

"What are you doing?" Brandon's question shot through her spine.

She turned around slowly, trying not to look guilty. "I was looking for you."

He dropped the metal waste bin. It clattered on the wood floor. He'd taken out the trash. That's where he'd been.

"It looks to me like you're reading my accounts."

What could she say? She had been. Despite shaky legs, she rose to face him.

"I'm sorry. I saw the ledger open while looking for you."

His displeasure didn't ease. "So you couldn't resist examining what wasn't yours."

Something horrible fluttered in her breast, threatening to take the air out of her lungs. She tried to find the right words, but none would come.

Brandon fought the bile rising in his throat. She'd been snooping. The Anna he knew would never have looked at his ledger, even though it was lying open. She would have trusted him, relied on him, believed in him.

Something had changed. She no longer accepted his word. Like everyone else in his life, she focused only on her needs and desires. Now, as he looked into her frightened eyes, he knew she'd lied. Just like Father and Reggie and every Landers before them.

She trembled visibly, but he would not let her distress get to him.

"I'm sorry." Her voice was thick. "I shouldn't have looked." She blinked rapidly. "I want to help. I want to help you save the store."

She had sincerely owned her mistake, and the frost that had built up around his heart began to melt. He'd been wrong to judge her by his family's standards, but he could not allow her to get involved in his problems.

"You've done enough," he said stiffly.

She looked even more distressed. "No, I haven't. I've been selfish." She blinked more rapidly.

Not tears. Please, not tears. Why did women break down at the slightest thing?

"I shouldn't have accepted such a large wage." Her voice clotted and roughened. "I knew it was too much."

The tenderness he'd tried to abolish returned with a vengeance. He couldn't see Anna suffer for his mistakes. He had to put a stop to this.

"It's what I offered," he said, "and I wouldn't change a thing. I'm sorry I couldn't do more."

She sniffled. "But I shouldn't have pressed you for the popular-novel section."

"It was a wise suggestion, and one I'll implement as soon as I can afford to do so."

"Then you're not closing the store permanently?"

He'd considered the grim possibility just minutes ago. "Not if I can find enough money to keep it operating."

"Find?" She bit her trembling lip. "Then you haven't found it yet?"

"No." He wouldn't get her hopes up. The bank might not give him a loan.

"And your brother hasn't found it either?"

"My brother? What does Reggie have to do with applying for a loan?"

"A loan?" Her distress changed to confusion. "What are you talking about?"

Now he was perplexed. "A bank loan. What are *you* talking about?"

She stared, wide-eyed, every bit the innocent he'd come

to adore. Faint pink colored her cheeks and made the freckles on her nose stand out.

Her lips trembled as she spoke. "Finding the lost fortune."

He could barely hear her. "The what?"

Her eyes sparkled. "I'll help you find it. Together we can do it."

Love battled with horror. Of all the things she could have said, none hit him harder. If she searched his library looking for clues, she'd discover the horrible truth.

"There is no lost fortune," he said emphatically.

"But Eloise Grattan told me that Sally and Reggie are looking for it."

"What?" He couldn't even place this Miss Grattan. "Tell her she's wrong." At least he thought she was wrong. Reggie wasn't looking. True, he'd come to Pearlman several times this winter, but he stayed at the Neidecker house and made no effort to call on him. But that didn't mean he wasn't visiting the house while Brandon was at the store. Suppose he *was* searching for the treasure? Brandon remembered the odd way Reggie had behaved last night in the library. He'd pulled dozens of books out of the bookcases and leafed through them as if looking for something stuck between the pages.

"But she seemed so certain," Anna said, almost pleading for him to change his mind.

He wouldn't.

"Tell her she's wrong. There is no fortune." His hunt through the family's records had led to that conclusion. The only thing his ancestors had hidden was how they'd made their fortune. That nasty little secret would stay buried if he had any say in the matter.

"Are you sure? Mr. Davis thought he'd found Tutankhamun's tomb, but he hadn't. What if there is money hidden somewhere? Wouldn't that solve everything?"

Brandon recoiled. Sure, he could use money, but not blood money.

Excitement danced in Anna's eyes. "We'd be like Mr. Carter, hunting for the lost tomb."

Disgust and something worse, shame, slammed into his gut. He could not have her looking into his family's past. "How many times do I have to tell you? There is no hidden treasure."

"But the money—"

"Stop talking about money," he shouted. "My business is mine alone. Not yours. Stay out of this."

Her expression fell, and she stepped back, as if afraid of him. The innocent excitement vanished behind a wall of hurt. She blinked rapidly to stem tears.

Brandon exhaled in frustration. He didn't mean to hurt her. He just wanted her to stop talking about this lost treasure as if it would solve all their problems.

"I'm sorry. I shouldn't have yelled." He reached out, but she shrank even farther away. Now he'd done it, ruined everything between them. Considering his past, maybe it was for the best. He retreated and gave one parting volley. "No lost fortune is going to save this store." He looked bitterly at the empty storage shelves. His dream was over.

Anna couldn't stop shaking after she left the bookstore. Brandon had changed. Gone was the tender soul who'd set aside his cane to whisk her onto the dance floor in front of Pearlman's elite. Something dark had seized him and wouldn't let go.

It had to be the business losses. A man like Brandon wouldn't admit defeat. He would try to carry the burden alone, even if it crushed him.

His denial of the hidden fortune only proved that it must exist. Eloise was right. Reggie must have been searching, and Brandon had joined him. Clearly they hadn't found it yet. Maybe they weren't looking in the right place. Maybe she could find what they'd missed.

If she did, he might forgive her for looking at his ledger. That little peek had cost his respect, and she bitterly regretted doing it. But he would never have told her the business was failing. The only way she could help was if she knew.

As she raced up the hill to the carriage house, she formulated a plan. Brandon would be tied up at the bookstore, and now that she was no longer working there, she'd have more time to clean his house—and more time to search. If she could find the fortune, she could give it to him—every last penny—and not only save his bookstore but also regain his confidence.

The ideas clicked together with each hurried step. She'd have to plan her search. The archaeology books and articles she'd read stressed the necessity of organization. She'd start in the most likely place—the attic. Next she'd search the little-used rooms on the second floor. The library was an ideal spot to hide things with its many books and old vases and such. No room had more nooks and crannies. The kitchen? Not likely. It had to have been added fairly recently. The parlor also seemed an unlikely spot. Something would have been discovered in such a well-used room.

"Where are you going in such a hurry, sis?" Hendrick pulled alongside her in Mr. Kensington's Packard.

She pulled her coat tighter, wishing she'd taken the time to button it when she'd rushed out of the bookstore. "Home."

"Give you a ride?" He inched the car up the hill, keeping pace with her.

"It looks like you're delivering a car. You shouldn't be taking me home."

He stopped the car, leaned across and opened the passenger door. "I'd like to talk with you."

Anna's stomach plummeted at his serious tone. "What's wrong? Is it Ma?"

"Nothing's wrong." He patted the seat. "Join me."

Though she'd rather start searching the attic, she got into the car. A fishing pole nearly stabbed her in the ear. "I didn't know Mr. Kensington fished."

Hendrick pushed the pole farther back. "I'm going to throw a line in the river after I drop off the car."

"Oh." She waited for him to say more, but he didn't. "I don't suppose you wanted to talk to me about fishing. What's wrong?"

"I am." He put the car in gear and headed slowly up the hill. "Or I might have been."

Anna stared. Her brother never admitted mistakes. "How?"

He swallowed hard, and his Adam's apple bobbed. "About your employer."

"Brandon?"

He cringed. "I'm having a hard time getting used to you calling him by his first name."

"He's more than an employer," she admitted, remembering the feel of his arms around her on the dance floor. "Well, at least I thought he was."

"Thought? Did he hurt you?" Hendrick practically shouted. "Because if he did…" He let the threat lie unspoken.

"No," she hurried to answer. "It's just that he won't let me help him." She hesitated, wondering if she should tell Hendrick that Brandon was in financial trouble. He was her brother and absolutely trustworthy, but Brandon wouldn't want anyone to know. Still, if no one knew, no one could help, and help was exactly what Brandon needed. "Please don't tell a soul, but I don't think he has the kind of money we thought he did."

Hendrick let out his breath. "Then what I heard is true. I've been hearing rumors of unpaid bills and requests for extension on credit."

Anna's gut knotted. She hated to think of Brandon struggling in any way. "He'll pay his debts. I know he will. He's the most honest and honorable man I've ever met."

Hendrick shot her a glare.

"After you, of course," she added. "Tell everyone that he'll pay."

Hendrick nodded as he pulled the car to a stop in front of the carriage house. "I want you to know that you and Ma will always be welcome at our house."

She jumped out of the car. "That won't be necessary. This is just a rough patch. Everything will turn out." Hendrick looked skeptical, so she added, "Thank you, though."

She slammed the car door shut and rushed into the carriage house. Ma looked up from her mending.

"Why are you home so soon, dearest? I thought I heard a car. Did Mr. Brandon close the bookstore early?"

Anna didn't have time to explain. "Hendrick brought me home. After I change, I'm going to the house to cook supper."

"At this hour?"

"I want to make a pot roast." Those took long enough that Ma might believe her. Anna didn't want to share her plan with her mother and get her hopes up.

Anna ducked into the bedroom and pulled her work dress from the peg in the closet. While the roast cooked, she could search the attic, which was bound to be dusty and full of cobwebs.

Quickly she changed, topped the dress with an apron and donned a sweater to ward off the attic's chill.

"Anna," Ma called from the other room. "Will you look

behind the dresser for my wedding band? It rolled there this morning."

"Why do you insist on taking off your ring when you wash your hands?" Anna grumbled. She was anxious to scour the attic before Brandon returned from the bookstore. After that angry denial, he wouldn't appreciate her looking for the lost fortune. Not until she handed it to him, that is.

"I don't want to lose it down the drain." Ma had feared drains from the moment Hendrick installed kitchen plumbing in their old house. To her it was a dark hole that swallowed up everything that came near the sink. That was no different here. So she took off her ring and set it on the dresser whenever she washed up. "Your father spent every cent he had to buy it for me."

Her wistful tone sent a wave of bittersweet regret through Anna. Papa. She nipped her lip to prevent tears. Why did he have to work on that old truck? Why did the jack collapse? It happened more than a dozen years ago, and Ma still thought of him every day.

She pulled up her stockings, stuffed her feet into her shoes and set about moving the chest of drawers. She pushed. She pulled. The heavy oak dresser wouldn't budge. She'd have to remove everything from it. That would take forever, and Brandon could return at any time.

"I'll do it when I get back," she informed her mother as she stepped into the sitting room.

Ma had moved to the table, where the late-afternoon light was better. She looked up from the mending, pins bristling from one corner of her mouth.

"Why don't you use a pincushion?" Anna reached into her mother's sewing basket and pulled out the cushion she'd made for her years ago. It still didn't bear one pin or pinhole. Ma kept her pins in a rusty old cold-cream tin.

"I don't want to ruin your handiwork." Somehow Ma

could speak from one corner of her mouth while keeping the pins in the other. "It's such a pretty cushion."

"No, it's not. It's lopsided and poorly stitched." Anna would never make a good seamstress.

Ma set down the shirt—the *man's* shirt—she was mending.

"Whose is that? Hendrick's? Is Mariah too busy with the orphanage to mend his shirts?"

"Now, Anna, I wanted the work. I need to work."

"Well, you don't need to be mending Hendrick's shirts."

"This isn't your brother's shirt. It's Mr. Brandon's."

Anna almost choked. "You're mending Brandon's shirts?" He was doubtless paying her. No wonder his finances were suffering. She had to put a stop to this.

"I asked him if I could do anything for him, and he was kind enough to bring me some mending."

Anna sighed. Her mother looked happy, and Anna hated to take away something that brought the color back into her cheeks. "We can't accept any more money from him," she said softly, sitting in the other chair. "I think he's in a bit of financial trouble."

Ma wasn't surprised or flustered. "I know, dearest, but I've been praying the Lord will provide his daily needs." She tilted her head slightly, the whisper of a grin gracing her lips. "And perhaps a bit more."

"I don't think it's working."

Ma smiled softly. "The Lord answers in His time, not ours."

Anna fought impatience. "Well, I hope He hurries. Brandon is so upset. It's as if he…" A thought darted into her head. "As if he's lost hope."

Ma nodded solemnly. "That happens when someone loses touch with the Lord."

"He's pushing everyone away." She'd felt that wall creep between them like the icy cold of a cellar.

"Oh, dearest, I'm so sorry." Ma patted her hand. "I'm sure it's just temporary. You'll see. Mr. Brandon cares for you a great deal, and that kind of affection never hides for long. Once things have settled a bit, he'll be back to his old self."

"He cares for me?" She'd barely let herself hope that he did. "How do you know?"

"A woman knows," she said coyly.

"But how?"

"It's in the little things. The way he looks at you when he knows you're not watching. The way he hurries to catch the door before you reach it. How he walks taller and surer when you're by his side."

Anna marveled at Ma's words. Could it be true? Did he really care for her? "Is that how Papa was with you?"

"Oh, yes, but I was too blind to see it at first." Ma chuckled, lost in memories. "He had to practically hit me over the head before I noticed him. Such a fool I was, looking for things that didn't matter."

"What things?"

"Oh, I thought I wanted the most handsome boy in town. He had money too. All the girls fussed over him." She shook her head. "But he was vain. I didn't see it at first, but thank the good Lord I came to my senses and realized your father was the man for me."

Anna swallowed the lump that had formed in her throat. She always got teary-eyed when Ma talked about Papa. How they loved each other. Though she was only seven when Papa passed, she remembered the way they'd hold hands watching the sunset from the front porch. That was their time together, and neither she nor Hendrick dared interrupt it.

Then it had all come to an end.

"I'm sorry, Ma," she said, her words coming out all teary.

"Oh, dearest." Ma dropped her mending and hugged Anna tight, which only brought more tears. "We had a good spell together, and we'll see each other again in the next life. Sometimes I think he's watching over us now." She gave Anna one last hug. "Now, you'd better head up to the house."

Anna wiped her eyes. "Not until I find your ring."

The house would still be there tomorrow. She could check the attic after Brandon left for the bookstore in the morning.

She and Ma had stuffed the four drawers of the oak dresser to the brim. That's what gave it the extra weight. She removed all their belongings from the drawers and set them on the bed. Then she slid out the drawers. She felt around on the floor inside the now-empty dresser but found only dust.

She'd have to move the thing. After wiping her hands on her apron, she tugged on one end of the dresser. It skidded ever so slightly across the rough plank floor. Goodness, this thing was heavy. She'd have to put her weight into it. At last, with a great deal of scraping and screeching, the dresser moved away from the wall.

Unfortunately, it also blocked the waning light. Anna struck a match and lit the oil lamp that they kept on the tiny table by the bed. She walked it across the narrow gap and held it low so she could spot the ring.

There it was, right next to the wall. In fact, it was jammed in the gap between the plastered wall and the plank floor, right where a seam rose vertically to...

Anna pushed the lamp closer. Why on earth was there a vertical seam in the wall? Upon closer examination, she found two seams, running parallel about shoulder-width apart. A door. It had to be a secret door. She followed the seams up. They ended at the chair rail—a long, rough board nailed across the entire wall. If it was a door, it should have a gap at the top, but she could find none below or above the chair rail.

How odd. Why would someone cut into the wall for no reason? It must be a door, even though it didn't have a handle, hinges or a visible top.

She pressed the side seam, and the wall rocked slightly. What on earth?

She knelt and pushed along the edge. Was this a secret passage? A hidden room? Could the lost treasure be right here? She looked for a knothole, a knob, anything that could serve as the mechanism for opening the door and found nothing. No matter how hard she pushed along each edge, the wall or door or whatever it was only jostled.

"Please, Lord," she whispered, "we need this."

"Are you all right?" Ma called from the other room.

"Yes, Ma. I found your ring." She scooped it up and put it in her pocket.

Maybe there was something in the floor that opened the door. She pressed every knothole, tried to wiggle each plank. Again the search led nowhere. Frustrated, she leaned against the chair rail. It shifted. Startled, she leaped away from the wall and examined what she'd thought was a single piece of wood. It wasn't. The roughness hid the seam. When she pressed downward on that piece of chair rail, the entire door moved inward a few inches. From there, she could slide it sideways behind the wall.

Anna's pulse raced.

This was it, the lost treasure.

Like Mr. Carter entering King Tutankhamun's tomb, she lifted her lamp and looked inside.

Chapter Sixteen

Brandon closed the bookstore and drove to the river. He needed to get away from town so he could think. He parked by the bridge and walked to the center of the span. Below, ice and snow covered the slower pools while the rapids still ran free. Raccoon and deer tracks dotted the banks.

Brandon had been drawn to rivers ever since the war. While soldiers and horses and artillery wallowed in the muck, the rivers flowed free, cleansing the land. In them he'd found hope. To the river he'd gone after the bloodbath in that ruin of a town. There he'd learned that water couldn't wash away everything.

Today he stared down at the black water edged with snow-covered ice. It burbled and flowed, tumbling on its way to some other place. Just like after the massacre in Europe, it didn't heal the raw spot in his heart.

His leg ached. His head ached. He'd thought until he couldn't think any longer. The bank had offered little hope. After Anna stormed out of the bookstore, he'd gone to Dermott Shea, bank manager. The gray-haired yet vital man had politely shaken his hand and ushered him into his office, but when Brandon explained his need for a loan, Mr. Shea's good humor had vanished.

Brandon replayed the encounter in his head.

"I'll need to see your profit and loss statement," Shea said.

Brandon pointed out the obvious. "I've only been open a little over a month."

"Then we'll take a look at that."

He knew what the result would be if Shea saw only the current books, so he offered an alternative. "I own the building outright. Perhaps that could serve as collateral."

Shea steepled his hands, appropriately somber behind his massive walnut desk. "Commercial-property values are low at present."

That was a polite way of saying Brandon shouldn't ask for too large a sum.

Brandon hedged, "I need enough to carry me through until the business turns a profit."

Shea frowned, silent for a long time. At last with a groan, he shifted forward in his chair. "Mr. Landers, has it ever occurred to you that Pearlman might not have a great need for rare books?"

Anna had said the same thing only in much nicer terms. He struggled to find the right words. "I am, that is, I *was,* going to add a popular-fiction section until I ran short on funds."

"It seems to me that should have been your first priority."

Brandon did not like being lectured to by anyone, even his elders, but he clenched his jaw shut so irritation wouldn't rule his tongue.

"What would be the cost to stock that section?" Shea asked.

"A hundred dollars. Two, if we add children's books."

"Two hundred might be doable." Shea rose and extended his hand in dismissal. "I'll run it past the board."

Brandon squirmed. A hundred or two wouldn't solve

his problem. He needed a much larger cash infusion. "It's not just the collection. Heating, light, employees. Those all figure into the cost. I'd hoped for a bit more, say three thousand." If he could recoup what he'd spent on Reggie, he should be able to stay in business long enough to attract steady customers.

"Three thousand?" Shea sat down with a thump. "That's another matter entirely. It will require collateral. I'm not sure your commercial building will be enough to sway the board." He paused, waiting for Brandon to offer more.

He didn't. His house would not go on the sacrificial slab.

After a long pause, Shea muttered, "I'll bring it to the board. Should have an answer for you by Friday."

Brandon should have been relieved, but he felt like a lead weight had been strapped to his back. Debt. No Landers had ever been in debt, except Reggie of course. Father always bragged how he'd stayed debt-free while others succumbed to bank runs and recessions. Brandon was about to end that legacy.

The only thing that might pull him out of trouble wasn't even his idea. Anna had persuaded him to add the popular fiction. She'd campaigned for the children's books. He hadn't wanted to run an ordinary bookstore. If not for her vision, he had no chance.

He knew he should be grateful, but his pride smarted. No Landers had ever fallen so low. Once the community learned about his financial troubles—and he had no doubt they would—credit would dry up, and he'd be scrambling to put food on the table. If he only had himself to feed, it wouldn't matter, but he couldn't let Anna and her mother suffer. In a way, they'd become his family.

So now he stared into the river looking for answers. Had he done the right thing? Would the store rebound? Could he sell enough popular books to repay the loan? Most of all, could he regain Anna's trust?

An acorn dropped from overhead, hit the railing of the bridge and bounded back onto the plank roadway. Brandon kicked it over the edge.

"Hey, watch it," came a cry from below. Moments later, a man emerged from under the bridge holding a fishing pole. He had removed his wool cap and was rubbing his head as if the acorn had struck him. Dressed in a thick wool jacket, he was tall and strong. After clearing the bridge overhang, he looked up.

Brandon froze. It was Anna's brother.

"Oh, it's you," Simmons said.

Apparently the day could get worse. "My apologies. I had no idea anyone was under there."

Simmons scrambled up the bank. "You must not fish much, then. This is the best spot this time of year."

"Is it?" Brandon had an uncontrollable urge to dip a hook in the icy water. "I haven't fished in years. Fish still biting?"

"Bit slow today, but I've caught my share this winter. You just gotta be patient."

Patience was not a word that Brandon would have associated with Simmons. He looked back at the water. "Trout?"

"Bass, mostly."

"That so? Maybe I should see if there's a pole in the carriage house."

Brandon realized his gaffe when Simmons drew in his breath sharply. He should never have reminded the man of his kid sister's housing arrangement. "I guess I should be going."

Fine snow had begun to sift down, dusting his coat. He took a step toward his car, but Simmons blocked the way. Intentionally or not, Brandon couldn't tell. He edged toward the center of the bridge, keeping his gaze on Simmons.

The man raised a hand to stop him. "I've changed my mind."

"About what?"

"You."

Apparently Hendrick Simmons was a man of few words. Brandon waited for him to explain.

Simmons shoved his free hand in a jacket pocket. "You're all right, a regular fellow."

Brandon guessed that was a sort of blessing. A lot of good it did when Brandon had just broken Anna's heart. "Thank you."

He started toward his car again, but Simmons wasn't done. "I don't ever want to hear that you hurt her."

Too late. Anna's crestfallen face floated before his eyes. He'd not only hurt her; he'd devastated her. The hand clutching Brandon's gut twisted even tighter.

Anna couldn't see a thing. She moved the lantern farther into the crawl space.

"What are you doing in there?" The telltale tap of Ma's cane drew near. "It sounds like you're rearranging the furniture."

"I'll be there in a moment," Anna called out before she stuck her head into the opening.

The lantern's soft glow revealed a small room, inky black. The floor was made of wooden planks like the rest of the apartment, but here they hadn't been planed smooth and varnished. The raw wood bit into her palms.

"What did you find?" Ma had wedged herself around the dresser and spotted the open crawl space.

"I don't know yet." She lifted the lantern to scan the ceiling. It was as tall as the bedroom but much narrower. The facing wall was only an arm's length away and made of stone. The mortar crumbled in places, but it was solid.

"Looks like a storage area," Ma said.

"Except there's nothing in here that I can see."

To her right, the crawl space ended abruptly in another stone wall. To the left was nothing but black, emptiness. The lantern's light didn't reach to the end. Maybe the treasure was hidden there. Probably not. It couldn't be this easy to find, or someone would have discovered it years ago. Nonetheless, Anna had to know.

She wiggled into the crawl space, making sure to keep the lantern ahead of her. Though she could stand, the tight area seemed to squeeze in on her, and she had to fight a moment of panic. The fire last summer had generated the same chest-tightening fear. She'd been in the upper-floor classroom when the wall of flame descended on the school. Whipped by storm winds, smoke soon filled the room. She'd had to help the teacher bring the children out of the classroom, down the stairs and through the narrow hallway to safety. By the time they got out, she'd wheezed and coughed from the smoke.

She leaned against the wall, trying to steady her breathing. This was not the same. There wasn't any fire. She wasn't in danger, thankfully, because that splintery plank floor would catch fire in seconds. She was in control. She could leave at any time, but if she did, she'd never know if the lost fortune was hidden here.

Curiosity drove her forward—that and the chance to win over Brandon.

Picking up the lantern, she inched down the length of the room. With every step she examined the lath-and-plaster wall to her left and the stone wall to her right. She tested each plank of flooring to see if it would move. Nothing but dirt, dust and cobwebs, though why spiders would inhabit such a dark space was beyond her.

At last she reached the far end, also constructed of stones

mortared together. Not one stone within reach moved, and she didn't have a stool to check the ones above her head. No gold. No hidden compartment. Maybe Ma was right, and it was just a storage area. But then why hide it behind a dresser and make the mechanism for opening it so difficult? Surely it had been intended to hide something.

Unless the treasure had already been removed, pilfered like most of the pharaohs' tombs.

Her heart sank. If so, then Brandon was right and there was no fortune to be found. The bookstore would fail. He'd leave Pearlman, and she'd never see him again.

The tightness in her chest worsened. Never see Brandon again? That hurt more than never going to college or failing to unearth a pharaoh's tomb. She slumped to the floor, the lamp at her side.

When had he got so important to her? Since that evening in the kitchen? Or during their waltz? All she knew was that she couldn't bear never seeing those gray eyes and dimpled chin again. That night he'd wanted to kiss her. She was sure of it.

How would that feel? She touched her lips. No man had ever kissed her, not romantically, that is. She'd seen kisses in the movies and read about them in the dime novels. She'd longed for just one, but not from just any man. That first kiss had to be special. It had to mean something. It had to come from a man she could love with all her heart—someone like Brandon.

"Mr. Brandon." Ma's exclamation sounded far away. "What brings you here?"

Brandon was here?

Anna shot to her feet and, in the process, knocked over the lamp. With horror, she watched the oil spill and the flames shoot across the floor.

"No," she screamed.

The fire. The school. It was happening again, only this time the flames stood between her and safety.

Chapter Seventeen

Brandon heard Anna scream and bolted into action. This wasn't a playful cry or even the shriek of seeing a mouse run across the floor. She was terrified.

He crossed the sitting room in few steps, but the chest of drawers blocked the bedroom entrance. He shoved it out of the way and started to push it against the wall until he noticed the crawl space had been opened. Wisps of smoke drifted out of the doorway.

Anna coughed. From inside. What was she doing in there?

He pushed the dresser against the bed and dropped to one knee to get through the crawl-space opening. His shoulders scraped both sides, even when he turned sideways. His leg and foot protested the act of kneeling, but he ignored the pain.

Anna was in danger.

Once he got his upper body inside, he saw the problem. A small fire, caused by a toppled oil lamp, burned across the floor from the stone wall to the plaster one. Anna crouched on the other side of the blaze, her eyes wide.

"Help me!" She panted, hysteria threatening.

Though panic wanted to propel him to her side, that would only put both of them on the wrong side of the blaze.

"Walk toward me," he urged as evenly as he could.

"I can't."

"Yes, you can. Just walk through the flames. They won't hurt you."

But she didn't move. She must be too afraid. He'd seen that in battle. A soldier would be all bluster and bravado before a fight, but once the shelling started, he froze, unable to act. Invariably that man fell.

If Anna didn't act soon, she *would* be in trouble. There was no other way out of this room.

"I'm right here." He spoke calmly despite the alarm beating on his eardrums. He balanced on his good knee and held out his arms. "You'll be fine."

If possible, her eyes widened farther. "My skirt will catch fire."

"Not if you jump over the flames."

She didn't budge. What was wrong with her? The fire was still tiny. She could easily step over it.

"I can't," she sobbed, and he knew she'd never move if he couldn't persuade her.

"Yes, you can. You can do anything. You're a brave explorer, just like Mr. Carter."

Even that didn't move her.

"It's just like before," she wailed.

Of course. The pastor had told him she'd been in a fire. Last summer, was it? She'd survived, but perhaps the scars still ran deep.

No amount of coercion would get her moving. He needed another tactic. He backed out of the crawl space to look for something to put the fire out.

"Where are you going?" Anna cried. "Don't leave me."

"I'll be right back." He gave her a smile of encouragement before ducking out to survey the bedroom. He could get a pail of water from the washroom or... The rug. It had bunched up when he'd shoved the dresser aside. That should do the trick. He tossed the rag rug into the opening and crawled in after it. The smoke had gathered enough to burn his eyes and throat. Anna crouched near the floor, her apron pressed to her face. Good. At least she had the presence of mind to get low, where the air was better.

At the sound of his reappearance, she lifted her head. "Brandon." The sound was muffled by the apron and her fear.

"Stay there."

With one motion, he threw the rug over the fire. The flames sputtered and died, but the searing hot lamp created a bulge that allowed air to creep under the edge of the rug. A tongue of flame licked out from underneath.

"It's not out," she shrieked.

Brandon stripped off his coat and threw it over the remaining fire. Within moments, the blaze died, leaving them in darkness. Only the dim light of the opening showed the way out.

"Come here," he commanded shakily.

She sniffled. "You must think I'm a coward."

"Not at all." Brandon fisted his hands to stop their trembling. "You're the bravest person I know."

She shuffled toward him but stopped at the smoldering remains of the fire. Her tear-streaked face lifted.

"I'm sorry." Her words came out in a sob. "Your coat."

He couldn't believe she was worried about something so insignificant. "It's just a coat."

But she only sobbed harder. "I've ruined it. Now you'll have to buy another. But you don't have the money." Each statement came with a gasp for air and a cough. "That's the last thing I wanted. Oh, Brandon, how can you ever forgive me?"

He didn't hesitate one second. He pulled her close and led her to the crawl-space entrance, where the air was clean. Only then did he collapse, cradling her against his shoulder. Her hair smelled smoky but still so very much like Anna. Dear Anna, the woman he thought he'd alienated, the one he could never quite get out of his mind. He breathed deeply, letting the smell and feel of her melt into his senses for just a moment.

Then he took her face in his hands and made her look at him. "Now you listen to me, Anna Simmons. All I care about is that you're safe."

And he meant it more than he'd ever meant anything in his life.

Her liquid blue eyes pooled with tears. Her lips trembled like flower petals in the wind. And he loved her. Not a passing fancy or crush. He couldn't imagine a day without her. With her, he could conquer anything.

Her lips formed his name, though nothing sounded, and he could hold back no longer. Closing his eyes, he leaned forward and lightly touched his lips to hers. They yielded at once, perhaps from surprise, but then she wrapped her arms around his shoulders and returned the kiss with an intensity that took his breath away.

He saw nothing but her, felt nothing but her, heard nothing but her.

That moment could have lasted forever if Mrs. Simmons hadn't called out, "What's happening? Are you all right? I smell smoke."

Anna pulled away. "Ma's worried."

Reality crashed in, and as the heat dissipated, so did his certainty. He should never have kissed Anna. That kiss would give her false hope of a future together, but he was even further from being able to provide that future than the day he'd met her. A woman like her deserved the world, and he could give her nothing. He should never have succumbed to temptation. Her glowing smile confirmed his worst fears.

"Anna?" Mrs. Simmons questioned from very near.

Brandon cleared his throat. "It's just the oil lamp," he called out. "Nothing at all."

Unlike the kiss.

Even after she'd been sitting at their little table for a quarter hour, Anna couldn't control her racing heart. He'd kissed her. Brandon had kissed her, and it was so much better than she'd imagined. She would never have guessed that a man as strong and reserved as Brandon could show such tender affection.

She had to keep looking at her tea to hide the glow in her cheeks while Brandon explained the mishap in the crawl space. Somehow he managed to make it his fault, that he'd startled her. His gallantry only made her heart beat more wildly.

"Thank God no one was hurt," Ma exclaimed when he finished. "No harm done."

Despite increasing blushes, Anna had to set the record straight. "I'm afraid his coat is ruined."

Ma's attention flitted back to Brandon. "We must get you another one, then."

"Nonsense." Brandon showed the scattering of burn holes in the lining. "They'll never show and don't affect the warmth one bit."

"Well, then, I'll mend it," Ma insisted.

Brandon, of course, refused. "It's nothing. I've put worse holes in coats with less cause."

Anna doubted that. Brandon was meticulous in every way.

"It's certainly more than nothing. Thankfully you arrived

when you did," Ma said for the umpteenth time. "I'm sure the Lord's hand was in it."

Brandon didn't recoil when Ma mentioned God. In fact, he seemed quite willing to deflect the praise elsewhere. "Anyone else would have done the same."

"No, they wouldn't. I was right here, but I couldn't squeeze past that dresser," Ma said, apparently forgetting that she'd done just that moments before Brandon showed up. "You're a hero, an absolute hero, and heroes deserve a little pampering. I'll tell you what. Why don't Anna and I fix you a nice supper tonight? I'll make some gingerbread for dessert. Anna said she was going to start a pot roast. Is there still time? Oh, dear, it has gotten late."

Anna let her mother babble on. She couldn't put two thoughts together, especially when she looked up and caught Brandon gazing at her. Then her cheeks would heat all over again, and she was sure Ma must know that they'd kissed.

"Maybe you should have waited to explore, dearest." Ma was clearly talking to her, but Anna had caught only the last sentence.

Brandon, though, must have heard the entire conversation. "Why *were* you in that crawl space? I'd blocked it off so you wouldn't use it."

Anna gulped. He knew about the crawl space? Then either he'd already taken the treasure from the room or there had never been any to begin with. Considering his insistence there was no lost fortune and the financial state of the bookstore, it had to be the latter.

She hoped she didn't look too guilty. "I was curious. After I discovered it, that is. Ma lost her ring." She was explaining things all backward, and Brandon looked confused.

"My ring!" Ma exclaimed. "I'd nearly forgotten with all the excitement. To think that old wedding band caused all this fuss. You must think I'm a silly old woman."

He smiled indulgently at her. "Not at all, Mrs. Simmons. A wedding ring is one of the most important things in a woman's life."

"And a man's," Ma hinted, none too subtly.

Anna hid her face in her hands.

Thankfully, Brandon didn't take the bait. "I'm sure your husband treasured his. I can't tell you how sorry I am that he passed at such an early age."

As always, Ma's eyes misted when Papa was mentioned. "He was a good man." She patted Brandon's hand. "As was your father. He took care of us after my Harold passed."

"He did?" Brandon and Anna said simultaneously.

After his initial surprise, a frown settled in. "Let me guess. He sent you money each month."

To her shock, Ma confirmed his guess. "And only charged a dollar a month for rent."

Percival Landers had rented them the house for next to nothing *and* sent Ma money? "Why would he do such a thing?"

Ma shrugged. "He said he wanted to make sure the garage stayed open. He wanted to help."

Charity. Anna felt the icy tentacles of pity wrap around her heart. Was Brandon like his father? Had he kissed her only because he knew she'd never been kissed? Her cheeks burned, this time with shame.

Brandon didn't notice. "That doesn't sound like Father. He always put money before people."

Ma clucked her tongue. "Now, now, we can't always know a person's heart. Clearly he felt responsible for us, and I thank God for your father's generosity. Now, what do you say we get busy with supper?"

Ma rose to her feet, putting an end to the conversation, but her revelations continued to tumble around Anna's mind. Why would a man who had sent them money each month suddenly sell their house without notifying them? And when had the payments stopped? Or had they? Hendrick resented Brandon's father. Maybe that's why. Brandon certainly looked as confused as she was. Only Ma seemed unfazed, as if life was percolating forward as normal, but it wasn't.

Everything had changed after that kiss.

In the days that followed, Anna scoured the house for clues while Brandon was at the bookstore. She had plenty of time to do so since Brandon worked late and refused to let her work without pay.

First, she crawled up into the attic, which was filled with cobwebs and nothing else. An empty attic? Who heard of such a thing? But there it was. Empty. So she busied herself with the second and first floors. She checked every inch of wainscoting for hidden doors. She looked behind every book in the library. She checked every drawer for secret compartments. In the end, she had to admit defeat. Except for the desk drawers that Brandon kept locked, she'd checked everywhere. Though she longed to see inside those drawers, she had to admit that they couldn't contain a secret compartment or he would have found it.

That left her nowhere. Maybe Brandon was right, and there was no hidden fortune. And no explanation for his father's odd payments to Ma. In any case, her efforts had run their course. Until she could think of another place to look, all she could do was clean and dream up some other way to save Brandon's bookstore.

He wouldn't talk about it, of course. Oh, she'd asked, but he'd brushed aside her concerns.

"Nothing for you to worry about."

But she *did* worry. She *did* want to help. She wanted him to trust her. If he'd just kept the popular-fiction section, he'd be turning a profit by now. She had no doubt.

Each day she lingered after preparing supper, hoping Brandon would stop in the kitchen and talk to her. She longed to hear about his day, to offer consolation, to be the partner that she was sure he wanted after that marvelous kiss. Instead, he bolted straight to the library and closed the door before she could get there, as if he was afraid to see her.

So she brought his supper on a tray and knocked on the door.

"Just leave it outside," he'd call out, and she'd reluctantly retreat.

"Why won't he talk to me?" she finally complained to her mother.

"He's under a great deal of stress, dearest. I'm sure he'll come around once this rough patch has passed."

Anna wasn't so sure it would pass. His expression grew grimmer by the day. His shoulders slumped. He looked like a man already defeated.

"You'll find a way," she would call out as he passed on his way out of the house in the morning. "Never give up. Mr. Carter didn't."

If he heard her, he never let on. He just retreated deeper and deeper into himself.

She had to find that hidden fortune. That was the answer. He must think so too because he spent all his time in the library. Sometimes he even fell asleep there. She'd hear him head upstairs when she entered the kitchen in the morning.

So she concentrated her efforts on that room. Each day, different books lay open on his desk. When she finished cleaning, she would sit at the desk and leaf through them. They were mostly journals and ledgers written by his ancestors. The dates ranged back into the late 1840s, when the house was first built. In an odd way, they were fascinating.

Soon she became engrossed in the details of their lives, reading until the grandfather clock struck five o'clock and she had to prepare supper for Brandon, who would be late, and Ma, who would be hungry.

The journals detailed daily purchases and expenditures. They noted incidents with servants, livestock or the stable. One day a horse might take a stone in its hoof. The next might list the number of calves born. Many days included commentary on the weather. At least she assumed the cryptic notes referred to the weather: "E2, 9, whiteside, midnight" or "S10 then E, 3, sunny blooms." Those she could explain, but not the ones that began "city of gold." What city of gold?

She sighed and rubbed the bridge of her nose. Plenty of frustration and unusual entries, but not a single clue. And no maps. She'd found nothing that could remotely be considered a treasure map, and nothing explained where to locate this city of gold.

Downstairs, a door banged shut.

Anna shot to her feet and hastily put the book back to the page that Brandon had been reading. It couldn't be six already. No, daylight still streamed through the window, and the clock read three-ten. What was Brandon doing home so early?

She rushed to the library window, which overlooked the carriage house and driveway. His car wasn't parked out front. Her heart pounded. Brandon wouldn't have walked home, nor would he have put the car away in the middle of the afternoon.

Then who had just come in the house?

Ma? Not likely. She wouldn't walk through the snow without assistance.

Anna moved to the fireplace and picked up the cast-iron poker. It had enough weight to knock out any man.

The hallway floor creaked. Whoever it was, he was coming straight toward this room.

She tiptoed to the door and stood behind it, positioned so she could crack the man over the head.

The knob began to turn. Heart racing, she lifted the poker.

The door opened, and a tall man strode into the room. She swung the poker downward but must have given herself away because he leaped aside, arms out in surrender.

"Goodness, girl. What are you doing?" It was Reggie, though not dressed as finely as normal.

She dropped the poker and pressed a hand to her waist to calm her tattered nerves. "Oh, Mr. Landers. I didn't know you were in town. I thought you were at college."

"Clearly I'm not."

"Yes, well, I didn't know that. I thought you were an intruder. I didn't see Brandon's car. I looked, but it wasn't out front." She was babbling, but at least he'd started to grin.

"No harm done. I didn't realize you were here either." He glanced around the room then at her. "Cleaning, are you?"

She swallowed hard. She'd taken off her apron. "I, uh, was…resting a bit." She forced a smile. "Brandon lets me read his books. We're both interested in archaeology."

"Are you?" Reggie looked skeptical. Considering no book was lying open other than the journals on the desk, he had every right to be.

She pressed her hands to her cheeks. "He loaned me Mr. Davis's book on his excavations in the Valley of the Kings." She truly was babbling, and he looked decidedly uninterested. "I should get back to the kitchen to prepare supper."

That was the first thing she'd said that he agreed with. "Sounds like a first-rate idea. I'm half-dead from hunger. What are you making?"

She'd planned a simple beefsteak, but that wouldn't take three hours to prepare. She scrambled for something that sounded like it would take longer. "A meat pie."

"I can hardly wait." He wandered over to the desk and glanced at the journals before looking up. "Is there anything else?"

"No, sir." She slipped from the room and hoped Reggie wouldn't tell Brandon that she'd been snooping.

Chapter Eighteen

Anna had to watch her step when Reggie was at the house. The tension between the brothers was thick. Something had happened to send Reggie home from college, but rather than discuss it, the two men appeared to be avoiding each other. Brandon left early in the morning as usual, while Reggie lingered in bed until eight o'clock. He then requested she bring a pot of coffee to the library. He seldom talked to her, simply waved at the table where he wanted her to set the coffee service. The moment she left the room, he locked the door.

He had to be searching the room, almost certainly for the lost fortune. There was no other explanation for his behavior. He never took a book out of the room. He never opened the daily newspaper. So as far as she could tell, he didn't read at all.

After the noon hour, he left the house and didn't return until late, well past supper. As far as she could tell, Brandon and Reggie seldom spoke. She doubted Brandon knew what his brother was doing.

One morning, Anna managed to catch Brandon before he scurried out the front door.

"You need to know something about your brother."

He paused, his hand on the doorknob, and for a moment

the gloom lifted and concern softened his features. "Has he done something to offend you?"

His tenderness melted her heart. "No. No." She shook her head. "But he is acting strangely." She glanced around to make sure Reggie wasn't standing on the staircase behind her.

Brandon's brow furrowed. "In what way?"

She took a deep breath. This felt awfully much like snitching, but Brandon needed to know that his brother was working behind his back. "He locks himself in the library all morning."

"And?"

"And then leaves the house until after you've retired for the night." The accusation sounded petty. "I'm sure it's nothing, but seeing as Eloise said he was looking for the lost fortune, I thought you should know."

Brandon looked exhausted, more than ever, and it was only seven o'clock in the morning. "Let him look. He won't find anything."

"Shouldn't you warn him that he's wasting his time?"

Brandon's lips threatened a smile. "Does your brother take your advice?"

"Well, no. Not usually." She cast around for one instance when he had. "All right, never, but that doesn't mean your brother is like mine. After all, you're older, and I'm Hendrick's little sister."

The smile broke through, warming his features. "Not so little anymore." He touched a finger to her jaw. "Not at all. If I were him, I'd listen to my little sister." He sighed. "I should have listened to you from the start."

Anna trembled under his touch. His gaze left no doubt that he cared for her, and his words confirmed it. "Then I can work at the bookstore again?"

"Patience." His eyes glistened in the soft light. "Give me a little more time."

She seized on the hope in his words. "Then my prayers have been answered. The bookstore will stay open."

His smile vanished. "It's going to take more than prayers to keep it open."

She wanted to tell him that prayer was exactly what it would take, but he wouldn't listen, not yet.

"It must be his decision," Ma had said last Sunday. "When he walks through the church door on his own, then you'll know he's ready."

Anna wasn't the patient type, yet that's what everyone wanted from her. Wait and see. Wait, wait, wait. She could barely stand it.

"Don't worry about Reggie," Brandon was saying. "He'll give up treasure hunting soon enough and realize he has to work to make his way in this world."

"At the bookstore?"

Brandon laughed. "Definitely not. I can think of no one less suited." He opened the door.

She missed the feel of his hand on her cheek and wished he did not have to leave so soon. "Am I suited?"

A peculiar mixture of longing and distress flitted across his face before the impassive mask returned. "You are suited for many things. Reach for your dreams."

He stepped onto the porch and hurried down the steps to his automobile. Anna stood a moment in the doorway, feeling every bit like the wife saying goodbye to her husband. The barriers of employer and maid had vanished long ago, and the kiss had confirmed it. He cared for her, perhaps even loved her, but before he could admit it, he needed to get the bookstore on its feet. Brandon was that type of man.

She stepped back and shut the door before the icy winter air filled the hallway. His departure always left a barren pit in her stomach that couldn't be filled except by him. She would wait anxiously all day and hope to see him at suppertime.

She leaned against the door and shut her eyes.

"Well, well, well." Reggie's voice set her nerves on edge. "Wasn't that cozy?"

Anna gulped. How much had he heard? Hopefully not the entire conversation. She had checked to make sure he wasn't up yet. He never rose before eight. So why was he here now?

She cast her eyes down, hoping he didn't see the guilt. "I'll bring your coffee at once. In the library?"

"Naturally." But he eyed her warily as she hurried to the kitchen.

Brandon could have stayed with Anna all day, but he had a nine o'clock appointment at the bank, where he hoped to learn if he would receive the loan that would keep the bookstore open.

Her concerns about Reggie amounted to nothing. The greater problem was Reggie's expulsion from college. In comparison, a little treasure hunting was child's play. Brandon had seen his brother poking around the house, but Reggie wouldn't find a thing. He'd told his brother that the so-called lost fortune was either hopelessly lost or had been discovered and spent years ago, but Reggie still insisted the fortune existed.

He sighed as he mounted the steps of the bank. Here was where the necessary money could be found, but it would come at a price. That's what treasure hunters always forgot—that any find had its cost. Mr. Carter was learning that in Egypt as the press denounced his exclusive agreement with *The Times,* dignitaries streamed in for a look and the antiquities service tightened its oversight. Any peace the man had enjoyed before the find was gone. Few men counted the cost. He liked to think he was one.

Mr. Shea showed him into the pristine office with the massive walnut desk. No loose papers littered the top. The polished wood reflected the bank manager's deep-set frown.

Shea opened the file before him. "The balance will be due in six months." He laid out the terms of the loan with precise detail.

Brandon tried not to show his dismay. The interest rate was exorbitant, the term of the note far too short. He could never turn a profit in that short a time, not if he employed Anna. When she'd asked if she could return to the bookstore this morning, he so wanted to tell her yes, but she needed stable employment, not the pittance he could offer.

"Six months?" Brandon needed some give on the bank's part, and he knew enough about business to realize he wouldn't get it unless he assured them his plan would benefit the bank in the long run. "Employment is key to Pearlman's growth, is it not?"

Shea nodded warily.

"I hope to rehire Miss Simmons." He searched his memory for some personal tie that would spark Shea's interest. The man was old enough for grandchildren. "And perhaps a stock boy."

Shea's somber expression flickered just enough to tell Brandon he'd hit on something, and just in time. He needed this loan.

"A stock boy, eh?" Shea stroked his chin. "My grandson might fill the bill. He's sixteen and the brightest lad in his class."

Thank God. Brandon could have kissed Shea for having a grandson. "Then you'll understand why I need a longer term. I'd rather put the profits back into the community through employment until the store has a solid toehold. I'm thinking five years would be adequate."

Shea countered, "One year."

"Four."

In the end, they settled on two years, which at least gave him a chance. He could order the popular novels and children's books and rehire Anna. She'd have brilliant ideas for promoting the new section. She would draw in customers.

"You do understand that a longer term will require greater commitment," Shea said.

His spirits fell. "What sort of commitment?"

Shea looked him in the eye. "More collateral. Your house, for instance, unless you have other property of equal value."

Brandon choked. If he defaulted, he'd lose everything. The bookstore would close. The house would go on the market, and he'd head for Detroit, where he'd lease a room and look for employment as a clerk. Not the sort of life he would ask any woman to endure, least of all Anna. At twenty, she had her whole life ahead of her. She didn't need to be tied to a man with no prospects.

On the other hand, he could only win her heart by making a go of the store. That meant taking the risk.

He nodded his assent. "The house it is."

"I'll have to take it to the board again." This time when he rose, Shea didn't smile. He knew what Brandon was laying on the table. "I won't lie to you, Mr. Landers. Some on the board feel there's no need for a bookstore, since the mercantile already carries a good selection of books."

Kensington Mercantile, owned by the same man who owned this bank. Oh, Mr. Kensington might be all smiles and handshakes at family dinners, but beneath that he must be a ruthless businessman. That's the only way one man could own half this town. No doubt Kensington chaired the bank board.

"To your benefit, one of the board members has always been fascinated by your house," Shea continued.

Brandon could guess which one.

Shea continued, "Putting it up as collateral should make the difference." He held out his hand. "I'd say you have a good chance."

Chance was not what Brandon wanted to rely upon, but at this point he had little choice. More and more he knew that he wanted a life with Anna. To get the reward, he must take the risk.

So, he shook Shea's hand. "Thank you for your help. I'll look forward to a positive response. When do you expect an answer?"

"Early next week."

Brandon breathed out. Soon he would know if he'd have a chance to claim that life. Soon he could tell Anna how he really felt.

Reggie left the house early that day, before noon. After he'd disappeared down the driveway, Anna rushed to the library to clear the coffee service and figure out what he'd done that morning. On every other day, she'd found nothing, but today she discovered the little book Ma had given Brandon sitting on the desk. Reggie had left it open and upside down as if interrupted while reading.

That was odd. The telephone hadn't rung. Nothing could have prompted him to rush away unless he suddenly recalled he had an appointment. That must be it. Or he telephoned someone who had demanded he come at once. She could imagine who. Sally Neidecker. Whatever the cause, he'd rushed off without replacing the book.

Naturally she picked it up to see what he was reading. The text was dense and footnoted, something she wouldn't have expected from Mrs. Neidecker. Her former employer, who now strove to outdo the Kensingtons, must have received a college education.

Anna sank into Brandon's chair. The soft leather warmed to her body, and she could smell him there. She closed her eyes and breathed in the scents of leather and lemon-oil mixed with something exotic that she couldn't quite place. It reminded her of antiquities and adventure and places she longed to explore.

The house creaked, and her eyelids flew open. She held her breath and listened, but nothing followed.

The house was forever creaking and groaning. She supposed that's what old houses did, especially old houses that hadn't been heated in many years. After two months working here, she should be used to it, but every time one of the sharper reports sounded, she wondered if the house would tumble down. Just to be safe, she opened the door wide.

No one was in the hallway, so she shook off her unease and returned to the book. Reggie had left off in the early part of the history, after Mrs. Neidecker's speculation on Indian settlements and her more definitive narrative of the first white settlers.

The town had apparently been founded in 1838 by a Mr. Norris. The town's original name had, naturally, been Norristown, but after drawing friends and neighbors to the settlement and building a mill, he'd absconded with the money they'd paid him to grind their grain. Those cheated neighbors had discovered the millworks incomplete and had nearly abandoned the town until the preacher, a Mr. Lyman, had declared the area a "pearl without price" and convinced the settlers to stay. They pooled what resources they had left and got the mill running. Their flour brought an unexpectedly high price, and in thanksgiving for God's providence, they renamed the town Pearlman.

The story was fascinating, but it certainly didn't have

anything to do with a buried treasure. She scanned the opposite page, and her eye caught a tiny pencil mark in the margin. Why hadn't she seen that before? That line of text referred to a specific book on the Underground Railroad.

She scrunched her brow and thought. She'd seen that title before, but where? At the bookstore or here? Brandon had a huge collection, enough to populate the store while still leaving his library's shelves half-full. The book in question had a green cover. That she could remember. She could recall the gold embossing of the title and the wear along the edge of the cover from being handled. It was a thick book, two inches wide at the spine, but short in height, like a novel.

She rose and walked around the library, scanning each shelf for the right color binding and thickness. My, he had a lot of books with green covers. When she reached each one, she checked the title. For the highest shelves, that required climbing the stool.

While examining a book on the highest shelf, the house creaked again.

That sounded like a floorboard.

She looked around nervously. What if Brandon returned and found her going through his books? He'd let her read them if she asked, but he did not want her to look for the lost fortune. That was the one thing they did not agree on, but he'd change his mind once she handed him the money. The bookstore could stay open. That worried frown would vanish from his brow. He'd take her in his arms and whirl her about. Maybe he'd even kiss her again.

She touched a finger to her lips, remembering the thrill of his touch and the incredible joy that had followed. Nothing could ever mean more than helping him keep his dream alive. That bookstore was his dream as much as searching for antiquities had been hers. So much had changed since he arrived. She no longer cared about antiquities except as an interest that she and Brandon shared. The most important thing was keeping Brandon in Pearlman. To do that, she must find the money before Reggie did.

Another creak came from outside the room.

She waited for what seemed like ages, breath bated, but didn't hear another sound. To make sure, she replaced the volume, which wasn't the book she sought, and checked the hallway.

Nothing.

It must be the house groaning. But she couldn't shake the jitters. The sooner she found this book, the better.

The clock now read eleven forty-five. By the time she got halfway through the shelves, it had chimed noon.

Then, like a pearl in the midst of sand, there it was, slightly pulled out, as if someone had hastily put it back without bothering to align the spine. That someone could not have been Brandon. He always made sure each book was exactly in line with the edge of the shelf. Anna appreciated that when she dusted. This book stuck out a half inch. Reggie must have shoved it back in a hurry. Maybe that's why he'd left so early today. He'd found a clue to the treasure's hiding place and needed to tell Sally.

Breathless, Anna pulled the volume from the middle shelf. The answer must be here, yet it was cryptic enough that Reggie couldn't figure it out without Sally's help. Anna's gut clenched. If Sally got her hands on the money, she'd never let it go.

Hands shaking, she carried the book to the sofa. Where to begin? She supposed in the early 1840s, since the Pearlman history had been left open at that date. She checked the table of contents and leafed to the proper chapter, which talked about the founding of stations on the Underground Railroad and how they used code names rather than actual place names to preserve their secrecy. One of the popular routes led north from various points and culminated in Detroit, which bore the code name *midnight*.

Anna grew more and more frustrated as she read. What did this have to do with treasure? It didn't even mention Pearlman. Most of the places listed were in states south of Michigan. No maps. No mention of hidden money. There were horrifying tales of slave hunters, a sort of bounty hunter who was paid to retrieve runaway slaves. When caught, the runaway faced brutal punishment.

She turned page after page, hoping for some clue to what Reggie had found, but it was all about the struggle between slave owners and abolitionists. In frustration, she slammed the book shut, dispirited. This didn't make sense. Why would Reggie care about the Underground Railroad and what did it have to do with hidden treasure?

Nothing, as far as she could see.

A tear trickled down her cheek and fell on top of the closed book. Oh, dear. It wouldn't do for Brandon to find tearstains on the edges of his book. He'd be furious. She brushed the dampness off the book and as she did, felt something rough. Upon closer examination, she saw a bit of paper a tiny bit higher than the edge of the pages.

That must be it!

Trembling with excitement, she opened the book and leafed through the pages until she got to the spot. Tucked inside, its edge barely above the top of the page, she found a yellowed newspaper article. It had been folded once.

Carefully she opened it. The headline, dated October of 1918, read, "Entire Platoon Lost." A photograph of the group of doughboys, young and eager, nestled amid the text. Her heart sank. This didn't have anything to do with treasure. It was a war story. She refolded the article and began to put it back in the book when she realized that one face in that photograph looked a little familiar.

She unfolded the newsprint again and held it under the lamp. Yes, that was Edward Naughton, but neither Brandon nor Reggie would know him. So why put a copy of this article in the book? Why keep it at all?

Curious, she read, and soon all thought of treasure vanished. She dropped the article to her lap, shocked. Now she knew what had happened to Brandon in the war and why it tormented his soul. His whole platoon lost.

Her heart ached for him. Now Reggie was spending time with Sally and working against his brother. Everyone was against him. Well, not her. She would stand with Brandon.

How, Lord? She lifted her concerns up in prayer and waited for God to answer.

When nothing came to mind, she read the article again, and this time a ray of hope darted into her mind. She could help him, but to do so, she must face Mrs. Neidecker and persuade her to help. It seemed impossible, but with God, all things were possible.

Again, a floorboard creaked, this time very close. It sounded like it came from directly behind her.

Her pulse raced as she whipped around to look.

Nothing.

She slowly scanned the room.

No one.

The library offered few places to hide. Even the heavy curtains didn't reach to the floor. The desk hid no one. She eyed the open door. Someone could be in the hallway.

She tucked the newspaper article in her apron pocket and put the book back on the shelf. Slowly, alert to every sound, she inched toward the open door. All she could hear was the sound of her heart pounding against her ribs. Every footfall echoed.

At last she reached the doorway. Her mouth was dry.

Her knees shook. She clung to the doorframe and leaned her head out just far enough to look.

Nothing to the left. Nothing to the right.

Naturally. She raced back to the window. Maybe the intruder had left.

Snow was coming down heavier now, creating a blanket of unbroken white. No car. No footprints. No one had come into the house since Reggie left. Even his footprints had filled with snow.

She laughed at her foolish imagination. Clearly she'd been spending too much time dreaming up mysteries where there weren't any and treasures that didn't exist.

The house was simply creaking and groaning in the coldness and dry air. After settling her nerves, she picked up the coffee service. She'd take this to the kitchen and rinse it out before putting the top-loin roast in the oven for supper. While it cooked, she'd consult Ma about the article. The housecleaning could wait until tomorrow. Something much more important needed to be resolved this afternoon.

Chapter Nineteen

Brandon whistled as he drove home. Despite the oppressive terms of the loan agreement, he felt a weight lift from his shoulders. He'd rehire Anna the moment he got back. He could imagine her smile of joy, that spark of excitement in her eyes.

Snow was falling heavily, coating the limbs with that sticky snow that looked like a Currier and Ives lithograph. Pearlman. Home. If events transpired as he hoped they would, he'd never leave here.

As he drove up the hill past all the regal homes of Pearlman's elite, it struck him how much he enjoyed having Anna and her mother so near. Those long discussions with Mrs. Simmons had stretched him intellectually and maybe even spiritually. She was a wily one, coming at him from every angle with her argument that he should rejoin the church. She never pressured and always spoke her piece with a warm smile. He'd known from the first day that he'd never win. Faith trumped persuasion every time. As soon as he signed the loan and had Anna back, he'd go to church. Anna and her mother would like that.

The tires skidded as he turned into the driveway. He'd have to choose his steps carefully between the car and the house. To be safe, he parked as close to the front steps as he dared. Lights blazed in the windows, welcoming him home. Home. None of his family had ever called this house home, but then none of them had a woman like Anna in their lives.

She could drive away the numbing chill of a winter's day. He had to admit he looked forward to seeing her, even on his worst days. Since he was arriving home early, she would be in the kitchen preparing supper. Usually he tried to stay clear and provide the proper distance so there wouldn't be any impropriety, but today was different.

Today he'd give her back her job. And when the loan approval came in, he'd celebrate properly by inviting her to dine with him at Lily's, the only restaurant in town. It might even be a sort of date. His heart warmed as he shut off the motor and prepared to exit the motorcar.

Though he wanted to bound into the house and call out her name, he took care he didn't fall, placing each foot firmly and using the cane for added support.

After negotiating the steps and porch without incident, he stepped into the foyer and shook off the snow. Lights glowed through the library doorway. Anna wouldn't be in the library at this hour. He peeled off his gloves and hat and then strode down the hall while unbuttoning his coat.

"Anna?" He poked his head into the room.

"Welcome home, brother." Reggie sat at Brandon's desk, feet propped on top.

Brandon wanted to wipe the smirk off his kid brother's face. "I thought you were dining with Miss Neidecker." He tossed his coat on the sofa.

Reggie whipped his feet off the desk. "I have more important business. Have a seat."

What impertinence. "May I remind you that *you* are in *my* chair?"

Reggie shrugged and vacated the desk. "I didn't realize that you were quite so attached to the furniture."

"It's a matter of principle, which you apparently don't have."

As always, the correction slipped off Reggie like rainwater off a roof. His brother absently ran a finger along the polished desktop, as if testing for dust. Finding none, he flopped onto the nearest chair.

"I have a bit of news."

Brandon reclaimed his desk. "The dean has reinstated you?"

Reggie waved a hand as if expulsion from college didn't matter. "More important news, something you'll find—shall we say—intriguing?"

Brandon gripped the arms of his chair, his good mood gone. "If it's not about college, then what?"

"That's what I love about you, brother. You're always direct. Rather a bottom-line sort of fellow."

Brandon glanced at the clock. If supper was simple, Anna would be finishing soon, and he'd miss her. "Time is valuable. Get to the point."

Reggie stroked the velvet-covered arm of the chair. "I believe we are not the only ones searching for the lost Landers fortune."

Brandon clenched his jaw. "There is no lost fortune. How many times do I have to tell you that?"

"Suppose you're wrong? I've been reading about the excavation in Egypt that has so captured your little Anna's imagination. Suppose Carter had agreed with everyone else and declared the Valley of the Kings tapped out?"

Little Anna? Brandon wanted to castigate his brother for those derogatory words. Anna was much more than the servant Reggie made her out to be, but arguing about Anna would only egg on his brother and do nothing to stop his infatuation with that vile lost fortune.

"The two situations have nothing to do with each other," he said as evenly as he could. "Even if money had been hidden away in the 1850s, it would most likely be state banknotes, which are worthless."

"It could be gold." Reggie drew a cigarette from his silver case.

"No smoking in this house."

Reggie ignored him and lit the disgusting thing. "Aren't you the least bit intrigued? The Brandon I knew would have leaped at the chance for adventure. You were the one who left Father hopping mad so you could become a journalist. Oh, he nearly burst a vein over that one."

"Your point?" Brandon tried to ignore the smoke.

Reggie tapped the ash into a tumbler that had undoubtedly contained brandy until recently. "My point is that if we don't find the fortune first—worthless or not—someone else will."

"Let him have it."

"You wouldn't think that if it was gold. I've seen your bookstore. A little capital wouldn't hurt either of us."

Brandon couldn't deny that, but neither could he place his faith on rumor. Or on the questions that finding such a cache might generate. From what he'd discovered, the family fortune had been made off the most despicable activities, which he hoped would stay hidden forever.

Reggie hopped to his feet and began pacing. "If she gets to the money first, we'll lose it."

"She? Your treasure hunter is a woman? Who? Miss Neidecker?"

"Sally?" Reggie laughed. "Certainly not. Ask yourself who has access to this house every day."

His words shot through Brandon's spine like a bullet from a German rifle. "You don't mean Anna."

Reggie snuffed his cigarette in the tumbler, leaving behind an ugly butt. "Who else?"

"She wouldn't," he protested, while recalling that she had wanted to do exactly that. But he'd told her there was no hidden fortune, had insisted she not search. She wouldn't go behind his back, would she?

Reggie leaned over the desk, both palms planted on the edge so he towered over Brandon. "I got suspicious when I saw some books out of place."

"She may read anything she wishes," Brandon snapped.

Reggie didn't budge. "As I said, I got suspicious, so I rigged a little test. I left a book on the desk with a mark in the margin referring her to another book in your library. Inside that book I tucked a little newspaper article that would interest her a great deal. Then I pretended to leave the house for the day."

"Pretended?" Brandon felt sicker and sicker with every word. "You trapped her?"

"I watched her from the room across the hall. You remember that knothole that slips out, how we would look through it at Father when he was raging at that Simmons fellow in the library?"

The memory came back in a rush. Father yelling at the man who must have been Anna's father. The man twisting his cap in his hands, promising better returns. Father demanding a greater percentage of the business. The man signing papers.

Brandon choked back the bile.

"Well, I slipped out the knot and watched her at work," Reggie continued. "She took the bait and did exactly what I thought she'd do."

Brandon shook with anger. "How dare you."

Reggie was unfazed. "I knew she'd hoodwinked you, but I didn't realize you were quite that bad off."

Brandon stormed to his feet, pushing his chair over in the process. "Don't you ever slander Anna Simmons. She hasn't a wicked thought in her." He poked a finger at Reggie. "She's not the one who runs through money. She hasn't failed at everything she tries. She's good and honest and the best person I have ever known."

Reggie stared at him, silent for long moments. "Then you *have* fallen for her."

Brandon picked his way around the desk, so furious that he could not account for his actions if he got hold of his brother. He couldn't let Reggie spread these abominable rumors about Anna. "She would never do anything behind my back."

"Are you sure?"

"Absolutely." He'd never been more certain of anything in his life.

"Then check her apron pocket." Reggie glanced at the window. "I see she's leaving now. If you hurry, you might catch her."

"I will not check her apron," Brandon growled. "I trust her, which is more than I can say for you."

"Very well." Reggie headed for the door but, just before exiting, turned for one last word. "The newspaper article Anna found is the one that tells what happened to your platoon in France."

Brandon's legs went numb even as his anger exploded. Reggie had given Anna that story? Of all the cruel, heartless acts.

"Get out," he growled, his blood pulsing hot.

"I am sorry." Reggie managed to feign regret. "I'd hoped I was wrong."

Brandon turned away from his brother, unable to look the

traitor in the eye a moment longer. Reggie must have hesitated, for a half minute passed before his footsteps echoed down the hall. No attempt to explain. No pleading for forgiveness. Not another word. Nothing could have stemmed Brandon's ire anyway, but he didn't experience the expected relief when he heard the front door open and close.

The deed had been done. After Anna read that article, she'd learn he was worse than a failure. She'd discover he was a murderer.

Anna turned the chair by the fireplace until it faced her mother and then sat.

Ma paused in her knitting, the ever-present smile upon her face. "Now tell me why you're back so early…and why you look so worried."

Anna took a deep breath. In the past two months, Brandon had spent many hours chatting with Ma. Perhaps he'd told her what had happened. "I found an old newspaper clipping today, from 1918, before the war ended."

Ma waited.

"It's about Brandon's unit. He was apparently a lieutenant and commanded a group of men."

"I see." She returned to her knitting. The deep blue strands looked like veins across her pale hands.

Anna leaned forward. "Did he tell you about the war? Did he explain what happened? How he ended up lame?"

Ma shook her head. "I'd think he'd be more likely to tell you than me."

Anna fought disappointment. "I thought you talked about everything."

"I let him guide the conversation." Ma finished the row before pausing. "The war never came up."

Anna blew out in frustration. Ma never stuck to the subject at hand. Why did she this time? "He said he was wounded in the war. The newspaper article said the unit was hit by heavy artillery. Did you know all his men died?"

"I suspected it. Something has been troubling him." She shook her head. "Poor man. That's a heavy load to bear without God's grace."

Ma's words touched her deeply. What if Brandon never returned to the Lord? "I want to help him, but he won't listen."

"Sometimes we must wait until people are ready."

"What if he's never ready? What if…?" She couldn't utter the unthinkable. What if he never recovered? What if he sank so far into darkness that he never came back? Unshed tears burned her eyes. Life without Brandon would be worse than empty and meaningless. She jumped to her feet and paced across the tiny room. "I have to do something."

"Then pray."

Anna groaned. "I do pray, but it's not helping. He's getting more and more anxious by the day. I can't just sit around waiting when I know what's bothering him. I have to help him. I have to *do* something. After all, words without actions are useless."

Thankfully, Ma didn't correct the poorly paraphrased scripture. "What do you propose?"

"I need to talk to him, tell him that I know what happened."

"Do you think that's wise? What if he gets angry?"

"He wouldn't." But Ma might be right. Brandon was a prideful man. He'd insisted she not search for the lost fortune, even when it could solve his problems. He'd exploded when he saw her looking at his ledger.

"Are you willing to lose him in order to help him?" Ma asked calmly.

Anna's eyes burned with determination. "I am." She

swiped away the moisture. "I'll do anything, even give up my dreams."

"Then you do love him. Sometimes love requires letting go of those we love."

"Like Papa?" Memories of her father's death rushed back with so much pain that she had to sit or her legs would collapse. She'd hidden in the tires, afraid to go to him. She'd let him die, alone. A sob fought its way up her throat, and no matter how hard she tried, it refused to be bottled up. "Like when Papa died." The words came out with a storm of tears. "Oh, Ma, I'm sorry. I'm so sorry." The last words wrenched out of her in convulsions that got even worse when Ma gathered her close.

"Hush, hush," Ma whispered. "It's all right."

But it wasn't and never would be until Anna confessed. Every inch of her quaked with fear. Ma had always given her whatever she wanted. She'd made Anna feel special, even though she had so much less than the other girls. What would she think when she learned what Anna had done? No small part of her wanted to continue soaking up Ma's love, but deep down she knew she must do what was right.

"No, Ma, it's not all right." She gathered what little courage remained. "There's something I need to tell you." She took a deep breath when she saw Ma's motherly concern, as if she expected a childish, trivial confession. This would hurt, but the truth must come out. "I saw Papa die."

"Oh, child." Ma gasped. A hand shot to her mouth. "You should have told me. How you must have suffered all these years. Dear Anna, say no more."

"No, Ma. I have to finish. I've been holding this in for far too long, and now I realize that I can never be what Brandon needs me to be until I own up to my mistakes."

Ma paled, sensing the solemnity of what Anna was about to say.

Blurting it out might be easiest but not fair to Ma, so she took the time to tell the whole story. "I knew it was wrong, but I did it anyway. I skipped school with—" For a moment she considered naming Sally Neidecker and her friends, but it didn't matter who had talked her into it. She'd made the decision. "I wanted to see the circus, but when we got there, I didn't have enough money to get in." She bowed her head, still ashamed of her actions. "I couldn't go back to school, and I couldn't go home, so I hid in the tires alongside the garage and waited for school to get out."

"Then you were there when the truck fell on your father," Ma whispered, barely audible.

Anna's throat had constricted so much that she could only nod for a second. She swallowed, trying to free up the words. "I—I—I saw the jack collapse. It fell so slowly." Her lips were quivering. "I could have gone to him."

"No, child, you couldn't."

Anna angrily swiped away a tear with the back of her hand. "Yes, I could have. I had time, but I just stood there, too afraid to do anything." She choked. "And he died." She sobbed. "He died. And I could have helped him. Oh, Mama, why? Why? Why couldn't I move? I loved him. I did. I did."

"Oh, dearest." Ma drew her close and kissed the top of her head. "I know you did. He knew you did." She held Anna's face in her hands. "Never, ever doubt that your papa knew you loved him. You were his little girl, his joy. You were everything to him. You are his legacy. Never forget that."

The pain that had been held in for so long finally came out, but it hurt. Oh, how it hurt, like knives slashing bone from bone. The good daughter that she had tried so hard to become was gone. In its place sat a broken, imperfect human being that didn't deserve the encouragements Ma was showering on her.

"I'm so sorry, so sorry," she blubbered over and over.

"That's all right." Ma patted her back as if she were seven years old again. "Let it all out. Only then can God work His healing."

Ma handed Anna a handkerchief—Brandon's, the one he'd given her that day in the kitchen. She must have left it here in the carriage house. The embroidered initials slipped beneath her fingertips. She couldn't use it. "Aren't you upset with me?"

"No, child. I wish you'd told me years ago so you wouldn't have had to carry this burden. It happened in the past. What counts is the future. Will you let God heal your hurting heart, or will you carry this pain with you the rest of your life?"

Anna had never boiled it down to such a simple decision. She pressed the monogram against her palm. "I want to be healed."

"Then let Him do the work. Tell Him what you told me and ask forgiveness. Then let go." Ma squeezed her hand. "It's the only way."

"I know," Anna whispered.

"It's the only way for Brandon too." Ma tucked a lock of hair behind Anna's ear. "Each of us must find our own way to forgiveness. For some, forgiveness is difficult to accept. I suspect it will be for him. He's carried the burden so long that he doesn't know how to set it down. Pray he won't wait as long as you did. Pray hard that God will heal his heart."

Ma was right. Some things only God could heal but, oh, how it hurt.

Chapter Twenty

Brandon paced the library. At each turn, he stalked to the window, where he could just make out the lights in the carriage house through the densely falling snow. Then he strode to the doorway and grasped the knob before letting go and returning to the window. Every circuit brought another conflicting thought.

Anna had devoured the archaeology books and articles he'd given her, but was her interest strictly academic? She'd harped on the rumored lost fortune, even after he'd told her it didn't exist. He'd asked her not to search for it, yet according to Reggie, she was still looking. Moreover, she hadn't told him what she was doing. That could mean only one thing—she intended to take anything she found.

The thought left a bitter taste in his mouth, which only got worse when he took into account that she must have read the article on his military disaster by now. She would despise him, just like Father had despised him. *Worthless. Coward.* Father's words still rang in his ears.

When his father died, Brandon expected nothing. Then MacKenzie informed him that he'd inherited the house. The boon soon turned sour. This house had sucked the life out of him, the way it had destroyed his father and the generations before him. All corrupt. All consumed by the love of money. He wanted nothing to do with it.

He'd hoped for a quiet life, but when he met Anna, that dream altered. She brought sunshine into the darkest day. Her lively curiosity made him want to reach for more, to cast aside the chains and step forth in courage. She'd made him a better man, but apparently her attentions had been a sham, and he'd nearly fallen for it. She was no better than the rest.

This time when he reached the door, he opened it. He would have this out once and for all. He pulled on his coat and shoved a hat on his head. Without bothering to don gloves, he stormed out of the house and headed down the hill to the carriage house.

The snow reached above his ankles but wasn't deep enough to impede his progress. With every step his fury grew until by the time he reached the carriage house, it threatened to explode out of him. He pounded on the door with his cane. Inside, he heard the scrape of a chair's legs, the hushed murmur of female voices and light footsteps None of it dulled his anger.

The door opened, and there Anna stood, more beautiful than ever, her eyes liquid in the dim light of late afternoon. She'd been crying.

His anger faltered.

"Brandon." Her voice sounded oddly strangled. "I was headed to the house to talk to you."

She'd read the article.

Embarrassment stuck its ugly talons into him. A hundred defensive statements rushed to his lips, yet one look at her, and he could not utter a one.

She stepped aside. "Please come in."

The room glowed with the golden light of oil lamps and candles. He'd forgotten that welcoming warmth after living with electric lamps for so long. The cozy room smelled of cinnamon and nutmeg.

Mrs. Simmons rose, a broad smile enlivening her rosy face. "Please have a seat." She motioned to her chair by the fire.

"Thank you, but I prefer to stand." He couldn't speak his piece in front of Anna's mother. "I wanted to speak with Anna."

"Of course, of course." The woman beamed. "I was just going to the bedroom to put on another sweater and wash up before dinner. Please take your time." She toddled into the bedroom, leaving the door open. No doubt she would listen. No doubt she expected words of love.

He motioned to the chairs by the fire and farthest away from Mrs. Simmons. "Would you care to sit?"

Anna looked pale, as if she knew what he was about to say. "I'll stand."

"Very well, Miss Simmons." He had to keep this impersonal or lose his nerve.

At first she started at the formality, but that surprise was soon followed by concern. "What is it? Is something wrong?"

He had to focus on the embroidered tablecloth. "I must ask to see the contents of your apron pockets."

"What?" Her concern flickered into confusion. "My pockets?"

"I understand you have something that belongs to me."

Dismay danced into place, but she didn't deny his accusation. "I found an article in one of your books." She pulled out the loathsome thing. "In fact, I wanted to talk to you about it."

He gripped the cane with all his might. "I am not interested in talking with someone who is working against me."

"What do you mean? I would never work against you in any way."

"Are you or are you not searching for the treasure that's supposed to be buried on the property and that I told you not to seek?"

She swallowed but again did not deny it. "I wanted to help you. I saw how badly the bookstore was doing. I—I believed the fortune was still here, and if I found it, you'd be able to keep the store running."

"Very altruistic," he said, not believing for one moment that she was telling the truth. "No one hands over a fortune, especially not someone who needs the money. Oh, I know what you were thinking. You'd find the fortune and then turn the tables on me. After all, I'm the one who took your house from you. It would only be fair to punish me by taking the money."

"That's not true. I would never—"

He bulled past her protests, the angry words flowing faster and faster. "I suppose you've already found it and squirreled it away."

"No, I didn't. All I found was the crawl space, which you've seen, and some meaningless scribbles in an old journal. Nothing more. You have to believe me. I would never hurt you."

He turned away. He'd heard that before. Mother claimed to love him but showered her affection on Reggie. Father only acknowledged his existence if he did what Father wanted. His commanding officer claimed superior knowledge, but not after getting his hands on a bottle of liquor. Vows of truth invariably turned to lies.

"Lies." The word shot out of him like a stone from a slingshot.

Anna reeled backward and grabbed a chair for support, but he couldn't seem to stop. All the frustration that had gathered over the years spilled out on her, culminating with the most hateful blow of all.

"You are hereby relieved of your housekeeping duties. I suggest you find other lodging as soon as possible."

Anna couldn't breathe. What had happened to Brandon? The red-faced, angry man before her bore no resemblance to the kind and loving Brandon she'd come to love. And all over a silly article. He might be embarrassed, upset even, but throw her out? She thought he cared for her. Was their time together a lie?

Clearly, she'd placed her hope in the wrong man.

So be it. She would not give him the satisfaction of knowing how deeply he'd hurt her.

She snatched her coat off the peg and faced him one last time. "Rest assured, Mr. Landers, I will leave your property at once."

Without waiting for him to answer, she darted outside and slammed the door behind her. The snow was falling heavily, and she struggled to don her coat before racing toward the gate. The afternoon light was dimming as twilight approached. She dug in her pockets for gloves but found none.

No matter. Anger would keep her warm.

She would let a room at the boardinghouse. If Terchie didn't have any rooms available, she'd go to Hendrick and Mariah. She and Ma would not stay one more night where they weren't wanted.

Oh, that man! How rude. How insensitive. How utterly unlike himself. Anna buried her hands in her coat pockets and scurried past the gate and onto the quiet street. No one was foolish enough to drive in the swirling snow, but she could make her way easily enough by foot. The snowfall barely came to her ankles.

He'd called her a liar. Anna did not lie. She certainly

hadn't lied to him. Yes, she was searching for the lost fortune, but it was all for him. Why couldn't he see it? She did everything for him.

A sob bubbled to the surface, and she wiped away the tears with her coat sleeve, which only made her face wet since her coat was crusted with snow.

"Fool," she cried out, releasing her anger into the swirling snow, though she wasn't sure which of them was the bigger fool. She'd believed in him. He should have believed in her.

Ma's words popped into her head. *He needs our prayers.*

Pray for Brandon after what he'd just done to them? Anna couldn't. She just couldn't. He'd thrown them out for the second time. What man would do such a thing?

A man who's hurting.

She had no idea where these thoughts were coming from, but it gave her pause. An hour ago, she'd understood why he'd turned away from God. The death of his men had wounded him far more deeply than a lost toe. He deserved compassion, yet she'd let his retaliation hurt her. Like a wounded animal, he'd merely lashed out in fear. He didn't know what else to do.

Her steps stilled. Jesus had been falsely accused many a time, yet he did not strike back. In fact, he insisted his followers accept a second blow to the other cheek.

Before Brandon arrived, she'd intended to help him. Pray, yes, but she would also act, no matter the consequences.

Off to her left, the lights at the Neidecker house glowed through the falling snow.

She wouldn't let hurt alter her course. Whether he hated her or not, she would help him.

Brandon stared at the slammed door. Anna had walked out on him. In the heat of anger, he hadn't quite realized it would end this way.

Mrs. Simmons stepped out of the bedroom. "Where did Anna go?"

The last bubble of anger popped, leaving him cold and empty. Anna's mother waited calmly for his answer. Surely she'd heard every word, but she didn't hurl accusations his way. No, she treated him with the same kindness as always.

Regret filled the vacuum left by anger's departure, just as surely as it had the day his men died. Anger was easy. Blame someone else. But the truth was never that clear. Doubts crept in. Even if Anna was looking for the fortune without his knowledge, she didn't deserve to be thrown out.

Mrs. Simmons waited. Calm, compassionate, kind. The opposite of him.

He swiped at his mouth. "I'll fetch her. She can't have gone far."

Above all, he had to escape. He grabbed the doorknob, but the elderly woman put a stop to his retreat with a hand to the door.

"We need to talk." It was not a suggestion.

Brandon felt like a boy caught in bad behavior. Like a boy, he tried to get out of the punishment to come. "Aren't you worried about her?"

"She'll come around. Like her father, she has a quick temper, but it cools just as quickly."

"That's not what I meant. She's out in the storm."

"Don't worry about Anna. A little fresh air will do her good." Mrs. Simmons patted his arm. "Let's sit before the fire. My hands are chilled."

He felt even worse for keeping an elderly lady in a cold bedroom while he castigated her daughter.

"Come." Mrs. Simmons took his arm, expecting him to lead her to the chair by the fire.

He did his duty and settled her in the chair closest to the fire, but he had no intention of joining her. "It's snowing harder. She might get lost."

"She's been out in worse." Mrs. Simmons pointed to the chair opposite. "Sit. What we have to discuss is more important."

His nerves snapped and crackled with the fire, so he tried to make amends. "I deeply regret what I said to Anna."

"You'll need to tell her that."

"I know." He stared at his large hands. Ineffective. What use were strong hands when they couldn't help a person? What use was a quick mind when it dreamed up insults and slights?

Mrs. Simmons got straight to the point. "You think she lied to you."

He sucked in his breath at the bald cruelty of his words. How foolish he'd been, but the impenitent boy inside couldn't admit fault. "She took the article."

"I grant you that she shouldn't have taken it with her, but the question you should ask is why. What could she possibly gain?"

He hung his head. "Nothing."

"Has she taken anything else from the house?"

He had to acknowledge she hadn't.

"Then why take an old newspaper clipping? It has no value."

"Except to me." The words came without thinking. He stared at the blazing fire, which hurt less than her piercing gaze.

"Why is it important to you?"

Brandon broke under her inquisition. Surely no sinner had faced worse. "It's not something...I'm proud of."

She nodded. "We all have done things that torment us. Why should you care that Anna saw it?"

"Because—" He fiddled with the lacy arm cover that Mrs. Simmons must have made. Because he cared for her. Because he didn't want Anna to know he'd made the worst mistake a man could. Because he didn't want to lose her.

Oh, the bitter irony! He brushed away the truth and dwelled on the hurt he'd experienced when Reggie told him what she'd done. "Because I trusted her."

"And you don't anymore?"

His face beaded with perspiration. "I'm not certain."

"In everyone's life there will come times when we lose faith with someone we trust and love."

A shiver ran through him at her words. Did he love her? Is that why this betrayal hurt so deeply?

"The true mark of character is how we deal with that loss of faith," she said. "Do we turn our backs on that person or do we forgive?"

"You make it sound easy."

She sighed. "Forgiveness is never easy. Let me tell you a story, something I haven't told anyone and never intended to tell anyone, but I think maybe it will help."

She leaned back, her eyes glittering in the firelight and her thoughts far away. "My husband was a wonderful man. That's not to say we didn't have our disagreements. I saw things one way. He'd see them another. It's inevitable when two strong-willed people come together. Anna is rather strong-willed, if you didn't happen to notice."

"I did," he admitted.

She didn't seem to hear him. "Harold could work miracles with his hands. He was always inventing something or other to make things work better. Did you know that?"

Brandon couldn't see how this had anything to do with him and Anna.

"One day he invented a new type of jack, one that would

raise heavy vehicles higher, and he took his idea to your father."

He could imagine where this story was headed. Father had made a fortune off automotive jacks. "My father stole it, didn't he?"

Mrs. Simmons smiled sadly. "Harold was never a businessman. He loved to share his ideas. Your father made the idea a reality. At first Harold was angry that he didn't get more money from your father, but he didn't dwell on it for long."

Something was left unspoken. "But you did."

"I was ashamed of myself, and I tried hard to forgive. I must have prayed a thousand times for God's help to forgive your father, but that anger wouldn't go away. Then Harold died."

Brandon wanted to bolt from the place, to go anywhere but to hear the rest of this story.

"The jack—his jack—had collapsed, and the truck crushed him."

"I'm sorry." Brandon fought the narrowing of his throat. "You must have hated my father."

"At first. Then the checks started arriving."

"Checks?" Brandon recalled the unexplained payments. "Guilt money."

"He told me it was the profits he'd earned from the patent on the jack. He paid us every month until just before his death, when the amount was paid in full."

"I never knew," he whispered. "I saw the entries in the ledger but I never knew why."

"Guilt is a hard taskmaster, Mr. Brandon. It is never satisfied. All your father had to do was accept forgiveness."

He looked up, surprised. "You would have forgiven him?"

"I already had."

He couldn't suppress a wave of irritation. "Then why didn't you tell him?"

Her smile was kind, patient. "Would he have believed me?"

He had to acknowledge Father wouldn't have. Neither would he in such a circumstance.

"Only when we ask can we truly receive." She touched his hand with fingers callused by years of labor. "The Lord works miracles in our hearts, doing things we could never do on our own. You see, I'd forgiven him years ago. I told him so, but he could never forgive himself."

"So he paid off the debt."

"He thought that would erase the wrong." She sighed. "How I prayed for him. I hope he found his way in the end."

"I doubt it." Father was too stubborn to turn to anyone—even God. Mother had discovered that.

She shook her head sadly. "I hope you're wrong. Forgiving yourself is the most difficult thing of all to do. Yet, we must if we are ever to move on."

Brandon had an uncomfortable feeling she wasn't talking about Father any longer. He slipped from her grasp and watched the fire. Flames licked the logs, occasionally shooting upward in tongues of gold.

"I should know," she continued. "You see, even after I forgave your father, I still blamed myself for Harold's death. I told myself that I should have pushed him to file the patent. I should have brought him lunch that day instead of pouting because he had to work through the dinner hour. Oh, the mind can think of a million ways to affix blame, but we can never know peace until we learn to forgive."

The fire had died down a bit, so he threw another log into the blaze before rising to take his leave. He understood full well what she was trying to tell him, that he had to forgive himself for losing his men, but it wasn't that simple. He *was* to blame. He had caused the deaths of his entire platoon.

"I must be going," he said.

This time she did not attempt to stop him. "Good night, Mr. Brandon. I'll keep you in my prayers."

That didn't ease the pain. In fact, it made him feel worse. He stepped out into the storm and was stunned to see the snowfall now reached to his knees.

Anna was out in this. Despite her mother's confidence, she could be in trouble. What if she'd fallen or lost her way? He could barely see the light from the house, and that was only a hundred feet away. His pulse raced, beating a steady thrum on his eardrums.

The dust and debris of the shell's explosion had been like this, blinding him so he couldn't see his men. When he'd finally stumbled forward, he'd tripped over the first lifeless body.

He had to find Anna before it was too late.

Chapter Twenty-One

Anna rapped the brass knocker against the cold wooden door. The sound rang out like a gunshot, but no one answered. Light filtered through the sheer drapes. Clearly someone was home. Perhaps she hadn't knocked hard enough.

The wind howled around the corner of the porch, and she scrunched farther into her coat. The brass felt like ice against her bare fingers. Once, twice, three times she knocked. Then blew on her hands to bring the feeling back.

Please let me in. Please listen.

Of all the people that might have held the answer to Brandon's past, why did it have to be Mrs. Neidecker? Anna's stomach fluttered. Evelyn Neidecker had every right to refuse to speak to her. After all, Anna had stormed out right before her Christmas party. She'd acted like a child. If Mrs. Neidecker would see her, an apology must come first.

The door opened. Graves, the Neideckers' butler, lifted an eyebrow before greeting her with stiff decorum. "The family is dining, Miss Simmons."

In her short tenure as housemaid, Anna had never got Graves to warm to her. He'd been with the family forever, at least as long as she could remember, and was loyal to a fault. Alas, that loyalty now stood in the way.

"May I wait in the parlor?" she asked, blowing again on her fingers for emphasis. "It's rather important."

He hesitated but at last stepped aside to allow her to enter. "I will inform Mr. Neidecker that you are here."

"Actually I need to speak to Mrs. Neidecker." Her face prickled when she stepped into the home's cozy warmth.

He closed the door behind her and glared at the clumps of melting snow that dropped off her coat onto the floor. Someone would have to clean up the mess. In the past, that someone would have been her.

"Your coat?" Graves barely lifted his hand, clearly affronted that he must handle her threadbare attire.

"Thank you, but I know where to hang it."

He sniffed, as if to say that her coat did not belong in the guest closet but ought to hang with those of the servants.

"I will let you know what Madame says." He waved her into the parlor before heading toward the dining room at his usual plodding pace.

Once he'd left, Anna pulled the newspaper clipping from her apron pocket and examined the photo again. It was blurry, but she was sure the third man from the left must be Edward Naughton. The article didn't name the men, but it had to be him. That would explain everything. It also offered the slimmest chance to help Brandon make peace with the past. She nibbled her lip and prayed that Mrs. Neidecker would listen and understand.

Her hands shook, and she had to put the article back in her pocket. *Lord, help me find the words.*

If she failed, Brandon might never come out of the abyss.

Where would Anna go?

Brandon scanned the space between the house and the

gate, but he could barely see ten feet ahead. The swirling snow and darkness obscured all but the intermittent twinkle of the light in the parlor window as he plowed toward the house.

He'd parked the car by the front door. If he could reach it, he'd have a chance of catching Anna, but the deep snow sapped his strength. Each step was an exercise in balance. By the time he'd taken a dozen steps, he was winded. Sir Edmund Hillary must have felt like this scaling Mount Everest. The wind, the snow, the bitter cold. His hands ached.

Ahead, a dark shape emerged from the wildly swirling snow. His car? He squinted as melting snow trickled into his eyes and stumbled forward until he bumped into the side of the Cadillac.

Thank God. He leaned against it, catching his breath.

Only a few steps more and he'd reach the driver's side. Halfway around, his good foot slipped and only the cane prevented a fall. Sharp pain burned up his leg to the hip. He bent over his cane to gather the strength to make the last few steps.

The snow pelted him. Large, wet flakes soaked his coat and numbed his hands. He turned and grabbed on to the car's roof before lowering himself into the driver's seat. Again, pain shot through his leg. He ignored it. Anna needed him.

He depressed the ignition. The car backfired violently.

He stifled the curse that wanted to come to his lips. This wasn't a time for the coarse ways of man. To save Anna, he needed higher help, God's help.

Please let the car start, Lord. It was a poor prayer, but the first one he'd tried since the day his men died.

Taking a deep breath, he tried the ignition again.

Bang!

Same result. Apparently prayer still didn't work.

He beat on the steering wheel in frustration. Worthless invention. Why wouldn't it work when he really needed it? He leaned his forehead against the cold wheel and felt the poke of the throttle and spark controls. He'd forgotten to set the throttle and retard the spark. What a fool!

This time the car started. He put it in gear, switched on the headlamps and inched forward. He couldn't see a thing. The headlamps reflected off the snow, illuminating a wall of white. At this rate, he would drive into the stone fence or the carriage house. He could put the car into a tree. Still, he pressed on, hoping he'd found the driveway. The mission must proceed. Anna must be found.

Thump.

The car rolled over something solid.

He stopped breathing. What if he'd run over Anna?

He braked. The car slid. He braked harder, and the vehicle finally came to a stop. He threw open the door and called for her.

No answer.

Dear God. What if he'd killed her?

Mrs. Neidecker strode into the parlor, her expression coldly reserved. "Your former position is no longer available. I've already hired Minnie Fox."

"I know." Anna managed to stand, though her legs felt like gelatin. "That's good."

Mrs. Neidecker stared at her as if she were mad.

Anna tried again. "I mean to say, that's not why I'm here." She struggled to pull together her thoughts. "I owe you an apology. I should never have resigned so suddenly. You needed my help for your party, and I—" Oh, how it hurt to admit fault. "I acted selfishly. I'm sorry. It was inconsiderate to quit without notice." Oddly, once the last word was out, the humiliation vanished, and a calm strength infused her with courage. She could do this.

Mrs. Neidecker's icy demeanor thawed a little. "Yes, you did leave me in a bind, but thankfully Minnie helped at the last moment. I must say, though, that you'll have difficulty finding *real* work with such an attitude."

She clearly felt Brandon had given her work merely from sympathy. Anna bit back the retort that rose to her lips. Once again unemployed, she couldn't risk further alienating Pearlman's elite.

Mrs. Neidecker glanced at the darkened window dotted on the outside with snow. "Surely you didn't come out of doors on such a night simply to apologize."

"No." Anna's heart inched up her throat. She forced it back down. Whatever the cost, she must try to help Brandon. When she'd left the house, she'd been certain this was the way, but now she wasn't so sure.

"Well, what is it? We are dining."

Anna swallowed hard and groped in her apron pocket until her fingers landed on the newspaper article. "I found something at Brandon's—the Landerses'—house today that I hope you can help me with."

Mrs. Neidecker looked at her oddly. "Wouldn't you go to Mr. Landers with that information?"

"Certainly not." Then, as Mrs. Neidecker's expression turned to confusion, she understood what the woman was thinking. "I'm not talking about the lost fortune. I found something else." She pulled out the newspaper clipping. "I think it's about Edward."

Mrs. Neidecker paled, and her hand clutched at the pearls around her throat. "My nephew?"

Apparently Edward had meant a great deal to her. Anna hesitated. Seeking forgiveness for Brandon wouldn't be as easy as she'd thought.

Mrs. Neidecker said, "Please have a seat on the sofa."

Anna fought the sensation that she was going on trial and sat at the far end. Hopefully Mrs. Neidecker would choose a seat across the room from her. Alas, the woman settled beside her, so close that their legs nearly touched.

"Now, what is it that you've found about my Edward?" She reached for Anna's article.

Not yet. Not until she'd explained. Anna shoved the clipping back into her pocket. "I think we should talk."

"Talk about what? Just show me what you've found. Is it about how he…died?" The last word was barely audible, and Anna could see the pain that she kept so well hidden the rest of the time.

"You loved him, didn't you?"

For a moment, Anna thought the woman would cry, but Mrs. Neidecker blinked rapidly and forged past the emotion.

"He was—" she cleared her throat "—like a son, the son my Ralph always wanted. Not that we don't love Joe, but he has no interest in the business, and, well, he lacks a bit of direction. Our nephew loved everything about business, had a head for it. He adored touring the cannery." She knit her fingers together. "He would be so upset to see how poorly it's fared since our competitors opened their cannery." She raised a handkerchief to her eyes.

Anna had never considered that the Neidecker cannery would suffer once the newer, more modern one opened in Belvidere.

"I'm sorry," she murmured.

Mrs. Neidecker shook her head just once. "Edward

would have found a solution. He was brilliant that way. Ralph had set his heart on Eddie following in his footsteps." She paused again to gather her composure. "Why did he have to go to war? He could have gone to college or at least gotten a commission, but he insisted on enlisting. A private. He should have been an officer. He could have been placed somewhere safe, but he wanted to prove he was no better than anyone else. But he was." She stifled a sob. "That wasn't Edward, though. So he went to France as a private, and he died." She crumbled on the last word, and the tears flowed.

Something urged Anna to reach out and hold the woman's hand, but it meant letting go of the article and allowing God to take control of what happened next. Either Brandon would be hurt even more, or he would be released from the past that tormented him. Whatever the result, he probably would never forgive her for bringing the article here today.

Courage and faith. Every woman of the Bible had acted with courage and faith.

She unfolded the article and handed it to Mrs. Neidecker. "I found this today. I believe it's about your nephew."

The bump Brandon had run over with the automobile turned out to be a stone that had tumbled out of the fence. Five more feet, and he would have run into the wall. The car was useless in such weather, so he abandoned it and set out on foot.

Not two paces away, he found Anna's red knit mittens and scarf. Fear knotted his stomach. Not only was she out in this weather, but she had no protection from the cold.

The temperature had dipped, and the snow had lost its greasiness. The smaller, finer flakes filled the air, howling around him with the increasing wind.

Anna could freeze to death.

He shoved the mittens and scarf in his pocket, hunched his shoulders and headed into the biting wind. She would have gone down the hill into town. Mrs. Simmons had told him Anna intended to rent a room at the boardinghouse before he offered the carriage house. She'd either head there or to her brother's house, which was only six blocks away. Any man, even one with a bad leg, could hike six blocks.

He made his way along the stone wall and, once through the gate, headed left and down the hill. The slope told him he was going in the right direction, though he could see nothing. Snow stung his narrowed eyes. It melted and ran down his neck. It crusted his eyebrows and coat.

Panting from exertion, he struggled against the wind. Once again he had a cause. Once again he was fighting against insurmountable odds.

"It's a trap," Pvt. Naughton had said. Edward Naughton had been a good man, the best. Every man who'd died tore apart his soul, but none more than Naughton. The private had the sense and courage to speak up. Brandon hadn't enough of either to act.

Naughton had been right. It was a trap. Worse, Brandon knew it. Or rather, he should have known it. He recognized the effects of excessive alcohol use: the too-bright eyes, the slight stagger, the belligerence. His commanding officer had exhibited all of those when he gave the order to drive deep into the ruins of that small town. Brandon should never have obeyed. Court-martial would have been better than what had followed.

The roar of artillery barely concealed the screams of his men as they died around him. Why hadn't he died too? He was supposed to die first and end this miserable life.

That day, the rain had chilled him to the bone. Today the

snow did. Something caught his worthless right foot, and he stumbled. The pain knifed through his hip, and he fell forward into a drift. Though the snow cushioned some of the blow, the impact still shivered up his arms.

His cane skittered out of reach. Once the shock wore off, he groped around in the snowy darkness until he found it, but his fingers were so cold he could barely grip the thing.

If he, a grown man, was succumbing to frostbite, how much more so would a slight woman in a threadbare coat? Tangled emotions—fear, love and despair—welled, threatening to freeze him to the spot. He could not give in to this. He must find her, help her, save her.

"Anna," he called out.

The snow muffled all sound. Pulling his coat shut against the cold, he listened harder. What if she lay near? What if she was calling out for him?

"Anna," he yelled with all his might.

In the silence that followed, he thought he heard something. It sounded dull and far away, soft thumping, like heavy footfalls or the distant thud of shells.

How could that be? He was in Pearlman, not the war. It was winter, not autumn. Yet that thump, thump, thump continued.

He drew in an icy breath, trying to calm the pain and the terror. When his platoon fell into the ambush, his men had scattered. He'd yelled out the order to hold formation, but only Naughton held. For that act of obedience, Edward Naughton had been the first to perish. Then the shells had torn through the rest, tossing them like leaves.

"No," he sobbed, pressing his frozen hands to his eyes. Why wouldn't it stop? Why must he lose everyone he ever cared for? His mother had slipped away with barely a protest. His father had stopped giving any affection when Reggie was born. His men had trusted him. And now Anna. He'd lost her too.

"Why?" he yelled at the fierce emptiness. "Why do I have to lose everyone?"

He heard no reply, just like in the war. But this time he felt something. Peace. It came from nowhere, pierced through the pain and misery as clearly as a regulation thirty-ought-six bullet.

Was it true? Had God always been with him, even when he'd turned his back on God? Is that why he'd struggled with whether or not to disobey the fateful order? Was He the small voice that pricked his conscience? Was He here now? Was He with Anna?

It didn't matter what Brandon wanted or needed, as long as Anna was safe. He bowed his head, unsure how to say a prayer that God would actually answer. This was too important to do wrong, but he didn't know how to do it right.

"Help me," he finally cried out. "Help me find Anna. I can't do it myself. I can't do anything myself, but Mrs. Simmons says if I just ask, You'll forgive me. So I'm asking." He sucked in a ragged breath. "I'm begging. Please. Please. Take me, if You want, but let Anna live."

Then he dropped into the snow, prostrate and sobbing like a boy. He could do nothing. Nothing. If God was gracious, death would come quickly.

It did not.

Gradually, after the anguish spent its fury, calm replaced the hopelessness, and the pain in his hip subsided. He opened his eyes and saw in the distance a lone light shining.

An answer to prayer?

He didn't know, but he had to trust it was. Using the last of his strength, he got to his feet and trudged toward this beacon.

Chapter Twenty-Two

Anna waited nervously while Mrs. Neidecker read the article. Apparently, she'd never seen it before. Maybe she didn't know that Brandon had been Edward's commanding officer, that he had led his men into the ambush that cost Edward his life. If so, Anna's task would be much more difficult.

Her heart pounded in her ears. She could hear nothing else in the deathly quiet room. Mrs. Neidecker's expression never changed. Perhaps the article told her nothing new.

At last Mrs. Neidecker set down the article, leaned back with a sigh and closed her eyes.

Anna was dying to know what she was thinking, but she had to wait for the woman to collect her thoughts. Her beloved nephew had died. According to the article, Brandon was at fault.

When Mrs. Neidecker finally spoke, her words came so softly that Anna could hardly hear her. "Why did you bring this to me?"

Anna hesitated. This wasn't about her or even Edward. It was about finding peace. She prayed God would give her the right words. "I hoped you could forgive him."

"Forgive who?" Mrs. Neidecker looked genuinely confused, and Anna wondered if she'd misinterpreted the article.

"B-Brandon." As she said his name, she felt the old heat suffuse her cheeks. "Mr. Landers, I mean."

Mrs. Neidecker didn't answer.

So Anna added, "He's hurting, and I think this is why."

"Survivor guilt." Her words carried no condemnation.

"What is that?"

"The survivor of a tragedy wonders why he didn't die too."

Anna marveled that Mrs. Neidecker could speak so calmly. "Where did you learn about this?"

Mrs. Neidecker glanced at the empty parlor doorway before answering. "Joe had promised Edward he'd enlist with him but changed his mind at the last minute. You can imagine how he felt when the news came back that Edward had been killed."

Anna had always thought Joe Neidecker lacked a moral compass, but after hearing this, she began to understand why. "He's trying to escape what happened, just like Brandon."

The woman's cheek twitched. "Survivor guilt."

Anna shuddered to think that Brandon might fall as deeply as Joe Neidecker if he couldn't get forgiveness. She had to get it for him at any cost. "Do you blame Brandon?"

"I did for a long time, but Ralph asked some questions, checked into the matter and learned the fault lay elsewhere. Even if he hadn't, what good would it have done to hang on to the anger? Edward was gone."

Anna hung her head in shame. This woman had forgiven a terrible loss, while she had held a grudge over the most insignificant slights. This woman acted with grace and dignity, while Anna had behaved like a spoiled child.

"I'm so sorry, so sorry." This time the apology came from the heart.

To her surprise, Mrs. Neidecker squeezed her hand. "What's done is done."

That sounded so much like Ma that tears rose to Anna's eyes. She brushed them away and mustered a smile. "Would you be willing to tell Brandon what you told me?"

"Will he listen?"

"I hope so." But she didn't know. He'd built so many walls around his heart. "He has to. His life, his future, even his store, depends on it."

Mrs. Neidecker nodded. "Ralph told me about the loan."

"What loan?"

"At the bank."

Anna knew Mr. Neidecker was on the bank board, but she had no idea Brandon had borrowed money. "If only I could have found the lost Landers fortune."

"It wouldn't have done you any good if you had."

"Why?" Her words startled Anna. "Did someone already find it?"

"Not that I've heard." Mrs. Neidecker smiled softly. "If I'm right, the fortune isn't anything you can spend."

Anna stared. "Then what is it?"

Brandon struggled toward the light. His cane had got so caked with snow and ice that it hindered more than helped. His hip burned and every few steps he gasped with pain.

None of that mattered. Anna was out in this without mittens or scarf. If he didn't get help, she'd die...the way his men had died.

Please, Lord, help me.

The light seemed so far away, and the need was so great. If the Bible was right, God looked after the least of his creatures.

Then keep Anna safe.

Why couldn't he find her? Why didn't God show him the way? Was He ignoring Brandon because Brandon had ignored Him?

"Please," he cried into the stormy night. "Take me, condemn me, but save Anna."

His legs ached. The icy air had frozen his face and fingers. The cane slipped from his hand, and he left it. Only the light remained, dim but growing stronger.

Hope rekindled. Perhaps he could make it there. Perhaps God had heard him this time. Maybe He was leading Brandon to help, to people who could find Anna.

Hope pushed him onward, up the long drive. Hope dulled the pain. Anna could be found. She would be saved. Thank God. He'd nearly made it to the house. Despite snow to his knees and an injured leg, he would be able to get help.

A rush of emotion overwhelmed him, and he halted, stricken. He loved Anna. He couldn't imagine living without her. Yet he'd hurt her terribly.

"Anna!"

He stumbled again but caught his balance.

What he felt didn't matter. After the way he'd treated her earlier, she would hate him. As she should. She would leave Pearlman, never to return. Her laugh would never lighten his day. Her smile would never again wipe away his fears.

Anna. He gasped for air like a fish on the riverbank.

Lord, I ruined everything.

What could he say? What could he do to right the wrong?

Again his lame foot caught on something, and he pitched forward. Yet somehow he didn't fall.

She could never love a man like him. Not now. Not after what he'd done.

He squeezed his eyes tight against the bitter cold that

numbed his fingers and made his lungs hurt with each breath. And he knew. The truth stared him in the face.

It didn't matter if she ever cared for him again. He loved her, and that meant giving all he had even if she never returned his love. He would summon a search party and bring her safely home to her mother. He would ensure she lived her dream. Even if it meant selling the house and his books, he'd send her to college to be an archaeologist.

This time when he drew a breath, it didn't hurt. His stomach had unclenched. He had a plan, one that would bring great joy to the only woman he would ever love.

The light was now quite near. Steps loomed before him. A warm glow from the front windows illuminated the door. He cautiously navigated the steps, crossed the wide porch and raised a hand to knock.

This door looked familiar. He'd seen that ornate brass knocker before. When? Now he remembered. The night of the Valentine's Ball.

God must have a wry sense of humor. Brandon had arrived at the one place least likely to help.

But he hadn't the strength to go farther. Somehow he had to convince them to help.

He lifted the knocker and let it fall.

A knock sounded on the front door just as Mrs. Neidecker finished explaining to Anna what she thought the lost fortune was.

"Who could that be?"

The heavy metallic clunk startled Anna from deep concentration. Everything Mrs. Neidecker had said fit with what she'd found. They'd pieced together the clues and come to the same conclusion.

"This isn't going to help Brandon's store." Anna sighed.

"Maybe it will." Mrs. Neidecker patted her hand before

rising to greet the visitor. "And the loan certainly won't hurt."

Graves hurried to answer the door, which would be unusual for the slow-footed butler, but then Anna saw Mr. Neidecker on his heels.

Ralph Neidecker poked his head into the parlor. "Seems we're mighty popular tonight. And in thick weather, no less. Good evening, Anna. Any trouble?"

"Not now." Indeed her jitters had vanished. "I should be getting home, though. Ma's probably worried." She also needed to talk to Brandon. Though all hope of finding a treasure was gone, the Neideckers' forgiveness had to erase the guilt he'd been carrying for so long.

She stood, and Mrs. Neidecker held out the article. "Do you want this back?"

"It belongs to Brandon."

Mrs. Neidecker nodded. "Perhaps it would be better if I gave it to him."

"Would you?" Anna's eyes dampened again. She couldn't believe the woman's compassion and understanding. How badly Anna had misjudged her.

Anna heard the front door open, followed by muffled voices.

Ralph Neidecker swiveled with surprise. "Mr. Landers."

"Brandon?" she whispered. "Or Reggie?"

Mrs. Neidecker shook her head. "Reggie came here earlier."

Of course he had. This must be where he retreated when he and Brandon had their quarrels.

"He and Sally went next door to spend time with friends." Mrs. Neidecker lowered her voice. "The two of them have grown close. I expect an announcement any day."

If Anna hadn't been so emotionally overwrought, that news might have distressed her. Just a few hours ago, she'd imagined a life with Brandon. If Reggie and Sally married, Sally would become Brandon's sister-in-law. Marrying Brandon would make Anna sisters with Sally. That would have sent her into conniptions, but she'd been wrong about the Neideckers. So wrong.

And about Brandon. He'd turned on her over the most insignificant thing. Tears stung her eyes. He didn't love her.

"You look like you've been through a war," Ralph Neidecker exclaimed from the front entry hall. "Come in out of the weather."

"I need your help." Brandon's ragged plea ripped through Anna.

Something was wrong, terribly wrong. Part of her wanted to rush to his side, but then she remembered how he'd dismissed her. The contempt. The finality. She froze, unsure what to do.

"Let me take your coat," Mr. Neidecker said as the door closed with a click. "We'll sit in the parlor."

Anna's mouth went dry. Brandon couldn't come in here. What would she say to him? He'd know at once that she'd shown the article to the Neideckers. She looked around frantically for an escape and found none.

"There. Isn't. Time." Brandon gasped for breath between each word.

Time for what? Brandon didn't sound angry. He sounded desperate, panicked.

"Help me please," Brandon cried. "S-she might perish."

Who? Anna's eyes widened as she realized she'd left him with Ma.

"Ma! What happened to Ma?" She rushed into the entry and saw Brandon in a shockingly disheveled and desperate state.

His eyes burned feverishly. His face was as white as the

snow covering his coat and melting off his hat. His bluish hands shook. He'd lost his cane.

He stared at her as if she was a mirage. "Anna? You're here?"

"Ma," she squeaked out, her panic matching his.

"Fine." He swallowed, never blinking. "She's fine, but you're here." Emotion shook his shoulders. "You're here."

"I'm here." Now that she knew Ma wasn't hurt, her terror subsided into puzzlement.

He reached out as if to confirm she was real but then dropped his hands. "I prayed." His voice came out clotted. "I asked Him, and then I saw the light."

"Poor man. He's half-mad from the elements," Mrs. Neidecker murmured, pulling aside her butler. "Fetch a blanket."

The butler vanished, and Mrs. Neidecker urged Brandon toward the parlor by wrapping her hand around his soaking wet arm. "We'll have a nice chat, and you can tell us everything."

He didn't move, didn't stop staring at Anna. His Adam's apple bobbed once, twice, until at last the raw words came out. "Can you ever forgive me?"

The sob rose to Anna's lips, and she had to stifle it with her hand. "Of course."

"I—I—I was wrong, so wrong."

He looked like as though he would fall, and she took a step toward him, but he held up his hand to stop her.

"I don't want you to leave." He swiped his mouth and turned his feverish eyes away. "Ever."

"I don't want to leave," she whispered, wondering if he meant the carriage house or Pearlman or even this house.

"But you must know." His gaze locked on hers. "I am not the man you think I am."

What did he mean? Her thoughts tumbled wildly. He

must be crazed from the cold. "You're good and kind and honorable."

"I'm none of those things. Look at me. I'm a failure."

"No, you're not," she said, but he didn't listen.

"I should have died. Me. I'm the one who led them to their deaths, but they were innocent. I wasn't. I knew. I knew it was a trap." His voice rasped with pain. "I deserved to die. They didn't."

"That's not quite true," Mr. Neidecker interjected.

Anna whirled around. She'd forgotten he was still there.

"Yes, it is." Brandon faced Mr. Neidecker and in doing so somehow found strength. His voice rang clearer, the pain replaced by determination. "I was their commanding officer. I knew there was something peculiar about the orders. I knew we shouldn't go to that town, but I didn't have the courage to speak up, and they died. They all died."

"You obeyed orders," Mr. Neidecker stated, "even though the man who gave them was drunk that day. He was, wasn't he?"

Anna held her breath. Then Brandon wasn't at fault at all.

Brandon, however, didn't let go so easily. His jaw clenched. "I don't speak ill of my commanding officers."

"I respect that, but the fault doesn't lie with you. You see, I know something about obeying orders, Lt. Landers. I'm a military man myself. Captain. Spanish-American War. I also happen to know how to cut through the static to get to the truth. Would you be surprised to learn your commanding officer was discharged after that incident?"

Brandon's lips formed one word. "Dishonorable?"

Ralph Neidecker shook his head. "Justice isn't always complete." He extended a hand. "I want you to know, Lt. Landers, that all the families know the truth, and no one blames you."

"How is that possible?"

"That's not to say we weren't angry. We all grieved, but it's been over four years. Time dulls the pain."

"It does." Anna hoped with all her heart that Brandon would accept this olive branch. "I cried for years after Papa died, but I held on to the guilt. It would have been easier if I'd asked for and accepted forgiveness."

He turned red-rimmed eyes to her.

"I blamed myself for Papa's death," she explained, "because I saw the accident and didn't go to him or tell anyone. I thought I could have done something to save him, but I know now I couldn't have any more than you could have changed what happened in France. The hurt's still there, but by accepting forgiveness, we move on."

Brandon absorbed her words silently and then looked back at the Neideckers. "Why would you go to all this trouble for me?"

"It was for us," Mr. Neidecker said, "for Evelyn and me. We felt the official reports weren't telling us everything, and we had to know the truth. You see, our nephew was in your platoon."

"I'm so sorry." He struggled for composure. "How can I ever repay you for your loss?"

"By making a go of that bookstore of yours. Evelyn says we've needed a place like that for years."

Brandon stared at them as if they were insane.

His wife nodded. "Edward loved to read."

"Edward? Edward Naughton?" Brandon paled and swayed. "Good man." His voice came out ragged with emotion. "The best."

Mrs. Neidecker wiped away a tear. "I know."

"He knew," Brandon whispered, "but I didn't listen. I didn't listen." He hid his eyes with his hand. "He should have been in command."

"If he had been, he would have obeyed orders also," Mr.

Neidecker said. "I knew my nephew well. He respected authority. He would have done the same."

Mrs. Neidecker nodded. "Please stop blaming yourself. It won't change the past."

Brandon swayed, and this time Anna went to him. Let him brush her aside or refuse help. She couldn't bear to watch him suffer.

"Let's sit," she urged softly, wrapping her arm around his. The coat was still wet, but she didn't care. She tugged gently. "I'm exhausted."

That shook him from his stupor if not his agony. He blindly came with her into the parlor while Mr. and Mrs. Neidecker tactfully drifted to another room Graves had left the blanket on the sofa, and after Anna got Brandon seated, she shook it out and draped it over his lap.

He shoved it aside and took her hands. This time when his eyes met hers, the stormy gray had calmed. He still looked haggard, but at last she could see again the man she loved.

"I regret what I said to you," he said again. "I was… wrong."

"Don't," she said softly, taking the hat from his head. His damp hair gleamed in the electric lights. "We've both been wrong in so many ways." She squeezed his hands, which had warmed. "I should never have looked for that so-called lost fortune without asking."

"So-called?" he lifted an eyebrow, his old self becoming more and more evident with every passing minute.

"I learned from Mrs. Neidecker that this fortune of yours isn't money or gold or even anything tangible."

"Then it's exactly what I thought." He rose and crossed to the window, where he pulled aside the sheer drape. Blackness stared back at them. "Gone. As dead as the man who buried it. Jeb Landers. The most despicable man alive. The rest were no better."

This time Anna blinked. "What do you mean? Your ancestors were noble."

He laughed bitterly. "I'm descended from the most miserable of men, the kind that would sell their souls for money."

She had no idea what he was talking about. "Do you mean your father?"

"He wasn't the first, only the latest in a long line. It goes back to the founding of the house. Do you know where my family got its money? From hunting down fugitive slaves." His lip curled bitterly. "That's right. Slave hunters. When Jeb Landers found a fugitive, he brought the man or woman back to their master in exchange for money. Just like Judas's thirty pieces of silver. That grand house was built on blood money. Any fortune he might have hidden away is not worth finding."

The entire time he talked, Anna shook her head, but he would not pause to let her speak until he'd pounded the final nail in his rickety coffin. "So you see, my blood is tainted."

"Why would you say such a thing? You're good and honest. I'd trust you with my life."

His red-rimmed eyes barely blinked. "You'd be a fool."

"No, I wouldn't." She faced off against him. "Moreover, I don't like being called a fool. I know you, and you're nothing like this Jeb Landers."

"Haven't you heard of the sins of the fathers being visited on the sons?"

"And they're all washed away by the blood of Christ. All you need to do—all any of them needed to do—is ask Him for forgiveness and let Him into your heart. Trust Him completely."

"The light," he muttered.

"What light?" She looked around. "All the lights are on."

"Not these lights. Well, actually these were the lights, but I'm talking about a more important kind of light. I prayed, and He answered. He showed me the light, His light. I was lost but now am found, was blind but now I see," he quoted from the hymn "Amazing Grace."

Anna's throat narrowed when she saw the expression on his face. Brandon truly had seen God's light, somehow, in some way that she could never understand. She closed her eyes and thanked God with all her heart.

"He brought me to you, just like I asked." Looking dazed, he leaned against the window.

Anna joined him, excited to spill everything she'd learned tonight. "And He revealed something to me too. After talking with Mrs. Neidecker, I believe there's another explanation for how the rumors of a lost fortune got started."

His gaze fixed on her then. "There is?"

"Do you remember that old ledger you've been poring over?"

He nodded. "The account book. Along with bushels of grain harvested, it also counts slaves."

"But Michigan was always free territory. They couldn't have owned slaves."

"They hunted them," he pointed out. "That's what the notes marked with an *S* meant—how many fugitives caught and returned."

"If so, then why did they also use the letters *N, E,* and *W?* I think they're for the four directions."

"Directions," he scoffed. "If only it was that pure and honest. The notes spelled out where Jeb found the fugitives."

She couldn't believe how stubbornly he clung to his interpretation. "Or where he sent them."

"North? Why would a slave hunter send captured slaves north?"

"To freedom."

He stared at her. "Are you mad?"

"No, I'm serious." She clasped his hands. "Mrs. Neidecker and I pieced it all together. The final clue was the word *midnight*. Remember seeing it in the ledger?"

"It's a time of day."

"It's also the code word for Detroit, the final stop on this branch of the Underground Railroad. If we're right, then your house was a station and your ancestors were conductors. They helped slaves to freedom. That's your legacy, Brandon, not slave hunting. Your family wasn't hiding treasure here on earth where it would only rot. They were storing up treasure in heaven."

He stared. "I wish I could believe it."

"We'll find the proof. I won't stop searching until we do."

"You won't?"

"*We* won't."

"We." A look of wonder settled over him. "You want to continue working with me after what I said to you?"

Anna tossed her head, a touch of impertinence taking hold. "No, I don't."

His shoulders slumped. "I shouldn't have—"

She cut him off. "I want more than work, Brandon Landers, and if you haven't figured out what I mean by that, then you're the blindest man on the face of the earth."

He looked at her, stunned. "You…? You…? You don't hate me?"

She braced her hands on her hips. "You must be blind."

Gradually, realization dawned, and, oh, what a wonderful moment. "You? Me?" he stammered in disbelief before straightening into the pillar of strength that she'd come to love and respect. "I do love you. I've loved you from the first time I saw you, but I didn't dare hope you could love me."

She tapped the end of his nose with her fingertip. "And that's where you were wrong."

"I was?" A smile gradually curved his lips.

"You were."

Then he swept her into his arms and kissed her as deeply and romantically as the most swashbuckling pirate in the best dime novel.

When he broke the embrace, he grasped her by the shoulders, hope shining in his eyes. "Anna Simmons, what would I ever do without you?"

She couldn't hold back a grin. "Not much, I expect."

Chapter Twenty-Three

Two months later

"Ouch," Anna complained as Brandon's heel struck her arm. The carriage-house crawl space was too narrow for them to enter side by side, so Brandon led with the lamp while she carried the old ledger. "I don't see why you had to go first. I'm the one who lives here."

"I'm the one who owns it," Brandon teased. "Besides, if I understand the Bible correctly, as the man of the house, I'm the head of the family."

"Man of the house?" A thrill ran through her. Was this his awkward way of proposing? Since that night at the Neideckers' house, they'd drawn closer and closer. They got the bookstore off to a better start by building on the excitement over King Tutankhamun's tomb. They hunted down clues to support Anna's hypothesis that Brandon's ancestors were conductors on the Underground Railroad. Each discovery elevated his spirits, but nothing could compare to the way he'd seized on his renewed faith. No one listened more raptly to the Sunday sermons. He even asked to join the church.

Still, he never came close to proposing. Yes, they spent hours together each day. Yes, she and Ma dined with him at the house. Yes, he treated Ma like a mother. Still no proposal. If this was his attempt, it was a pretty poor one.

"You aren't the head of my family," she shot back. "Hendrick is. If you want to take over that job, you'll need his blessing."

"He gave it weeks ago."

"He did?" If so, Brandon must be waiting for a sign from her that a proposal would be accepted. She jutted out her chin. "Then you know what you need to do."

"Ask you and your mother to move to the house?"

"That's not what I meant, and you know it."

"Maybe I'm afraid." He actually sounded serious.

"Of what?"

He didn't answer right away. "A man must be able to meet his obligations."

He *was* talking about marriage. Her heart pounded harder. "Finances will improve once we find the real fortune."

He halted. "You think it's gold?"

"It had better not be. I don't want to marry a millionaire."

His laugh sent warmth clear to her toes. "You don't have much to worry about, then."

He said no more, just crawled ahead in silence. Had she been wrong? Impossible. Ma had hinted she should expect a proposal, and Ma was never wrong in that department.

At last he stopped. "Here we are. If we're right, our lives will never be the same after today. We can stop now, seal up this crawl space and never mention it again. You decide."

She couldn't bear not knowing. "We're already certain there's no gold or money hidden here."

"But there might be a map. Who knows where that might lead?" He gingerly rose, stepped over the charred remains of the rug that had caught fire months ago and turned to face her, so the lamp was between them.

She pointed to the odd *X*s that had been penciled on the stone wall. Knowing what she now knew, these marks took on new meaning. "See? Three of them. Like the three crosses on Calvary. Right here where we had the fire."

He held out his pocketknife. "Would you like to do the honors?"

She took it and began scraping away the ashes below the marks. The crevices in the wood plank floor revealed nothing, but as she removed the dirt and ash next to the stone wall, the knife caught an edge of paper.

"That's it," she said, excitement pounding in her chest. Her hand trembled. "I don't know if I can get it out without damaging it."

"Do you want me to do it?" he asked just as breathlessly.

"No, I've got it." With a little effort and a lot of patience, she slid the blade under the paper and wriggled it from its hiding place.

She picked it up and held it out to Brandon. "You open it."

"You found it."

"It's your house." She placed it before him.

His hands trembled as he moved the paper exactly midway between them. "We'll open it together."

While she held one edge, he unfolded the paper. It crackled, brittle, and he had to open it carefully. When at last it lay open, she was no closer to an answer. Odd markings were scribbled all over the paper. She pulled the lamp closer and looked from every angle.

"It might be a map."

He laughed, the nervous sort of excited laugh. "Of course it's a map. See? This is the Blackman farm and here's Green Lake."

"The Blackman farm? Is that where the Highbottoms live now?"

He nodded.

"But this says Africa and Emerald Pond."

"Exactly. Code names for locations. Remember? Let's see the ledger."

She opened to the page she'd read before and pointed to the odd entries. "Where are Whiteside and Sunny Blooms?"

"Perhaps a white barn and a field of sunflowers."

"They're not on this map." She ran her finger along the line connecting the locations. "If that's Green Lake and that's the Highbottom farm, then your house must be the City of Gold."

He sat back heavily. "City of Gold? Why would it be called that?"

Anna nibbled her lip, deep in thought. The old brass lamp cast a steady but dim light on the map. She grabbed the polished metal base to move it closer, probably leaving fingerprints that would later tarnish.

"Tarnish. That's it," she exclaimed.

"What?"

"The roof. It's green."

"Copper."

"But it wouldn't have been green when the house was first built."

Realization dawned on his face. "It would have gleamed in the sunlight like gold."

"City of Gold."

"City of Gold," he repeated. "No wonder the rumors started."

She shook her head, marveling at the myriad rumors that had caused so much grief. "How the truth has been twisted through the years. If only you'd known."

He touched her cheek, soft as a whisper. "I know now, thanks to you. Some treasure hunter I am."

She drank in his dimpled chin and broad smile. "The

best ever, Mr. Brandon." She laughed when she used Ma's name for him, but somehow it felt right.

"Think of all we can do. We'll unearth the stories of those who hid in this crawl space on their way to freedom. We'll print a book of those stories. Tell the world about their lives. Everyone will want to see this place. We could turn it into a museum. The bookstore can have exhibits. It'll be famous."

"Whoa." He chuckled. "You're getting ahead of yourself."

"Am I?" She couldn't stifle her excitement.

"Well, you're a bit ahead of me." He rifled through his jacket pockets until he unearthed a simple gold band. "I have something to ask you first."

Anna sat back with a thud. Even though she'd expected a proposal, she'd anticipated nothing like this. Why, her heart had practically stopped, and her ears were buzzing.

He took her trembling hand. "Anna Simmons, will you join me on the greatest adventure of all, a life together? Will you let me take you to exotic lands and faraway places? Will you work beside me to unearth life's secrets? Will you marry me?"

With every word, she felt lighter until she thought she would lift clear off the floor. "I will, I will." She flung her arms around him, knowing she had found the one and only man for her.

After a kiss, he slid the ring on her finger. "It's not a proper engagement ring, but someone insisted I give you this until we pick out your ring."

Anna's eyes widened. "Ma's ring?" Tears sprang to her eyes.

"Yes, dearest," Ma said from behind her, where she must have been waiting for Brandon's proposal. "Your father always wanted to be part of your wedding."

Anna hugged the ring to her heart. "Then I will always wear it."

Then, though the space was not quite large enough, they all hugged and laughed and made countless plans. All Anna knew was that she'd found the best treasure of all—family.

* * * * *

Dear Reader,

Archaeological finds have always fascinated me. I love to read about recently discovered tombs and monuments. Like Anna, I dreamed of being the first to open an ancient tomb. As a child, I conducted "digs" in my mom's gardens and occasionally unearthed an arrowhead. When I learned that this month marks the 90th anniversary of the discovery of King Tutankhamun's tomb, I had to include it in this story. Though I'd read about Howard Carter's excavation years ago, I found that rereading the story of that monumental archaeological event renewed my childhood desire to unearth something special. I hope you have enjoyed Anna and Brandon's search for lasting treasure. They have many more adventures ahead of them.

I love to hear from readers. You can write to me through my website at http://christineelizabethjohnson.com.

Blessings,

Christine Johnson

Questions for Discussion

1. Anna's life turns on end when she and her mother must move from her childhood home. She lashes out at Brandon, while her mother responds with understanding. Why do they react differently? How have you reacted to a stressful event?

2. Wealthy Sally Neidecker denigrates Anna, putting her down for being poor. Why would Sally behave that way? Today, there's a lot of focus on bullying. Would you consider this bullying or a precursor to bullying? How would you deal with this if you were Anna?

3. Why does Anna initially refuse Brandon's offer of the carriage-house apartment?

4. Brandon is especially uncomfortable around Pastor Gabriel. Why? What might have happened in his past to make him this way? What does he need to do to get over this discomfort?

5. While Mrs. Simmons wants to celebrate Christmas to its fullest, Brandon tries to shut himself away from all celebrations. Why? What does he fear?

6. Brandon is frustrated by his kid brother's attitude and reckless behavior, and tries to instill a sense of responsibility in him. Why do Brandon's efforts fall short? What could he do that would get better results?

7. Brandon fears emotional attachment. Why? How does Anna break through that barrier?

8. After Brandon invites Anna to the Valentine's Ball, she worries about her dress and hair. Why does she place so much stock in how she looks? What would have happened if she'd worn her Sunday best instead of a ball gown?

9. Brandon consistently denies that there is a lost fortune hidden in his house. Why? Why doesn't he embrace Anna's desire to find it?

10. Why does Anna proceed with the search for the fortune without Brandon's permission? Do you think she did the right thing? Why or why not?

11. While Anna grasps at the hope of finding lost treasure, Brandon turns to the bank—a practical solution. How would you deal with a similar financial difficulty?

12. Why didn't Anna tell her mother years ago that she saw her father die? How does that secret affect her life?

13. When Brandon accuses Anna of going behind his back to find the treasure, she reacts differently than she did early in the book when he gave her the eviction letter. That time she reacted with anger. How does she react this time? What do you think changed her?

14. To help Brandon, Anna must swallow her pride and talk to the woman she wronged at the start of the book. Have you ever faced this sort of situation? How did it turn out?

15. What changes Brandon's attitude toward God? How does this reconciliation affect his interaction with people?

REQUEST YOUR FREE BOOKS!

2 FREE INSPIRATIONAL NOVELS
PLUS 2
FREE
MYSTERY GIFTS

Love Inspired.
HISTORICAL
INSPIRATIONAL HISTORICAL ROMANCE